Everything Under the Moon

Fairy Tales in a Queerer Light

EDITED BY MICHAEL EARP &
ILLUSTRATED BY KIT FOX

FOREWORD

Queer people have always existed. In the world, in stories.
But in one much more than the other.

A collection such as this might have asked its authors to create original fairy tales in the traditional style, but, you know, with LGBTQIA+ characters. How glorious that would be! But I wanted to ask authors to look at what fairy tales have given us and reflect these narratives back from their own perspectives. To take a traditional story of their choice and queer it in every sense. To use the craft of storytelling to question the very idea that queer sits outside of 'normal'. To explore how that world view is reinforced by casual acceptance of stories set down in bygone eras. To interrogate who these stories keep in power, and who they keep from it. To ask what 'happily ever after' means and what other endings are out there.

Tales that capture our collective fascination do so at their own peril. Stories passed down in the oral tradition can be edited and revised as society learns and grows, but they are frozen at the moment they are set down in ink. All these years later, traditional fairy tales are ripe for scrutinising. Their (supposedly) universal truths about life need to be plucked out, examined and challenged in the retelling. They beg to be retold, to continue to evolve as they would have done in the mouths of storytellers.

Readers might not know all the stories that have been given a new life in these pages. That's neither here nor there. You'll find stories full of bright and vivid characters who reflect the people around you regardless of knowing the original. An upstart Cinderella who has bigger concerns than some prince. Boys who set out for a new life and find something else entirely. Sisters fighting to stay together in the face of malevolent men. Sons loved by their fathers no matter what. A rescuer who needs to reassess her objectives. Brothers divided by schoolyard jealousy. A mermaid who offers an escape from a loveless

The Dog and the Sparrow, Jacob and Wilhelm Grimm · She was unable to resist, and, trembling, she took the little key and opened the door. *Bluebeard*, Charles Perrault · The old man's garden was suddenly transformed into a beautiful picture of spring. *The Old Man Who Makes the Trees to Blossom*, Yei Theodora Ozaki · Rapunzel's voice had stirred his heart so powerfully that he went out into the forest every day to hear her. *Rapunzel*, Jacob and Wilhelm Grimm · Mirror, Mirror, on the wall, who's the fairest one of all? *Snow White*, Jacob and Wilhelm Grimm · 'I don't like the sound of that. Come with me,' said the mermaid. *Mary Bell and the Mermaid*, Virginia Hamilton · But it's delightful not to be forgotten! *The Old House*, Hans Christian Andersen · Just this. When bad boys become good and kind, they have the power of making their homes gay and new with happiness. *The Adventures of Pinocchio*, Carlo Collodi · Tomorrow, at the crack of dawn, let's take the children out into the deepest part of the forest. *Hansel and Gretel*, Jacob and Wilhelm Grimm · By chance, he put his eye to the keyhole. *Donkeyskin*, Charles Perrault · Here was a well-known face at last – a round, friendly countenance, the face of a good friend I had known at home. *What the Moon Saw*, Hans Christian Andersen · She did not mind as long as it meant that she would be able to free her beloved brothers. *The Wild Swans*, Hans Christian Andersen · They said they had not seen anyone leave except a girl who was poorly dressed and looked more like a peasant than a lady. *Cinderella*, Charles Perrault · Off they started now upon the highroad; but it being very warm weather, they had not walked far, when, as they came to a corner, the Dog said, 'I am tired and must go to sleep.' *The Dog and the Sparrow*, Jacob and Wilhelm Grimm · She was unable to resist, and, trembling, she took the little key and opened the door. *Bluebeard*, Charles Perrault · The old man's garden was suddenly transformed into a beautiful picture of spring. *The Old Man Who Makes the Trees to Blossom*, Yei Theodora Ozaki · Rapunzel's voice had stirred

*For Teague, who showed me I had the power to re-write
my own happily ever after.*
M. E.

First published by Affirm Press in 2023
Boon Wurrung Country
28 Thistlethwaite Street
South Melbourne VIC 3205
affirmpress.com.au

10 9 8 7 6 5 4 3 2 1

Anthology and foreword © Michael Earp, 2023
Individual stories © retained by the individual copyright holders

The moral rights of the anthologist and contributors have been asserted.
All rights reserved. No part of this publication may be reproduced without prior written permission from the publisher.

 A catalogue record for this book is available from the National Library of Australia

ISBN: 9781922863645 (hardback)
Cover and internal design by Kit Fox and Mika Tabata © Affirm Press
Cover and internal illustrations © Kit Fox
Printed and bound in China by RR Donnelley Asia Printing Solutions Ltd.

home. Aromantics who carve a space for themselves. Boys whose desires defy wooden hearts. Siblings searching for scraps of themselves in the shadow of the forest. A crush-triangle in a nightclub. An exiled royal sharing secrets with the moon herself.

In much the same way you can take a solid beam of white light and see that it is, in fact, a rainbow, retelling is the prism that uncovers the ways that we've always been here. It's all in the telling, and each of this baker's dozen of authors has their own way of dividing the light.

Isn't it about time we showed our colours?

CONTENTS

FOREWORD — ii

IF THE SHOE FITS
Lili Wilkinson — 1

THE INSTANT I DIED
Gary Lonesborough — 20

LUZ AZUL
Alexandra Villasante — 34

THE CHERRY BLOSSOM QUEEN
Maggie Tokuda-Hall — 52

LET DOWN YOUR H.A.I.R.
Meagan Spooner & Amie Kaufman — 65

FAIREST OF ALL
Will Kostakis — 86

ALDA, AYSEL & THE EDISTO RIVER
Amber McBride — 103

SEEING COLOUR
Jes Layton — 120

THE WOODEN BOY
Abdi Nazemian — 139

MORSEL
Helena Fox — 153

THE KEYHOLE
Michael Earp — 171

MOONFALL
Alison Evans — 188

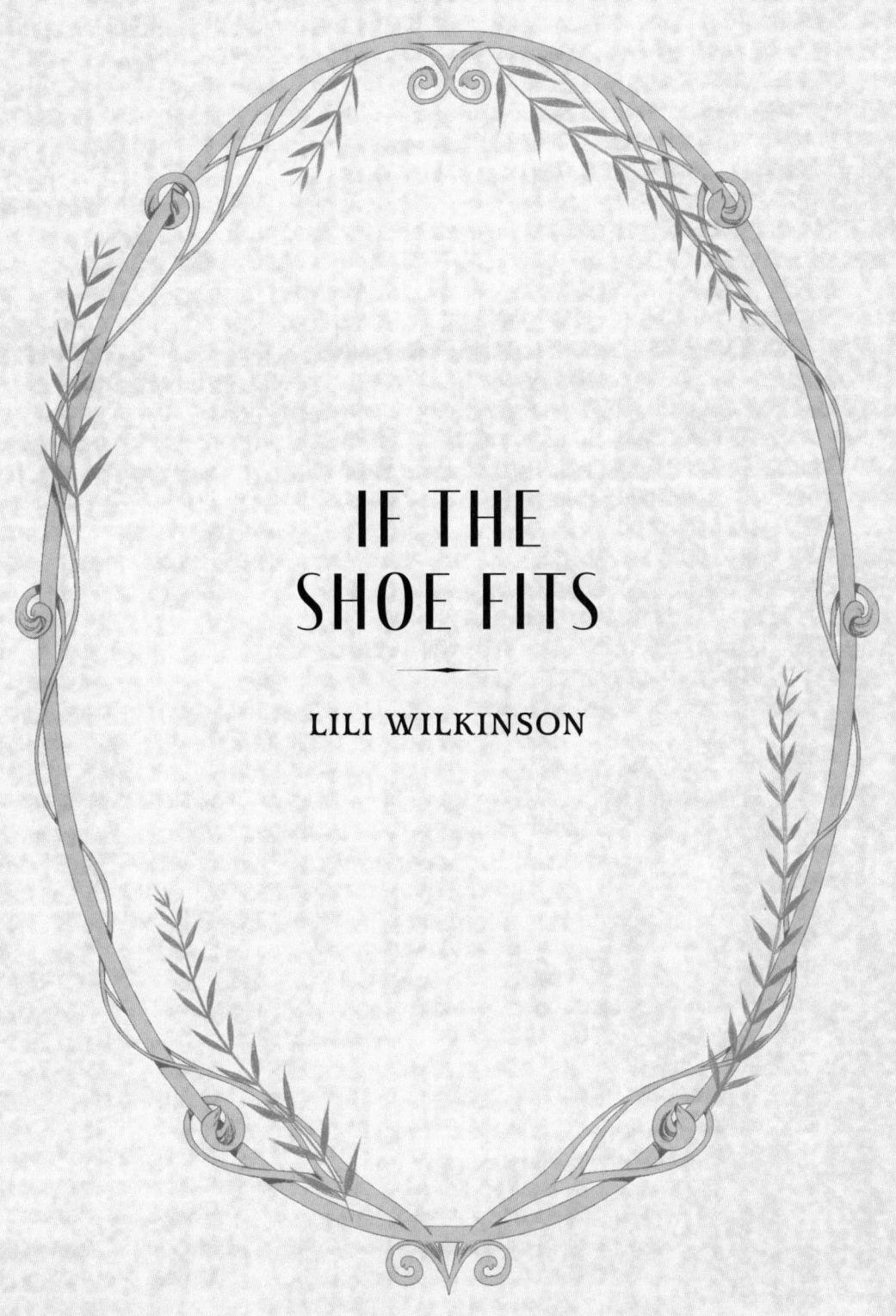

IF THE SHOE FITS

LILI WILKINSON

Every morning, I get up before dawn to shave the moss from my skin. It grows in soft fuzz all over my body, thicker under my arms and between my legs. It's the most vivid emerald green and smells of rich, damp soil.

It doesn't make me beautiful, or gifted, or special. It's just a pain in the arse.

The Prince has just turned twenty-one, so of course it's time for him to settle down and marry. There was a big ball last night for him to choose his twelve candidates.

Ridiculous time to hold it, if you ask me. We're on the brink of war with Canenae, there are rumblings of a growing rebellion, and the Prince is buggering off into his pleasure gardens for a fortnight? I know it's tradition, but maybe hold off a year?

But nobody in the palace wanted to talk about impending war and rebels and famine. All anyone wanted to talk about last night was the new girl.

I was on my hands and knees, scrubbing the kitchen floor clean. But I still got a glimpse of her, out with all the fancy folk.

Who is she? The question went rocketing around the room in whispers and murmurs.

Cendrillon, the answer came back. Cendrillon, and nothing more. Rumours ricocheted around the other servants. Her father was a wealthy merchant, a wicked ogre, a king. Or she had no parents at all, but sprung fully formed from a moonbeam. I ignored it all, of course, but even I knew this girl was all but guaranteed a pair of glass slippers in the morning.

Long after all the guests went home, after every dish and pot was sparkling clean, I tumbled exhausted onto my thin polyester mattress with a groan. But despite my weary bones, I couldn't fall asleep. I couldn't stop thinking about her. *Cendrillon*. What a charmed life she must lead, being so beautiful, so adored. She can have anyone and anything she wants.

What I wouldn't give to have that.

Which is why the next morning, when horrible old Master Thule thrusts a box at me and demands that I take the seventh pair of glass slippers to Anais Giada, I keep them for myself. I'm pretty sure I won't get caught – not at first, anyway. The pleasure gardens are forbidden to anyone except the Prince and his candidates. Not even servants are allowed in – the whole place is staffed by magical poppet-people.

I shave off the moss, put on my cleanest jeans (not very clean) and my nicest T-shirt (from The Baboon Section's latest tour), and gingerly slip my lumpy, bunioned feet into the glass shoes.

They fit, of course, because magic shoes always fit.

Twelve candidates, chosen by the Prince. Twelve pairs of glass slippers, required for admission into the pleasure gardens. Twelve nights of luxury and decadence. On the first eleven nights, a girl gets sent home. On the twelfth, there is a wedding.

Don't worry. I am under no delusions that the Prince will pick me. I wasn't born yesterday. I'm nothing but a kitchen bitch, callused and scarred from too many years of hard work. Nothing but a quarterblood woodwose, with green fuzz sprouting from me like damp fur. I know there's no happily ever after in store for me.

(I mean, I wouldn't turn him down, don't get me wrong. Because even if he's a bit of a jerk, I'd still get to live in luxury for the rest of my life. I'd have servants of my own, bringing me my breakfast every morning on a silver platter. He'd have to be a real monster for me to say no to that.)

I'm doing this for one reason, and one reason only.

I need a holiday.

I have worked all day, every day, since I was old enough to hold a scrubbing brush. My hands are raw from scrubbing dishes. My back aches. I'm always hungry.

In the Prince's pleasure gardens, I might be able to score a night or two off. Maybe even three or four, if I'm lucky. A few nights where I get to be a princess. It's totally worth the trouble I'll get in for missing a few days' work.

I get to the gates early and linger under a beech tree to watch as the other candidates start to arrive. Rosamel is first, in a huge, sleek car shaped like some kind of monstrous phallus. Her father is there, orange-skinned and dripping with jewels. She kisses him goodbye (on the lips, is that weird? I think it's weird) and struts through the gate with the kind of confidence that can only be bestowed by truly hideous amounts of wealth and privilege.

Milly-Mae is next. She arrives on a bicycle, apple-cheeked and sweet-tongued. She greets the poppet footmen at the door like old friends and thanks them for their help as they guide her inside. They bow and smile. They almost look human.

Then Radegunda, in boiled leather armour and braids, with a broadsword strapped to her back, astride a mighty black boar.

Gwenllian emerges from a taxi in a close-fitting dress made of iridescent fish scales, her hair still damp from the ocean. Her pearlescent skin glistens and her black fishy eyes are wide as she takes in the golden gate.

The twins arrive – Sophronia and Octavia, arm in arm in scarlet satin dresses. They are as thick as thieves, whispering and giggling even before they set foot inside the gate.

A motorcycle roars, and Nadiva pulls up, all silver zippers and latex, her eyes sporting a perfect electric blue cut-crease. (Yeah, I know what it's called. I'm not an animal.)

Yutika comes next, on a sled pulled by mountain dogs. I can smell her stinky elk-pelt jacket from here. Then Jadwiga, in a lace gown stitched from cobwebs, wrapped in a cloak made of moth wings. Then Xenia, their skin dark against a dress that is even darker and as insubstantial as smoke.

Then ... nobody.

Of course Cendrillon wants to be last. I bet she's hiding around the corner, waiting for the eleventh girl to go first.

I guess that would be me.

I take a deep breath and totter up the driveway to present myself to the footman. Will it know I stole Anais Giada's shoes? Will it turn me away in disgrace?

How do women wear shoes like this all the time? I'm likely to break an ankle.

The footman doesn't raise its eyebrows at me. It doesn't demand to know what I'm doing there. It just bows and ushers me inside. Up close, its skin is too smooth, its features too symmetrical.

The pleasure gardens are stunning. There are swathes of flowers, rolling emerald lawns, and trees hung with perfectly formed, ripe fruit. There is some *very* impressive garden magic going on in here. Brilliantly coloured birds are perched on every branch, and the air is thick with jewel-like butterflies. Everywhere I look there's another statue or pavilion or bower. Tinkling fountains spill into pools bursting with carp who probably eat better than I do.

I ignore it all and head straight to the buffet.

It's everything I ever dreamed of and more. There's roast bonnacon drenched in garum cream, hyssop and lovage. Starlight oysters garnished with saltbush and crushed pearls. Lichen cheese with bitterling and Pettavel wax. Persimmon and pink peppercorn sorbet, glittering with fairy dust.

I grab a plate and dig in.

Fancy food is better than I ever imagined. The flavours blend together, creating layers and levels that shift and evolve as they move through my mouth.

How am I ever going to eat gruel again after this?

A poppet approaches, bearing a tray featuring the finest in Oenotrian wines. I select a sparkling vintage and close my eyes in bliss as the bubbles fizz and pop on my tongue.

I'm halfway through my second plateful when Cendrillon arrives. I glimpse her carriage through the gardens – all gold and glass. Terrible design for a carriage if you ask me. What's the point of having one if it doesn't give you somewhere private to scratch your bum?

She hovers near the gate, away from the rest of us. I get the feeling that she doesn't really want to be here. The other candidates eye her jealously.

'I hear she sold her bastard son to a witch in exchange for that dress.'

'I heard she *is* a witch.'

'Typical.'

'I think she looks nice,' says Milly-Mae staunchly, which is on-brand.

'She's clearly a gold-digger,' says Rosamel, and I snort.

Ten pairs of eyes turn to me. 'What?' I say. 'We're all gold-diggers, aren't we?'

'I don't know how you can *eat*,' Octavia says with a sniff. 'What if the Prince arrives and you're stuffing your face?'

I shrug and snag myself a seared skvader fillet seasoned with matcha and just a hint of brimstone.

I'm not going to let these basic bitches ruin my holiday.

I wish I could take off these bloody shoes.

The Prince arrives ten minutes before midnight, looking like he'd rather be anywhere else. I've worked in the palace my whole life, but I've never actually seen him up close before. He's handsome enough, although his chin is a little weak for my taste. Rosamel, who has drunk too much sugar plum nectar on an empty stomach, goes charging up to him.

'I'm soooo glad you're here. I mean, finally? You and I are totally meant to be together because we understand what a burden it is to be rich.' She giggles. 'Regular people just don't understand, but *you* do, because you're my soul mate. I can tell.'

The Prince winces.

Rosamel laughs, so shrill and forced that it sets my teeth on edge. The other candidates hang back, letting Rosamel sign her own eviction notice.

'I'm the *complete package*,' she slurs, running her hands over the curves of her body.

She *does* have perfect breasts.

A passing poppet tops up my drink. 'Keep 'em coming,' I tell it with a wink.

This is great.

The clocks strike twelve, and Rosamel suddenly stumbles as her glass slippers crumble into glittering powder. She looks around, horrified, but the Prince is already gone.

'This is a mistake! You'll regret this! Don't you know who my father is?'

A pair of poppet footmen gently but firmly escort her out the gate, and then we are eleven.

I'm awoken midmorning on day two by one of the Prince's poppets opening my curtains and presenting me with a tray of delicate pastries and Abyssinian coffee.

Now *this* is what I'm talking about. Luxurious bedlinens, the longest sleep-in I've ever had, and breakfast in bed.

Except there's something I have to do, first.

I slip into the marble bathroom, hoping the poppet isn't looking too closely. I pull off my nightgown and inspect the night's growth.

I reach for a razor and get started.

'Ma'am,' the poppet says through the door.

I didn't know they could *talk*. 'Don't come in!' I tell it.

'Very well, ma'am. It's just – apologies, ma'am, but we don't know your name.'

I hesitate. 'Mossy.'

'We seem to have misplaced your luggage, Miss Mossy.'

'Just Mossy is fine. And I didn't bring any.'

There is the smallest pause as the poppet processes this. 'Very well, ma'am. If you'll permit me, I shall bring in some clothing options for today.'

'Knock yourself out.'

I laugh out loud when I see the gowns the poppet has selected for me. All flounces and tucks and frilly bits.

'Hard pass,' I tell it. 'Find me something more comfortable.'

We go through a few more rounds, and I finally settle on some wide-legged culottes and a tunic, both made from butter-soft Belfarsad linen. The poppet tries to do something with my hair, but I wave it away.

Then I sigh and put the stupid shoes on again. I guess every holiday has its downsides.

We are escorted to the far side of the pleasure gardens, where perfectly manicured lawns spill onto a white strip of beach and a boat the size of a city is awaiting us.

The yacht is well stocked with food and drinks, so I make myself comfortable on a deckchair and settle in for a very pleasant afternoon. Radegunda and Yutika position themselves at the prow, whooping as salt spray explodes around them. The twins are clad in impossibly impractical swimwear and drape themselves fetchingly over railings. Nadiva clutches a chair miserably. She comes from landlocked Khinvali and had to be coaxed onto the boat by sweet Milly-Mae, who held her hand patiently and murmured comforting things into her ear. Cendrillon stands apart from everyone, staring out to sea, the wind lifting her hair around her like a golden cloud. It's like she can feel me gawping, because she turns to look right at me, and I feel my cheeks grow hot.

The yacht moors beside a coral reef, and Gwenllian really comes into her own, diving from the yacht in a smooth arc and slipping beneath the surface of the ocean like a seal. She dives deep and returns to the surface with treasures for the Prince to inspect – a seven-pointed starfish, a bouquet of living coral, a giant pearl nestled in an oyster bed. The twins scowl at her and exchange bitter hisses. Milly-Mae makes sure that Nadiva has a cracker to nibble on, and a bucket, just in case.

I dangle my feet in the water, watching tiny fish nibble on my toes. A poppet presents me with a plate of cured featherfish with lemongrass and sargassum and a glass of sparkling elderflower wine. The sun is warm on my back, and I don't know how I'll be able to bear it when I get kicked out of here.

We return through the most stunning sunset I've ever seen, the wind in our faces and the ocean rolling beneath us.

Just as the yacht moors at the jetty, Nadiva spoils the perfection of the day by vomiting spectacularly all over the Prince, who chokes out a curse and flees.

Nobody is surprised when her shoes disintegrate at midnight.

On the third day, we are split into three teams for sports. I'm with Cendrillon and Milly-Mae. Cendrillon smiles at me as I move over to stand next to her.

'That colour suits you,' she says, gently brushing the shoulder of my waistcoat.

The waistcoat is green velvet with bone-and-gold buttons, each one carved into the shape of an animal. It's the first time Cendrillon has ever spoken to me, and it's like I've been bewitched. My throat closes over and my heart starts to pound. I can feel myself blushing – me! *Blushing!*

What even.

But despite my bumfuzzlement, I still notice Cendrillon's hands. They're not smooth and elegant like Gwenllian's or the twins'. Her hands are callused, with chewed nails and burn scars. They're the hands of someone who works for a living.

The plot thickens.

It is very difficult to complete an obstacle course in high heels. Gwenllian is as clumsy on land as she is graceful off it, much to the frustration of the twins, who are her teammates. They exchange murderous mutterings when they are eliminated.

'Come on, everyone,' cheers Milly-Mae, her cheeks glowing adorably. 'We can do it!'

We put up a valiant effort, but with Radegunda, Xenia and Yutika on the other team, we don't stand a chance. We're eliminated, and the three of them compete in an individual challenge that nobody is surprised to see Radegunda win.

The Prince arrives to crown her with a laurel wreath. He looks bored.

'I have proven myself the superior warrior,' Radegunda declares. 'Now you must face me in single combat.'

The Prince blinks and looks suddenly uncomfortable. 'Um,' he says. 'No?'

Radegunda bellows in fury. 'If you wish to marry me, you must honour *my* traditions. I could never marry a man inferior to me with a blade.'

She draws her broadsword and spits into the dirt.

'I'm very sorry,' the Prince says with an air of exhaustion, then turns and walks back towards his rooms.

'You would turn your back on me?' Radegunda yells, outraged. 'Coward! Jellyfish! Limpworm! I hope the rebels turn your balls into a door-knocker.'

She kicks off her glass slippers in disgust. 'Ridiculous hobbles,' she growls, sheathing her sword. 'May he be crushed under the boots of a thousand furious women.'

Amazing. I live to lounge another day.

I'm hopeful that we'll have a quiet fourth day, but we are woken early and herded onto a sleek bus with velvet upholstery and perfectly packaged individual breakfast boxes. We are taken to a shopping mall that has been cleared of regular people. One of the Prince's poppets explains to us that we are to curate an outfit for tonight's banquet. How this is supposed to help the Prince choose a future consort, I do not know.

The twins squeal with joy and scurry off.

I do a few laps of the shopping mall, past plastic mannequins with blank faces, and rack after rack of fiendishly expensive, impractical clothing. I hate everything about this place. I could never afford any of these clothes in a million lifetimes, and I wouldn't want to.

We reconvene at the bus. The twins are laden down with bags. The others mostly have one or two. I have nothing, because I like my green velvet waistcoat and I hate shopping.

Gwenllian can't stop scratching. 'It's the air-conditioning,' she explains. 'It dries out my skin.'

I see the twins exchange a glance. 'You *poor thing*,' says Octavia, her voice dripping with concern. 'That must be *so uncomfortable.*'

'You know what she needs?' Sophronia says to her sister. 'That special ointment we use. It always helps when we have dry skin.'

They produce the ointment back at the pleasure gardens – a suspicious-looking paste in an old jam jar. I wasn't born yesterday but clearly Gwenllian was, because she thanks them and smears the ointment all over her arms and shoulders and neck.

By the time we get to the banquet, her skin is flaking off in giant papery strips, and she's in tears.

The Prince looks at her with some degree of sympathy. 'Are you ready to go home?' he asks.

She gives a tiny nod and hiccups.

The twins titter as the clock strikes twelve and Gwenllian's shoes turn to powder.

On the fifth day, we all paint portraits of the Prince. I make mine as forgettable as possible. Cendrillon's is clumsy but adorable. Xenia's is almost photorealistic. One of the twins 'accidentally' bumps Milly-Mae's hand as she passes, giving the Prince a second nose. But Jadwiga has no skill with a brush, and her painting looks more like a potato than a prince. She goes home at midnight.

I awake on the sixth morning with a very strong feeling that I'm on borrowed time. I should have been sent home by now. But I shave the moss from my skin as usual and put on a cream linen shirt, loose trousers and the green velvet waistcoat.

We are each given a scheduled private interview with the Prince. I'm to go last, after Cendrillon. I assume that's when he'll realise that I'm here under false pretences. Better make the most of the buffet today.

When Octavia emerges from her interview, she whispers something to Sophronia and they head over to Cendrillon, who is sitting demurely by a stream, tossing crumbs to the giant koi.

'*Dear* Cendrillon,' Octavia says. 'Can we join you?'

'We *really* want to get to know you,' says Sophronia. 'You are just *so* interesting, and we're *desperate* to be friends.'

Octavia nods and holds out a box of chocolates.

Cendrillon hesitates, but she seems to know that she can't refuse without offending the twins. So she takes a chocolate – the smallest one in the box – and slips it into her mouth.

Octavia's lip curls in a smile.

When Cendrillon heads off to her interview with the Prince, I slip away from the buffet and follow the lanterns up a hill to the secluded spot where Cendrillon and the Prince are talking.

Or at least, are supposed to be talking.

They're sitting side by side on an ornate carved wooden bench, under the fragrant boughs of a cedar tree draped with jasmine. I lurk behind a gardenia bush and watch.

Cendrillon sits demurely, almost glowing with beauty in the golden afternoon.

The Prince doesn't seem captivated by her, though. He doesn't even look at her. He is gazing off into the distance, lost in his own thoughts.

The silence stretches on interminably.

At last, the Prince sighs. 'I suppose you should tell me something about yourself.'

Smooth, buddy. Real smooth.

Cendrillon opens her mouth to reply, then shuts it again, clapping a hand over her face. Her expression is alarmed.

'Are you okay?' the Prince asks.

Cendrillon convulses, and I wonder if the Prince is going to get thrown up on again. Her jaw is clamped closed, but I can see her cheeks bulging as if something is moving inside her mouth. The Prince edges away from her just as Cendrillon's mouth is forced open and a fat, warty toad slips from between her lips and plops into her lap.

The Prince lets out a horrified noise and leaps to his feet. He's gone within moments, leaving Cendrillon sitting there, her cheeks flushed with embarrassment.

The toad hops down from her lap and disappears into the undergrowth.

I wait a few moments, then step out from my hiding spot and offer her a peppermint from my waistcoat pocket. She hesitates.

'Don't worry,' I tell her. 'It's not enchanted. You should know better than to take gifts from the twins.'

Tears slip from Cendrillon's glistening eyes, like shining stars falling through the night. 'I don't want to go home,' she whispers.

Me either.

I head back to the buffet. The twins are lounging on a swing, looking triumphant.

I hesitate.

I shouldn't get involved. The Prince won't want to see me now. This is my chance to keep flying under the radar. To stay an extra night.

I'm still trying to talk myself out of it as I head to the Prince's chambers. A poppet guarding the entrance tries to stop me.

'I didn't get my interview,' I tell it.

'Apologies, ma'am. The Prince isn't taking any more interviews today.'

I draw myself up and try to channel some of Radegunda's confidence. 'I *insist*.'

It works. Maybe I should try being assertive more often.

The Prince is wearing a dressing gown and looking like I am the last person in the world he wants to see.

'It was the twins,' I tell him without preamble. 'They slipped her something. Hence the toad.'

He blinks, surprised that I've spoken. Frankly, I'm surprised too.

'Fine,' he says, moving to shut the door.

And again, I can't help myself. 'Aren't you wondering who I am?' I ask him. 'Haven't you noticed that Anais Giada isn't here?'

His brow crinkles in confusion. 'Who?'

'Did you even choose the candidates?'

He shrugs.

'You don't want to be here,' I say.

He shrugs again, but there's something in his eyes. He looks exhausted. I guess he's worried about the war, the rebellion.

'Why do it, then? If you don't want to marry any of us, then why go through the whole parade?'

His expression grows cold. 'I think we're done here.'

So that's me done, then. Oh well. It's been a good holiday. And I'm *so* ready to take these shoes off.

I head back to my room. Lie down on the feather-bed one last time. Stuff myself full of dates and blackcurrant wine and crumbly bellarmine cheese. Open my wardrobe and let my hands run over the buttery linens and silks. My hand pauses on the green velvet waistcoat with the gold-and-bone buttons. Each button is exquisitely carved in the shape of a different animal – fox, rabbit, crow, mouse and hedgehog – and surrounded with gold filigree. Each animal has a twinkling green emerald eye.

They are tiny works of art.

And just one of them is worth more money than I could earn in a lifetime.

Would anyone notice if a button disappeared? Buttons fall off clothes all the time. It could have been lost anywhere – the mall, the gardens, the yacht.

One button would be more than enough for me to get out of here. To slip over the border to Lothian, where there are no princes and no courts. I could rent a little shop or something. Live my own life and leave this beautiful, awful world behind.

I emerge just before midnight, wearing my old T-shirt and jeans. I can't say I'm ready to go home, but I know when my number is up.

The prince appears just after I do.

Cendrillon is tear-stained, standing in the shadows. The twins look triumphant, right up until the moment that the clock strikes twelve and their shoes crumble to dust.

Both of them.

Everyone is totally silent.

The prince glances at me and gives an almost imperceptible nod before turning and heading back inside.

No girl goes home on the seventh night. The prince doesn't appear, and we have a quiet evening in our own chambers. This is exactly what I wanted – a fabulous dinner of roast guineafowl with tansy and crow corn, and only myself for company. But I feel restless. I go out for a walk in the moonlight and bump into Milly-Mae, who seems unsettled as well, her eyes darting around me as if she's looking for ghosts.

'You seem nice,' she says, which is meaningless because Milly-Mae thinks everyone is nice. 'Can I tell you something?'

'Sure.'

'Maybe don't stick around here for too long. Things are going to get ugly.'

They've been ugly all along, if you ask me. But it's sweet of Milly-Mae to look out for me. I bid her goodnight and head back to my room. As I pass the waterfall, I spot

Cendrillon gazing up at the moon and weeping.

I don't disturb her.

Yutika goes home on the eighth night after a humiliating singing contest, and Xenia on the ninth after their sponge cake fails to rise. I keep catching Cendrillon staring at me. Does she know that I told the Prince about what the twins did? Does she know about the mouse button I've got tucked into my underwear? Does she know that I had a filthy dream last night, and she was a special guest star?

I assume the tenth day will be my last.

Milly-Mae, Cendrillon and I get a speech from one of the poppets about how we will be expected to lay down our lives to protect the Prince and his children, should we be chosen. Then we sweat through a series of self-defence drills – or Prince-defence drills, I guess. The Prince reluctantly emerges after lunch, and a hilarious pantomime ensues where the poppets pretend to be assassins and the three of us fight them off. The poppets aren't trying very hard, and frankly neither am I. But Cendrillon and Milly-Mae are giving it their all, cheeks becomingly flushed, mouths set in determination.

The twist comes unexpectedly. Milly-Mae effectively disarms a poppet-assassin, then whirls in a blur of movement towards the Prince and buries the knife in his chest.

'For Sassenach, and the revolution!' she hisses, giving the knife a savage twist.

I am totally frozen in shock.

Milly-Mae? A forreals rebel assassin? Apple-cheeked, wholesome Milly-Mae?

She speaks some complicated string of words I don't understand, and the poppets suddenly go limp and floppy, like their bones have turned to jelly. They crumple to the ground, and the Prince does too, his face white as bone. Milly-Mae turns and flees, vanishing into the thick greenery of the pleasure gardens, and, despite my shock, I'm genuinely impressed at her ability to run in the ridiculous glass slippers.

Cendrillon comes over all efficient, and she crisply orders me to help her gently lift the Prince and carry him to his chambers. I don't know if she's done this sort of thing before, but she seems totally in control, organising boiling water and clean towels. She rips the Prince's shirt open and inspects the wound.

'Get me that,' she orders, pointing at a bottle of Taaffeite whiskey on a nearby shelf. I hand it to her and she uncorks the bottle with her teeth, pouring the contents onto the Prince's wound, where it sizzles and steams.

I choke a little, and it isn't just the smell of caraway, myrrh, and burning flesh. A single swallow of Taaffeite whiskey is worth several king's ransoms.

I like this version of Cendrillon. She's a boss, no longer hiding behind shyness or demure reticence. We work hard to save the Prince, cleaning and stitching the wound. Cendrillon's brow beads with sweat, and I wipe it for her. She flashes me a grateful smile, and my knees tremble a little. I make sure she stays hydrated and bring her the things she needs and hold the things that need holding. His breathing evens out, and we wait by his side until the sun starts to creep over the horizon, staining the world pink and violet.

Then something goes wrong. The Prince heaves a great, bubbling cough, and I notice that the bandage over his wound is soaked dark with blood.

Cendrillon makes a frustrated noise. 'I don't know what else to do,' she mutters. 'The bleeding has started again and I can't make it stop.'

Everything is slippery and red.

I don't know much about medicine.

But I do know a lot about moss.

Cendrillon hasn't noticed the green fuzz that sprouted all over me as we worked through the night.

I rake my fingers through it, lifting it off in chunks. I gently elbow Cendrillon aside and press the moss into the Prince's wound, packing it tight. He moans a little, his body trembling.

But the bleeding stops.

I glance over at Cendrillon, expecting disgust, but I find only respect and curiosity.

'Does this happen a lot?' she asks, nodding at my mossy limbs.

There's no point in lying. 'Every morning. The mistress at the boarding house where I grew up said it was a curse, but I think it's just annoying.'

'I think it's beautiful,' she says, softly, and reaches out a hand. 'May I?'

I nod, and she touches a gentle hand to my arm, running her fingers down the green velvety growth. It sets my flesh tingling.

I clear my throat. 'Milly-Mae, huh?' I say. 'Who'd have thought?'

'I know. I guess it's down to you and me now.'

I chuckle. 'I don't think I'd make a very good wife,' I say.

'I would,' Cendrillon says bleakly. 'I'm obedient. A great housekeeper. I only speak when I'm spoken to. And beautiful to boot.'

She says it like she has a curse of her own.

'What's your deal?' I ask. 'You're not rich, are you? You're like me. You've lived a hard life.' I glance down at her chapped hands.

She sighs. 'Evil stepmother,' she explains. 'Fairy godmother. You can fill in the rest.'

'Huh. Landed on your feet, though, didn't you?'

'I guess so. I didn't ask for any of this. I would have preferred a small bag of coin and a fast horse.'

I think about the mouse button with its glittering emerald eye.

Perhaps I should give it to her.

Perhaps I should ask her to come with me.

We gaze at one another, each one working through private calculations and hypotheticals. Cendrillon's eyes dart to the Prince.

'He'll be okay now,' she says. 'The Royal Guard will be here soon.'

I swallow. 'They'll have a lot of questions for us,' I say.

Cendrillon nods.

'For me, in particular,' I say. 'I didn't really get chosen. I stole the shoes.'

She doesn't look hugely surprised, which is fair. 'You probably don't want to be here when they arrive.'

I swallow, then flee back to my room. I don't have time to shave the moss away, but I rinse the dried blood from my hands and change clothes again, back to my jeans and T-shirt. I kick off the glass shoes for the last time. I'll have to go barefoot.

The mouse button is in my pocket.

I have to run, even though every ounce of me is screaming to go back to Cendrillon's side.

I slip out into the hallway, but I'm too late.

The sound of soldiers is everywhere. Boots stamp down the hallway, and rough voices bark orders.

I don't think I can get out.

I head down a corridor, then another, not even sure where I'm trying to go.

Someone reaches out and yanks me into a small closet. Seconds later, the tramping feet pass right by the door.

'You smell amazing,' Cendrillon whispers. 'Like mossy stones and icy streams.'

We're pressed right up against each other. I can feel her chest rise and fall with her breath. Her heart thuds against mine. Nothing has ever felt so right.

I kiss her, because why the hell not? And to my utter delight, she kisses me back, a deep kiss that involves teeth and tongue and hips and makes me think that perhaps Cendrillon isn't nearly as sweet and innocent as she looks.

I guess this is goodbye.

The footsteps recede. We break off the kiss and step out into the corridor.

Cendrillon is wearing loose trousers and a button-up shirt, her hair tied back in a braid and her face scrubbed of makeup. She's never looked more beautiful.

'Ready?' she asks me.

I'm confused. 'Are you—' I notice she's holding a pillowcase that clinks as she shifts it from one shoulder to the other, like it's full of candlesticks or goblets or something.

'Oh, I'm coming with you,' she says. 'Did I not make that clear?'

I reach out for her hand. Our fingers interlace.

I can't believe this is happening.

We race down the hallways to the entrance to the gardens. The sound of the soldiers has dimmed, and for a moment I think we're going to make it.

But the Prince is there, blocking our way. He's grey-faced and half-dressed, leaning on the wall, but the bandage is still white. The moss worked. He takes us in – our travelling clothes, our clasped hands. Cendrillon's pillowcase.

I'm pretty sure we can't lie our way out of this one. I open my mouth, hoping an excuse will emerge. But instead, truth spills out.

'The thing is,' I tell the Prince, 'neither of us want to be your princess. I'm sure you're very nice – actually, I have no idea what you're like. But we're both regular people with shitty lives, looking for something better. It doesn't need to be a palace full of luxuries. But you have so much, and we have nothing. I – I stole a button. I apologise for that, but I'm not sorry.'

The Prince listens.

'I don't want you to be my princess either,' he says. 'Honestly, I don't want a princess, or a prince. I'm trying to prevent a war. Getting married is the last thing on my mind.'

'Why do it, then?' I ask.

He shrugs. 'My father believes in tradition.'

Cendrillon speaks up. 'You could run away with us.'

The Prince shakes his head. 'Not today. Thank you for the offer, though.'

He looks around as shouts ring out and footsteps start to grow loud again. 'Follow the hill up past the big alder tree,' he says, 'and then down to the blue rockery. There's a hidden door in the wall there, behind the largest rock. You can get out that way.'

Cendrillon reaches out and brushes his cheek with her delicate fingers. 'Thank you,' she says.

He nods. 'Go.'

And we go. We follow his directions as the tranquil beauty of the pleasure gardens is shattered by the clanking of armour and the stink of horses. We find the hidden door, and we slip out.

The border is only a few miles away. Cendrillon has thoughtfully included a cold pie, two apples and a skin of fresh water in her pillowcase. We can be free by nightfall.

Between Cendrillon's pillowcase of fancy tableware and my gold-and-bone button, we'll have enough money to make a fresh start in Lothian.

We. The thought of it makes something inside me roar. I've never been a *we*. It's always just been me against the world.

Cendrillon reaches out and takes my hand. I glance at her, and she grins, and there's a wickedness to it that I really, *really* like. I can't wait to start a life with her.

Perhaps we'll open up a shoe shop.

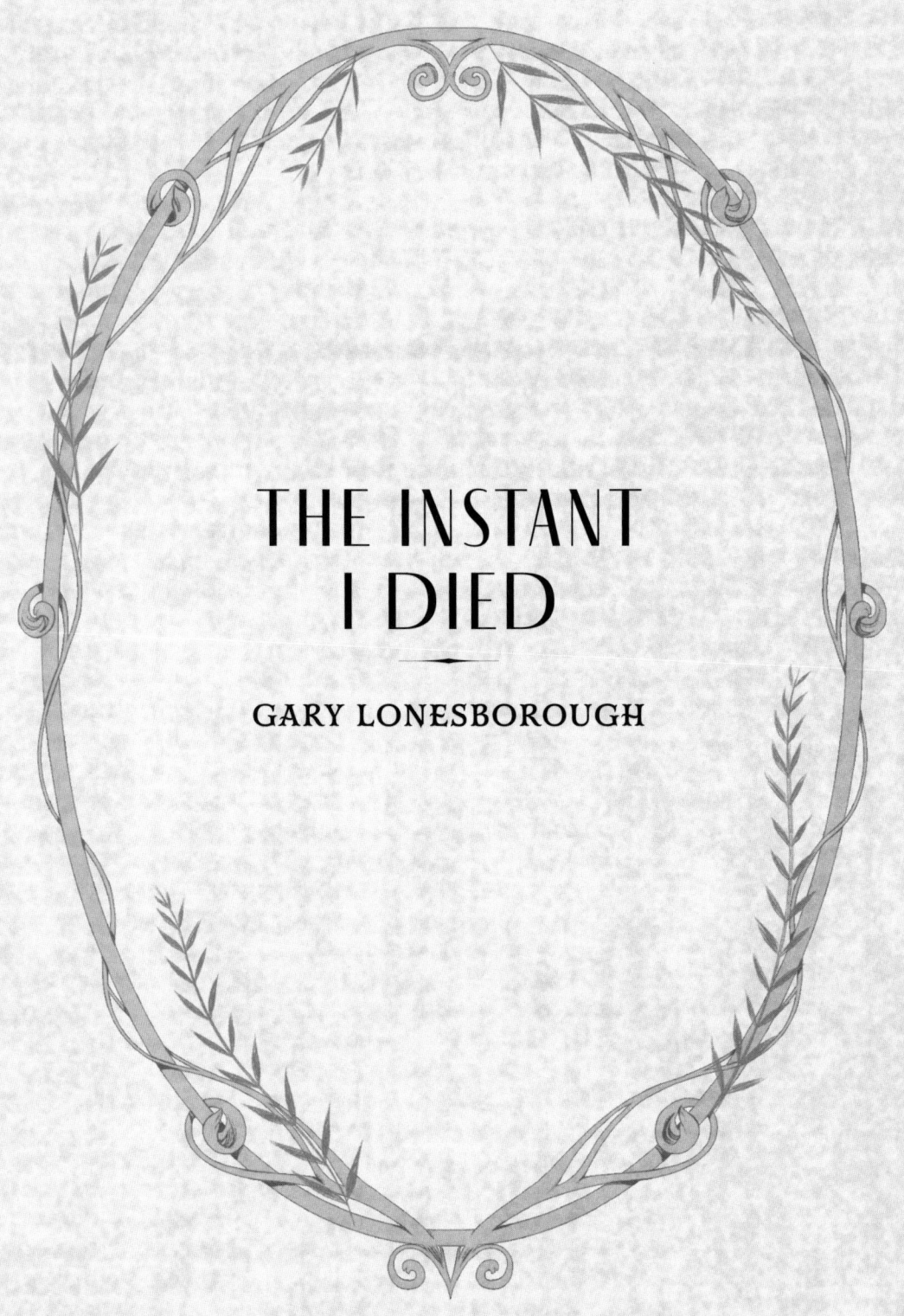

THE INSTANT I DIED

GARY LONESBOROUGH

The instant I died, I saw black smoke. It swirled around me like fog. There was no sky, no ground … nothing. Just thick black smoke.

Shapes began to emerge. Squares. Windows. Windows showing moments – moments that led me to here.

The sun was beginning to rise as I creaked open my bedroom window. The rays shone over the grassy hill above and looked like the gates of heaven opening.

I lowered my bag to the dirt below and let my legs follow. I fastened my bag over my shoulders and took one last look at the green hills of the farm where the sun rises in the morning.

I walked quickly for the gates at the end of the long dirt driveway.

This is it, I thought. *The last time I will walk down this driveway.*

My heart thumped hard in my chest when I saw the green hood of Robin's Ford Laser waiting for me behind the gates. Its engine rumbled like the stirring in my stomach as I climbed over the steel and my shoes hit the dirt. Robin was resting his head against his window. I slid my bag onto the back seat and climbed in the front.

'Finally,' Robin said. 'I've been sitting here for ten minutes.'

'Sorry.'

Robin swept his brown hair to the side and smiled to me. He was wearing his jean jacket, and he smelled like Dove men's deodorant. I looked at the freckles on his brown face and thought: *god, you're beautiful.* I leaned over and kissed him. His lips tasted like toothpaste.

'You sure you're up for this?' he asked.

'If you go, I go,' I said. 'Besides, I've had enough. If Dad tells me one more time that I need to mend my relationship with god, I'm gonna blow up a tractor.'

'Yeah. Forget him, ay?' Robin said, cupping my cheek. 'You're destined for big things.'

Robin put the car into drive and we set off along the road. I turned up the stereo and it played just what I needed to hear to begin my escape: Kylie Minogue. It reminded me of how I met Robin. I had sat across from him at a desk in the school library. It was lunch and I needed to finish my biology assignment, which was due next period. Robin had his earphones in, reading *Animal Farm*. His music was up loud enough for me to recognise the tune. He was listening to Kylie's 'In Your Eyes'. He was the first person I'd ever met who listened to Kylie like me.

In the car, I turned Kylie up to full volume. We passed the farmlands and turned onto the highway, heading for Sydney, for Robin's cousin Maureen's place. Robin said we'd be safe there – that we could finally start our lives together. We wouldn't have to be a secret in Sydney. We could be in love anywhere we went in Sydney.

We stopped at McDonalds for breakfast.

'I just realised it's our anniversary,' I said to Robin as we ate hotcakes in the carpark.

'Holy shit. Really?'

'Yep. I remember it was three days before my seventeenth.'

Robin smiled at me then reached over to take my hand.

'Well, happy anniversary, then,' he said.

At a service station, Robin bought me a box of Cadbury Roses. 'To celebrate,' he said as he handed the chocolates to me.

We passed the town of Albion Park, which was as far north as I'd ever travelled before. The stereo entered hour number four of Kylie Minogue. We were still singing along to every song.

I took over the driving for an hour, then settled in for a short nap while Robin drove. With my eyes still closed, I reached out my hand and rested my palm on Robin's forearm. He took my hand and held it against his knee. I was drifting off to sleep and I wasn't so alone anymore – I had my boyfriend right beside me. We were going to move to Sydney, share a room at Maureen's place and eventually, get our own flat. I was going to study acting part-time like I always wanted to, and Robin was going to do his certificate in community services. Most importantly, we could be boyfriends without those guys from school throwing around slurs, without my dad telling me I was going to hell, without feeling like my brain was wrong and all messed up.

I woke as we passed Wollongong. I turned on my phone for the first time. There were three missed calls from Dad, followed by a text: *Where are you? Call me.*

I turned my phone back off and slipped it into my pocket.

'Mum called me,' Robin said. 'Said your dad dropped by, looking for you.'

'What did she tell him?' I asked.

'Just that she hadn't seen you, but that you might be with me. She told him I was going camping with a couple of friends and that you might have tagged along.'

I loved Robin's mum. She was fully supportive of Robin taking me with him. She knew the way the community looked at me and Robin.

The car began to jolt. Robin accelerated, then the car began to jerk and sounded like it was coughing. Smoke started to puff from beneath the hood.

'Crap,' Robin said. He steered us onto the dirt by the side of the highway and we came to a stop at the top of a little hill surrounded by bushlands. I checked my phone. *SOS ONLY*.

I began to chuckle.

'What's so funny?' Robin asked, rubbing his temples.

'I mean, it's pretty romantic, right? Being stuck in the middle of nowhere with the boy I love.'

'We've never said we *love* each other,' Robin said.

'Well,' I said, placing my hand on his knee. 'I *love* you.'

Robin smiled, sucked in his lips and looked out the window for a moment. When he turned back to me, his cheeks were red. 'I love you too.'

He kissed me. All thoughts of our predicament disappeared as our shirts and shorts came off and we moved to the back seat. I grasped Robin's shoulders as he shuffled on top of me, his waist between my legs. It was hot as hell in the car and his face was wet with sweat, but I didn't care.

We lay there in each other's arms with the car windows down. It wasn't long before it was pitch-black outside and cold had come in. Robin pulled a blanket over us.

'Definitely never thought I'd spend an anniversary in a broken-down car in the middle of nowhere,' Robin said, with his head resting on my chest.

'Really? This was always a goal of mine,' I teased, running my fingers through his long, straight hair. I knew he liked it when I did that.

'I guess we'll have to walk into town in the morning,' Robin said, checking the map he had downloaded on his phone. 'Forty minute walk. I'll give mum a call and we'll figure something out.'

'Mmm. I need to piss.'

Robin sat up and I pulled on my shirt and shorts and shoes. I got out of the car and had goosebumps immediately. It was freezing and so dark ahead, but with the light of the full moon I could make out the bodies of the tall trees as I walked to them.

After I pissed, I started back for the car. Robin's face was half-lit by the moonlight as he sat on the backseat. The shadows over the left side of his face made him look dangerous and sexy. A smile came to my face – I was so lucky I found him. On the road, I spotted an echidna. It was just standing there by the centre lines. There was a distant rumble of a car, so I headed to the road.

'Hey, little buddy,' I said to the echidna. 'You better get off the road.' The echidna stayed still. 'Little buddy,' I said, knowing full well it couldn't understand what I was saying. I stepped towards it, hoping to scare it away.

'What are you doing?' Robin asked from his window.

'There's an echidna on the road,' I said. 'A car's coming. I can hear it.'

I took a step closer to the echidna and it shuffled across the road away from me.

'See?' I said to Robin. 'Just wanted to scare him off the road.'

Robin shook his head with a smile. Light beamed over the hill. A truck came speeding, like a giant moving Christmas tree.

High beams.

Roaring engine.

Screeching tires on the bitumen.

I screamed because that was all I could seem to do. Robin screamed.

I closed my eyes.

Blackness. Endless blackness.

Black smoke.

I didn't understand.

I was somewhere else.

A flash in the distance caught my eye.

Windows.

Windows emerged from the smoke. In one window, I saw two red lights. The red lights belonged to the truck that killed me. It was pulled over to the side of the road, by the bush. There was red all over the road – spilt wine from the back wooden tray of the truck.

I guess the bottles shattered with the frantic braking.

I couldn't reach through the window. I was stuck at the glass – the glass between me and the real world. I didn't understand. I thought I might be dreaming. A nightmare.

There was a man on the road. He had a goatee and wore a flannel shirt and jeans. His eyes were wide and teary. His lips were shaking, like he was shivering.

A scream rang out – Robin's scream. I saw him on his knees on the road, kneeling in red, but it was not wine. Blood covered his knees as he knelt beside a body. His hands were on the body, crying like I'd never heard him ever cry before.

'Robin, what's happening?' I asked. He didn't answer. He didn't seem to hear me. 'Robin!'

I recognised the brown legs now painted red: they were mine. It was my body in the road. It was me. The bloody puddle Robin was kneeling in was growing with each passing second.

'What are you doing?' Robin yelled. 'Help us! Help us!'

The man with the goatee was startled by Robin's calls. He took a step back, shaking his head, tears flowing from his eyes.

'Help us! He's dying!' Robin shouted.

The man with the goatee turned and ran back to the truck. He got in and drove away, spinning the tyres as he accelerated. Robin raced for the car, took out his phone and called for an ambulance.

As Robin rushed to my body again, his knees on the bloody puddle, I began to think maybe this was the afterlife. Maybe there would soon be some kind of white light coming to take me away.

I began to imagine what the papers would say: *Aboriginal teen hit by truck while crossing highway*. Maybe there would be no story at all. Maybe the story about the gay Aboriginal teen killed on the highway wouldn't really be newsworthy.

'Robin,' I said. 'I'm sorry.'

Robin recited the truck's licence plate number to the person on the phone, still crying. I just wanted to tell him I was still there.

'Robin!' I yelled, but he didn't hear me. 'Robin, I'm here.'

He placed his phone beside my body and rested his head on my chest. My blood was all over his face, his arms, his clothes. 'I'm sorry, Robin,' I said.

Smoke descended over the window. Blackness came over me again. In the black smoke, I waited for the white light.

There was nothing. No pain, no drifting smell, just blackness.

A new window appeared in the smoke.

A police car.

It was morning in some neighbourhood, in some town I didn't know. The truck that killed me sat in one of the driveways, and the police car waited at the gutter. The front door opened and out came the man with the goatee. He was crying. His arms were behind his back. Two police officers led him out of the house. Behind them walked a woman in a suit.

They took him to the police car and loaded him in the back. He was still crying. Now that he was closer to the window, I could hear him saying he was sorry. He looked smaller than he did when he stood on the highway and watched me die.

As the police car drove up the street, cries rang out from the house. At the open front door was a toddler trying to race onto the lawn, but a tall woman with red hair was holding them back.

'Dad!' the toddler called.

They were crying and so was the mother. She wrangled the child back inside and closed the door. I didn't get it. Why was I seeing this?

The image in the window flashed in a puff of smoke, then another appeared and showed me the inside of the police station. The man with the goatee was being placed into a holding cell. The officers left, then it was just me and the man with the goatee. He was hunched forward on his little steel bench, his elbows on his knees, his face in his hands.

'Can you hear me?' I asked. He kept his face in his hands. 'You killed me. I'm dead because of you.'

He didn't respond.

'Hey!' I shouted. 'You killed me!'

He glanced up, looked around his cell. He shook his head, then returned his face to his hands. Maybe he heard me.

I turned away from the man with the goatee, and then black smoke consumed the window again.

More windows emerged from the smoke. One showed Robin in the back of the car, on top of me. He was breathing heavy and fast. I could smell his shampoo as his hair messed all over my face.

The sound of something smashing dragged my attention to another window. Through it, I could see a phone shattered on the kitchen floor at home. Dad was standing there at the sink, crying.

He wiped away his tears and screamed, though it sounded like a roar. He roared so loud it burned through the black smoke around me. He swung his arms at the dishrack and all the dishes smashed to the floor. Dad rushed to the wall and punched a hole in it, roaring again. Then he slumped to the floor and lay on his side. He brought his knees to his chest and held them.

I couldn't watch him cry like that. I turned away to another window. It showed me the end of the driveway, where Robin picked me up. I wanted to cry myself. I was not ready to die. I wanted to be with Robin. I needed to be with him.

I searched through the smoke, looking for a window with Robin's face in it.

Within the black, I could see a small beam of orange light. It sliced through the smoke like a knife, growing stronger and nearer with each moment passing. I wondered what was coming for me. Maybe heaven. Maybe hell. Maybe something else. Maybe nothing. All I knew was I was not ready to go yet.

I turned away from the light and moved deeper into the black smoke. A window emerged from the dark and in it, I could see Robin. He was walking up the steps to a small, brown-bricked house. He knocked on the door and a tall Aboriginal woman opened it. She was wearing a black shirt with the Aboriginal flag across her chest. She smiled at Robin as she looked over him, then she hugged him.

'I'm so sorry, little cuz,' she said. It must have been Maureen – the cousin of Robin's we were going to stay with. She hugged Robin tight. She loved him. She was going to give him the love he needed. Somehow, I could feel it.

I kept watching Robin through the window as the afternoon turned into night. He ate dinner with Maureen and her partner, Jay. He was this towering Samoan guy with the biggest muscles I'd ever seen. They ate quietly at first, then Maureen and Robin took turns telling stories about growing up together in the country before Maureen moved away. Robin laughed and smiled and his eyes didn't look so red anymore.

Bedtime came and Robin slept on the futon in the lounge room. I watched him for a while. He was snoring quietly. His eyelids looked heavy.

'I'm right here,' I whispered to him. 'I love you.'

Morning came. Robin was woken by Maureen and Jay, and they all had bacon and eggs together. I was still there. The window hadn't disappeared and the orange beam hadn't returned. Maybe I'd be stuck there forever, watching through the window. Maybe that was okay, because it meant I could be with Robin.

The days drifted past almost without me noticing. The window followed Robin everywhere he went. I was with him as he took a barista course and had a job interview at a café. I was with him when he answered the questions and forced the smile on his face. He undid his top button as soon as he left the café.

I was with Robin when he turned eighteen. I was with him when Maureen dragged him out to a queer nightclub with a few of her friends. He looked so hot as he danced in his loose white singlet and jean shorts. A tall white guy with a beard danced with him. He kissed Robin but Robin pushed him away and kept dancing. When he got home, Robin cried. He looked at a photo of me and him on his phone as he cried quietly to himself.

'It's okay,' I whispered to him. 'I'm always here.'

The days flowed by like a steady river.

A new day arrived and the window showed me Robin and Maureen travelling in Maureen's car. Robin was dressed in a white shirt and black pants. They drove a few hours south to a small town. They parked outside a tall building with white bricks and glass doors. Inside, they walked through a foyer and a security screening. I followed them into a big room with white walls – it was the courthouse. The door opened and the man with the goatee entered, guided by two court officers. His goatee had been trimmed and his hair cut short.

Robin stood at a podium. His hands were shaky and there was sweat seeping from his forehead. He took a piece of paper from his pocket, unfolded it and read his words to the courtroom.

'As I knelt by my boyfriend's bloody, mangled body, you just stared,' Robin said to the man with the goatee. 'When I called to you for help, over and over and over, you just stared. When you realised what you had done, you didn't help. You got in your truck and drove away. You left my boyfriend in the middle of the road to die.'

Tears escaped Robin's eyes as he spoke, but he didn't stray from his words. He and Maureen left when he was done.

Night came and Maureen stood at the door of the spare room, which had become Robin's room. He was lying on his bed, watching *Friends* on his laptop.

'The verdict was set for the thirteenth. You want to go?' she asked. Robin nodded.

Another day arrived and the window stopped following Robin – now it showed me only his empty bedroom. Another day passed and Robin had not come home. I searched through the smoke for more windows, but I couldn't find Robin in any of them, so I stayed by the window showing me the empty room.

Days passed. Robin had not returned. He was always a clean-freak, but now, dirty clothes were scattered on the floor. There were scrunched receipts on his desk, and his desk was a little dusty. He hadn't made his bed in weeks.

It was the day before the thirteenth when Robin came home late. Maureen spoke quickly and loudly, telling Robin to text her when he's not going to be home for dinner and that she doesn't like worrying about him. Robin just said he was sorry, then he went to his room. He locked the door behind him and took off his black hoodie. He sat on the side of his bed and unzipped the pocket on his hoodie. He pulled out a gun. It was a small black revolver with a brown grip.

The window moved closer to Robin as he clicked open the barrel. From his pocket, he took six little gold bullets and loaded them into their slots.

'What the hell have you done?' I asked. 'What are you doing, Robin?'

He didn't answer. He closed the gun and took it to his desk, where he placed it into his drawer.

The thirteenth arrived, and Robin and Maureen dressed up again in their white shirts and black pants. Robin wrapped the gun in his hoodie and held it in his lap as they drove out of the city and back to the small town.

'Don't be a fucking idiot,' I said to Robin as they pulled up at the courthouse. They got out of the car and Robin pulled on his hoodie. He reached his hand into the pocket and gripped the gun.

He walked with Maureen into the courthouse. Ahead, he saw the security screenings.

'Can I get your keys?' Robin asked Maureen. 'I want to put my hoodie back.'

Maureen handed him the car keys and he took his hoodie and the gun back to the car, then met Maureen back inside the courtroom, where they sat towards the back. Robin was sweating. His hands were shaky as he tried to hold them between his knees.

The man with the goatee stood before his sentencing. Robin's fists were clenched on his knees. I wanted to place my hand on his shoulder, tell him it'll be okay.

Judge read out the verdict for the man with the goatee: *not guilty*. Judge said the man couldn't have avoided hitting me and killing me, that it was my fault for standing in the middle of the road in the middle of the night. Judge said that the driver couldn't have had enough time to react when he got over that hill. It was wrong – all wrong.

If only my skin was white.

Robin stood and left. The man with the goatee was crying tears of joy at the front of the courtroom. The window followed Robin.

Outside, Robin was leaning against the passenger door of Maureen's car, crying but wiping the tears away before they could escape his cheek. I stayed with Robin while he stood there. I wished I could wrap my arms around him, let him know he was not alone. But I couldn't. All I could do was be near him.

'I'm sorry, Jack,' Robin whispered.

'Robin? Can you see me?'

Robin wiped away another tear as he spotted Maureen coming out of the courthouse. 'He's not getting away with it.'

Maureen came to the car and gave Robin a hug. She held him tight.

'It's alright, little cuz,' she said. 'You'll be okay.'

'No, I won't be,' Robin said, breaking from the hug.

Maureen nodded. They watched the man with the goatee when he came out of the courthouse with his wife. He got into a black car with his wife and someone else, then they drove away. Robin reached into his pocket and pulled out the car keys. He got in the driver's seat and quickly locked the doors.

'What are you doing?' Maureen asked. 'Robin?'

'They don't care about Jack,' Robin shouted back through the closed window. 'They don't care about the gay black kid who got killed in a hit-and-run. Jack's dead. He took Jack's whole life away from him.'

'I know,' Maureen said. 'We'll fight it. You just have to be patient.'

'I need to tell him. I need him to know I'll never give up on Jack,' Robin said, then he started the car and drove after the man with the goatee.

We came to the house – a house I had seen before through the windows in the smoke – where I saw the man with the goatee get arrested.

Robin parked the car a few houses away and watched as the man with the goatee and his wife got out of the car in their driveway and walked inside.

Robin took a deep breath, holding the hoodie in his lap.

He got out of the car. Before he closed the door, he threw the hoodie back on the car seat. He shoved the gun down the front of his pants and began the twenty-metre walk to the house.

I was jolted away from the window like something had yanked me back. The black smoke flew through me like bullets. I stumbled through the smoke, peering into the windows emerging around me.

I saw Robin shooting the man with the goatee in the chest. The wife screamed and ran out of sight.

Robin went to prison – just one in an ocean of black faces.

In his fifth year, he got into a fight, spent weeks in hospital and almost died.

Robin got out of prison when he was thirty-five.

He tried to get a job, but he couldn't.

In his eighth month out of prison, Robin was evicted from his apartment. He went to Maureen, but she didn't let him back in. She yelled at him, saying she felt guilty about the man with the goatee's death because she drove Robin to court.

Robin lived on the streets, begging and stealing food to survive. He was caught shoplifting and went to prison again.

On his tenth day back in prison, he pricked his finger on a piece of metal in his cell. His finger became infected, and the infection spread into his blood and then his heart.

Robin got terribly sick, then died alone in a hospital bed inside the prison. There was no one around when he died, and no one realised he was dead until an hour later.

I had died in an instant. It took Robin years to die, but it all started here. I wasn't going to let that happen.

'Robin!' I shouted again. 'Robin! Stop!'

In the smoke, a window rose in front of me. Robin was walking to the house. I was shouting with everything I had, everything I was. With every shout, the window grew bigger, scattered the smoke around me like a wind.

'Robin!'

Robin stopped as he reached the lawn at the front of the house. He turned around.

'Don't do it, Robin!'

Robin was staring right into my eyes. Tears came to his.

'Jack?' he whispered.

'Don't do it,' I said. 'You'll ruin your life if you do this. This is not how you get revenge. You get your revenge by living.'

Robin shook his head. The tears flowed again.

'I love you,' I said. Robin's eyes travelled down to the gun.

'This isn't the way,' he said.

Robin wiped his tears. I didn't know if he could see me. He stood there for what seemed like hours, then took a deep breath and started back for Maureen's car. He got in and drove away from the front of the man with the goatee's house. As the car disappeared around the corner, smoke enveloped me again, but this time the smoke was white. In the smoke, windows returned. I could see Robin's whole life in the windows – his smiles, his tears, his best memories, the mistakes he had not yet made and the friends he had not yet met. I could see his pride, how he'd grow.

The smoke felt lighter around me, and I began to drift by the windows. The orange light reached through the smoke. I was weightless and free, like a leaf that had fallen onto a river, resting on the water and floating steadily downstream. Robin would live without me. I was done, and that was okay. There was no longer anger within me, no desire. The only thing left was *surrender*, and I surrendered to the stream.

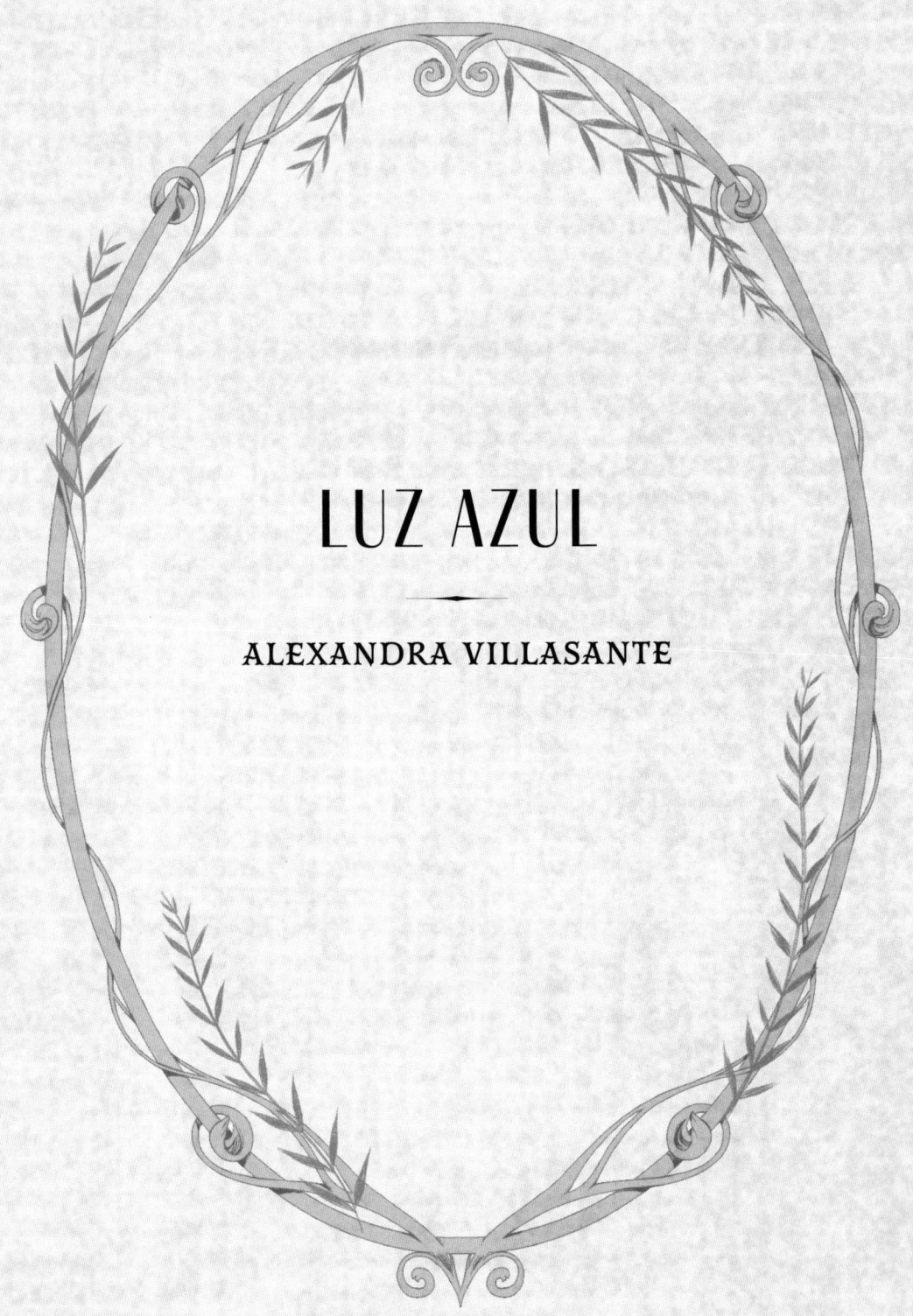

LUZ AZUL

———

ALEXANDRA VILLASANTE

DECEMBER 30TH, 1.00PM

'How much are these?' a young girl with an American accent asks. I want to say, *don't spend your money, these are knock-off sunglasses*, but that's a sure way to get fired.

I need this job.

I need to stay close to Casa Azul.

'Twenty-five dollars,' I answer in English. She frowns and I direct her to a yellow T-shirt, thin as gauze, with a graphic of a whale and *Punta Ballena* stamped in chunky letters across the top. 'That's only twenty dollars, and a much better souvenir.' Minutes later she buys the sunglasses, two T-shirts, and a *Punta del Este* keychain.

Ananda waits until the customers leave before letting the smile drop from her face. She slides in behind the cash register and makes puppy eyes at me. Ananda is beautiful with flawless, deep brown skin she likes to flaunt, and with her summer hair in waist-length locks. It's not any kind of secret that I like girls and I guess that radiates off me because, fifteen minutes after being introduced to me, she felt the need to tell me that she's straight. Then I felt the need to tell *her* that I'm demi.

'¿Que es eso?' she had asked.

'It means I'm not gonna hit on you. Or at least not unless we fell in love. I don't do sex without love. Not judging, just not my thing.'

'Sometimes the best sex is the kind without love.' She smiled condescendingly, like I'm una bebecita. I almost made the mistake of disliking her then. Now I know she was just ignorant. Straights can be real smug about what they think queer people know and don't know.

'We've worked hard enough,' she says, fiercely batting her lash extensions. 'Time for a break?'

'Roosevelt will have a fit if he finds out,' I say. Our boss frowns on breaks, even a smoke break. But I give in because I need to talk to Ananda about the heist.

This is a fairytale. This is a heist.

There's a beautiful girl locked in a castle and a menacing villain keeping her against her will. The castle is a puzzle, an illusion, and a trap. The villain is unpredictable and dangerous.

Before Roosevelt's surf shop, I worked inside the castle. Casa Azul, it's called, and I think that's why I was hired in the first place. My name is Azul and my hair is blue. I lied and said I was eighteen; you don't need more qualifications than that to walk around a bar delivering drinks. I never planned on being there forever.

The girl trapped in the castle is my sister, Luz. The villain is my ex-boss. The castle is a nightclub overlooking the Atlantic Ocean, and I have a plan to get Luz out. I always have a plan.

'Let me make sure I've got this straight,' Ananda says, lighting up a cigarette. We sit in the white-washed alley that runs alongside the outside of Surf's Up!

'You and your sister worked at the fancy castillo on the hill. She fell in love with the boss, who gives you the creeps. When you sensibly quit to get away from said creep, your sister wouldn't leave with you. And this is why you think she's a damsel in distress needing to be rescued?' She exhales a cloud of smoke in my face, underscoring her scepticism.

'Last week, Luz sent me this text.' I show her my phone.

You wouldn't understand, you're just a child.
El Capitán has captured my heart
I don't want to be anywhere he isn't
At night or day or any time
Do not look back. For the 31st time I have to tell you not to come for me!
I don't want to go home
You don't need to rescue me.

She tilts her head. 'Okay. Seems harsh, but pretty clear, ¿no?'

'You know how some siblings are best friends one week and worst enemies the next? Well, the same is true for twins, but al máximo. When Luz and I were little, every fight was like Armageddon. When we were close, there was no one else on earth that mattered.

And when we were worried that our mood swings would put us at odds when we needed each other the most, we created a code. Luz would say to me, *You wouldn't understand, you're just a child*; or I would say to Luz, *You wouldn't understand, you're too old.* That was the clue, the sign for us to listen up; *the next words you hear from me need deciphering.'*

I highlight the important words from the text and show Ananda again.

You wouldn't understand, you're just a child.

El Capitán has captured my heart

I don't want to be any**where** he isn't

At night or day or any time

Do not look back. For **the 31st** time I have to tell you not to **come for me**!

I don't **want to go home**

You don't need to **rescue me.**

Ananda quirks an eyebrow at me. More scepticism. 'You think she's sending you a coded message?'

'Yes.'

'Why wouldn't she just leave? Or ask you to call the police? Why the cloak and dagger stuff?'

'You don't get it.' I exhale, frustrated. 'Luz – she's the swan on the water, the one that looks peaceful and perfect, the one that doesn't need help. Only I know how hard she's struggling underneath. We understand each other.'

Ananda shakes her head. 'You're not chiquilinas anymore,' she says. 'Playing spies, princesses and knights, or whatever twin fantasies you concocted. She's happy there. She's found someone she's mad for and she wants you to stop pestering her.' Ananda stubs out her cigarette and throws it into the cenicero at the door. She gets up and holds out a hand to help me up. I smack her hand away and stand.

'Are you gonna help me or not?' I ask.

'Of course. Cien dolares is not nothing, and anyway, I like you. I just don't want you to get in trouble, nena.'

DECEMBER 31ST, 9.00PM

An hour before the front entrance opens for New Year's Eve revellers, I'm at the delivery door wearing my old uniform, a baseball hat low over my face, and carrying a large basket of limes on my hip. I'm sweating like the devil in church.

A guard – thankfully a new one – opens the door, and I smile at him in what I hope comes across as benignly appealing.

'Soy idiota,' I start with a weak laugh. 'I got lost in the service passage with these stupid limes and then got locked out of the two o'clock. Stewart needs these for the caipirinhas and mojitos – he'll be really mad if I'm late!'

'Got your ID?' he asks lazily.

'You don't recognise me,' I tease.

'Of course I do. But rules are rules,' he says. He doesn't recognise me, but he can't admit that. I hand him my doctored ID. The QR code is smudged – deliberately, because otherwise it would take the guard to the menu for the restaurant next door to Surf's Up! instead of the employee database – and won't scan. I'm relying on the guard blaming the notoriously poor internet reception at this spot in the back of la Casa.

Behind me, a party supply company is trying to deliver an oversized bouncy house.

'What's that for?' I ask.

'Some nonsense. Nikki thought it would be fun to have an American-style carnival,' he says with disgust. Nikki Pazos is El Capitán's accountant, who's got a sideline as a professional sneak. 'Hey,' the guard shouts at the delivery men carrying the half-inflated monstrosity, 'take that to the far side, down over there.' He points to the south end of the maze before turning back to me.

'Bueno,' he says when the scanner on his phone gives an unsatisfactory beep. I give a childish giggle and a little curtsey and he swipes a hand towards my ass.

'Save me a caipirinha, guapa,' he calls after me.

I'll save him a kick en las nalgas the next time I see him, the piglet.

Even having worked for weeks in the oddly shaped compound, I only understood the intricacies of la Casa after getting the architectural plans from Roosevelt – it cost me cincuenta dolares and a promise to be nice to Roosevelt's niece, Laura, who's visiting from California.

Casa Azul is built like an interlocking puzzle: a dodecagon enclosing a triangle, enclosing a henicosagon. That's a 12-sided building on the outside, a three-sided building inside that, and a 21-sided building (the sides so minutely defined, you can't even see it on the plan) inside of that.

Why? Why the actual hell would anyone build a structure that looks like an evil eyeball?

Because 12321 is a palindrome. El Capitán is obsessed with palindromes.

A palindrome, for the uninformed, is a word or a sentence (or a sequence of numbers) that is the same forwards as backwards. Examples include: racecar, radar, borrow or rob, never odd or even, ojo, reconocer, yo de todo te doy, amó la paloma.

And of course: Luz Azul.

Luz, then a scant three minutes later, Azul. We were born juntas and whichever way you see us, we're a palindrome. A continuous circle.

But only when we're together.

Outside the palindromic building is a round maze garden, just tricky enough to get you lost if you're drunk, which everyone at Casa Azul is at some point. For the camareras that work there, delivering drinks, handing out freebies to long-time patrons, and picking up dirty glasses, there's a hidden passage that laces through two and a half metre-high rosemary bushes of the maze. Moving clockwise through that passage, you can bypass the maze and get from point A to point B quickly and easily. If the outer maze were a clock, and the time were 2.32, the hour hand and the minute hand point to exits out of the maze and directly onto the road that encircles Casa Azul. That's where Ananda will be waiting with transportation.

In the cool of the first building – the dodecagon – I repeat the plan in my head. I have to time it perfectly. When El Capitán is on the south side of the maze, making his speech to the well-heeled crowd, I have to be underground, finding the secret room.

And before any of that, I need to find a flute that is also a key.

DECEMBER 30TH, 3.00PM

After closing Surf's Up! and extracting a promise from Ananda that she'll be in the right place at the right time tomorrow night, I catch a bus to Piriápolis, to the address of a former Casa Azul camarero. The dirty white sticker on the doorbell to the apartment reads *Massam Retter*. I press the buzzer and count to ten before buzzing again, like the text told me to. The glass door to the apartment building unlocks and I pass through a foyer with sunken tiles and piles of mail growing cobwebs in a corner.

Massam's flat is on the second floor and when I climb the last set of stairs, an anxious face peers out at me behind a chained door.

'Azul?'

'Yes, I'm Azul Camacho. Massam, right?'

'Did you bring what I asked for?'

I lift up the carrier bag so he can see the six-pack of Fanta Limón inside. Only then does he open the door and let me in.

The apartment is neat and sparse, with no art on the walls or plants on the shelves. Just the very basic things of life, some mismatched furniture, some books – the same kind of temporary vibe as a youth hostel. Coffee and a box of bizcochos from the panaderia are laid out on the little table. We sit and it's awkward, even after he serves me coffee and places a media luna on a plate for me.

'You must think I'm so weird, making you do all these things before I let you into the apartment.'

'I think you're careful.'

He scoffs. 'If I were careful, I wouldn't be in the mess I'm in.'

I wait, drinking my café slowly. This is his story to tell.

'I wasn't going to talk to you. But when you told me of your sister, still there, en esa puta casa, I knew I had to say something.' Massam's hands tremble; he has to put his coffee cup down.

'I don't want to rake up the past. I want to go home to Paysandú and forget any of this nightmare happened. But I can't go home without Otto. And he's still in Casa Azul.'

I sit up straighter. I never met anyone named Otto in my time at Casa Azul. There were some male service staff, mostly bartenders, but waiters too, subjected to the same exactitudes of dress and attractiveness as the females. Enby beauties need not apply at la Casa. El Capitán might be an asqueroso with a relentless eye, but he's a man with little imagination. For him, a world outside binary boxes doesn't exist. Pobre cretino.

Massam and Otto first came to Casa Azul in spring, hoping to find jobs near Punta before the flood of student workers came for the high season. El Capitán himself interviewed them both and was charmed by Otto's blond-haired, blue-eyed good looks, and by Massam's night-dark eyes. They were hired immediately.

'I can only describe it like a virus, like I had immunity and Otto didn't,' Massam says. 'El Capitán just seemed a little …' Massam waves a tired hand. 'You know the old story, El Traje Nuevo Del Emperador?' I nod, because it was the same for me. El Capitán was just like the vain man in The Emperor's New Clothes, and to me at least, he was showing his ass. The more Luz rhapsodised about El Capitán, the more I tuned it out.

'Otto adored El Capitán. He spent hours on his appearance, followed the captain around like a lost puppy. Any little mistake he made, any time El Capitán was displeased, Otto was crushed.'

Tears run down Massam's face. I'm afraid of how his story ends, but I have to know everything. I hand him a napkin.

'When the season started, la Casa took on more people, mostly students from Montevideo, some, like us, from further away. Otto took on double, triple shifts. I don't know why I wasn't worried when he stopped coming back to the house. I thought, he's almost six feet tall and strong, what could happen to him? Qué idiota,' he says quietly.

'It was November 11th – a palindrome, so a big deal at Casa Azul, you know – and there was a big private party, all service staff working, the garden and the maze filled to bursting with guests. I saw Otto talking to El Capitán at the two o'clock maze entrance and something looked … off. I don't know. I was suddenly worried about him. When they walked off together, I followed, picking up dirty glasses and garbage on the way so I wouldn't be noticed.'

Massam followed Otto and El Capitán to the wine cellars that are built into the caves that pockmark the cliff under Casa Azul, the ones that house special vintages for special guests, the ones that smell of must and ocean water. He followed them down a staircase carved from stone, deeper into the foundations, until he couldn't follow them anymore without being heard or seen. From the hidden recess of the curved stairway, he watched as the captain reached into the breast pocket of his black coat and took out what looked like a thin white flute and blew two notes from it.

'I didn't know what I was looking at, honestly. It looked like performance art. When he sounded two notes, a door appeared in the wall. I won't say it's magic because I'm not that crédulo. The door was probably activated by sound or something. El Capitán and

Otto stepped through it, and the door sealed behind them, as if it had never been there. Like a horror movie.'

The next day, when Otto didn't come home again, and when Massam couldn't find him at work, Massam confronted El Capitán.

'He told me Otto had quit and left. I stood there, stunned that he would just lie to my face. I told him I knew he was lying – that I'd seen the secret room. I told him I would go to the police. He didn't even bother to laugh at me. He told me to do whatever I wanted, but that I should at least finish the work I'd been paid to do. He placed two drinks on my tray and told me to deliver them to table 22. I was in a fog. My mind was whirling with plans and calls and action. And then I saw who was sitting at table 22.'

At table 22, the National Director of Police sat next to the Minister of Tourism. They accepted their drinks with a smile and thanked Massam. *By name.*

'I moved to Piriápolis, as far as I could get from that evil place while still being close in case Otto ever got out. I'm waiting for him. It's all I can do.'

I'm not interested in waiting for El Capitán to get tired of my sister, though I don't say that to Massam because he's already fragile.

'Can you draw me a map? So I can find that door you talked about?'

Massam carefully draws a map on a piece of scrap paper. When he's satisfied, he pushes it across the table to me, as if he's exhausted.

'I don't know how you'll get your hands on the flute-key thing. I don't even know if what I saw was what I really saw. Maybe I'm crazy.'

I thank him and stand. I wish I could hug him, but I think he'd fall to pieces if I did. At the door he tells me to take the six-pack of Fanta with me.

'Didn't you want it?' I ask, confused.

'I hate the stuff,' he says with a bitter laugh. 'It was Otto's favourite drink. I wanted to make sure the person I let into my home was the same person I was texting, that's all. Please take it with you,' he says and turns from me. I let myself out.

DECEMBER 31ST, 10.45PM

This is the dangerous part of my plan. I have to get El Capitán to take off his voluminous jacket without him seeing me. Or at least without him *knowing* me.

I slip into the tech closet, a room kept icy cold so that the servers that run all the electronic systems in Casa Azul don't overheat. I dig into the basket of limes and pull out the clothes and accessories I've hidden there. My hands shake as I wipe off the first face of make-up I applied – bubblegum lipstick, frosted eyeshadow, obvious highlighting – and begin to build a new face. This one is sophisticated and layered, the foundation put on with a delicate brush, the eyelashes magnetic and expensive, a flawless cat-eye, and a red mouth as lush as suede. I put on the sequined gown, a deep teal with a thigh-slit that can be undone with a zipper, and then step into sharp heels. My face, my body, my height, all of it has distorted to look as different from my usual self as possible. Except for my blue hair.

When I dyed it blue the first time – painstakingly stripping the brown, then applying the royal blue hue – Luz cried a little.

'We won't look exactly the same,' she'd said.

'We're not the same,' I replied. I was eager to show the world that I was Azul and not a reflection of Luz.

It's vanity that has kept me from dyeing my hair black or brown or red – anything to disguise myself. Instead, I bought the best-quality wig I could. Above a skull cap and several painfully tight pins, the wig, honey-brown and waved, sits on my head like it came there honestly. The mirror reflects someone unlike me or Luz. I'm ready.

Luz and I are supposed to be identical, but something must be off in me because I cannot concentrate – never could. Because Luz does amazing at school and has no problem focusing, people assume that I'm just lazy. But I really can't focus for longer than a few minutes at a time. When I try, other thoughts boil up through my consciousness, trying to distract me, so I spend all the attention I have on thinking of how caracoles move shells when they get too big for the ones they're in, or why Luz has a deep purple fleck in the iris of her right eye, but I don't. I wonder if that's why she can do things I can't.

Luz always told me that I'm exactly as I should be. I do the wondering for both of us, and she pays the strict attention for both of us. As long as we stick together, we're perfect.

But I broke our deal.

We got jobs at Casa Azul together – hired on the spot because we're twins and because our names make a palindrome. There was a long training process when we had to watch boring videos about the history of la Casa, which was really the history of how wonderful El Capitán is. Luz watched it for us both, and I snuck off to swim and explore. Which meant I wasn't there to wonder what any of it meant, to suspect where things might lead.

I skipped out on many training hours, only arriving, slightly out of breath, in time for work. It wasn't difficult work: pick up orders, deliver them to tables, avoid grabby hands, smile at everyone – even when they're terrible. In the small hours, we'd help sweep up, eat free food from the kitchen, then ride our bikes down the promontory to the large, homey place where all the Casa Azul service staff lived. It felt like camp, friendly and communal and fun. I thought it suited us, laying on la playa in the morning, napping in the afternoon, working in the evening. Saving lots of money because everything was provided. I thought Luz was feeling the same way.

'What are you saving your money for?' Luz asked. We were in Punta del Este on a Tuesday, the night Casa Azul is closed and staff get a day off. She was trying to convince me to try on designer swimwear with her. I told her I didn't have that kind of cash.

'When we go to university,' I explained, 'I want to have enough saved so I don't have to work so much. I don't want to take ten years to finish a degree.' Even though university is free in Uruguay, we tend to take a while to finish degrees – if we even do – because life is expensive. Ananda has been doing a pre-med degree for nearly six years, and she's only halfway through. Life gets in the way.

The look Luz gave me, standing outside the storefront of Desigual, was one of pure puzzlement. That's when the shadow began to spread over Luz – or at least, when I could see it. She'd stopped thinking about the future, of anything beyond Casa Azul.

A week later, we were all made to watch as El Capitán humiliated Anna, another new camarera. He abused her and took her apart with his words until she was prostrated on the dirty floor like an overzealous priest, face pressed into the drink she had thoughtlessly spilled. Instead of being frightened or indignant like I was, Luz was unmoved.

'If Anna can't do what is required, why is she here?' she said. Anna disappeared that same night.

When I quit, barely making it to my one-month anniversary, Luz refused to come with me. In the end, she closed the door to Casa Azul on me herself.

DECEMBER 31ST, 11.11PM

The bar in the triangle is the least busy. People desperate for a drink hit the first long bar in the dodecagon; people eager for privacy travel deep into the henicosagon to find it. I walk lazily – as lazily as I can in sky-high heels – to the bartender in the triangle. At twenty-one, Laura is the oldest employee here. Even though it's not usually part of the uniform, she's wearing a royal blue bow tie, and looking damn fine doing it.

'Punta Sunset, por fa,' I say with a soft smile. As if I'm not terrified, as if I'm not faking everything.

She nods and starts preparing the frozen house specialty by layering a rainbow complement of frozen vodka and juice slush into a tall glass.

'You're new, aren't you?' I say, pretending I don't know exactly who she is.

'Yes, Ma'am. Still looking for a place to stay for the summer.'

'And how is the housing market these days?' I drawl, as if affordable housing concerns are for other people.

'Inflated,' she says with a wolfish smile and pushes the finished concoction towards me. I pay for my drink, slip Laura a little something for her trouble, then make my way into the henicosagon.

El Capitán is holding court by the grand stairway to the terrace, where select special guests will watch the fuegos artificales from an enviable vantage point. He never drinks, so his hands are free to linger a second too long on any pretty people around him. And Punta del Este's elite society are always pretty.

When I'm a few feet behind the captain, I stop a waitress carrying a tray of dirty glassware.

'Excuse me, there's something wrong with my drink,' I say, weaving in place.

As she was trained, she immediately offers to get me another one. I shake my head sloppily, like I've had five too many.

'No, I want you to taste, here, try it. Mmm, tastes funny,' I slur, pushing the candy-striped straw towards her face. Under no circumstances are service staff allowed to drink while on duty. As she pulls away from me, I tip my hand under her tray and push. It wobbles, then falls, half-filled cocktail glasses trembling and clinking on their way to crash on the floor. As she leans forward to try to mitigate the mess, I get in her way, so she tumbles against my hand, sending my sunset-coloured cocktail splattering against the back of El Capitán's long black coat.

I can't worry about the waitress, I know that, but the fear I see in her eyes as the captain turns on her is almost enough to stop me. Luckily, he's surrounded by people and can't lose his temper.

'Boluda,' he grunts as he strips off his black coat and tosses it to the waitress. 'Be useful, if you can't be careful, and give this to Nikki, then have him bring me a clean one.' I melt into the crowd of guests, a simple onlooker, then make my way around the periphery of the room to intercept the waitress. She's visibly upset, an embarrassed blush on her face.

'This is all my fault,' I say, taking her cold hands in mine and pulling the captain's coat from her grip. 'Please, let me take care of this for El Capitán. I'm an old friend of his.' I put a hundred-dollar bill in her hand – nearly the last of my savings. Her eyes connect with mine and I try to convey the warning.

'Go on,' I say with a shooing motion.

'I'm not coming back,' she says, defiantly.

'Good.'

After pulling the flute-key from the captain's inside breast pocket, I leave the coat on the bar where Laura, turned away and busily shaking a cocktail, will eventually find it and take it where it belongs.

I ditch the heels to go down to the wine cellars and now the dress is way too long. I scoop the tail up and tell myself to hurry, but not to trip. I find the hidden stairway exactly where Massam told me it would be. *Be careful. Be quick. Be careful. Be quick.*

The flute-key is an off-white colour, long and surprisingly lightweight. It has seven holes, and there are grooves covering the surface. I stand in front of a blank wall where Massam said a door magically appeared. Math is hard with a wandering mind like mine, but I know there's a finite number of two-note combinations I could play. I'll stand here and play them all if I have to.

I raise the flute to my lips, but before I can play my first note, my attention locks on the carved lines of the flute, the minute blemishes – really, tiny holes – dotted along the surface. Once, when we were little at the beach in Atlántida, I found a sun-bleached stick and waved it at Luz like a sword. Until she told me it wasn't a stick at all; it was a bone.

I flung it into the ocean, and refused to go swimming for the rest of the day. I know the feel, the pits and aching lightness of bone.

I look closely at the flute, curved asymmetrically on both ends, and begin to perceive delicately carved letters, then names:

Ada. Otto. Anna. Viv. Asa. Luz. Azul.

The names of other camareros are engraved into this bone flute and the thought paralyses me. Without having to blow a single note, a doorway lights up in the wall and opens. Inside a round room with seven doors, dressed all in white, stands my sister.

'Hello, Azul,' she says.

DECEMBER 31ST, 11.50PM

Luz and I hold hands as we walk up the steps back to the world of the party. I used all the words I had, every argument and bit of reason I could think of, to convince my sister to leave with me. But her face stayed impassive, as if she were listening to other voices only she could hear. When I finished, she took my hand and told me to follow her. I can't tell if she's pulling me or if I'm pushing her. My hand cramps, holding on to her so tightly. Through our entwined fingers I feel her shaking – with fear, adrenaline? I don't know. Maybe Ananda was right; Luz is going to take me straight to the captain. Maybe this was un fracaso from the beginning. But now that I'm with my sister again, I can't let go.

Instead of taking me to El Capitán, Luz leads me to the edge of the terrace that overlooks the hedge maze. She gazes out over the ocean, while the crowd and music swells around us. Bursts of laughter and drumbeats build and fall. The anticipation is palpable. In a moment, El Capitán will make a speech and then the fireworks will go off, and my chance will be over.

'Come home with me.'

'This is my home,' she says. We're actors in a play with no script. Still, I have to get my lines just right.

'I don't want to lose you. I'll stay here with you,' I say, though the words taste bitter. It doesn't matter that I was wrong about Luz, that she didn't want rescuing after all. It only matters that we are together.

Luz turns to face me, placing her other hand in mine too. We're linked together like

when we were little and danced La Rueda de San Miguel in a circle.

'You would do that for me?'

'Of course.'

'He said you wouldn't.' Luz lets go of my hands and sits on the low wall of the terrace. 'He said you wouldn't even come, but I told him I knew you.'

I'm nearly crying now. 'You know I'd do anything for you, Luz, right?'

She smiles at me, her real smile, not the serene, plastic smile she uses on guests, or the captain or the staff.

'And *you* know you wouldn't understand, you're just a child,' she says, using our childhood code to let me know she's made her choice.

Under the dying sky of the old year, I push Luz off the terrace.

She screams as she goes down, drawing attention from some in the crowd. I break the glass over the fire alarm and pull, setting off the blaring sirens. Some guests look up as though expecting fireworks and others blearily look around for an exit. I unzip the slit in my sequin dress, the better to scramble over the terrace wall. El Capitán has his angry eyes on me, but he's much too far away to reach me. I salute him with my middle finger and jump off the terrace.

JANUARY 1ST, 12.20AM

I slide off the much-battered bouncy house, landing with a soft thud. Laura's waiting for me. She takes off her suit jacket and drapes it over my shoulders. I kiss her, a fleeting but grateful one that I hope lets her know I love her, and that I can't believe I'm lucky enough to know her.

'Was the royal blue bow tie too much?' she asks.

I try to frown, but my heart is too happy. 'You know that bartenders only wear black ties, not royal blue ones. I told you that.'

'Do you know how many boring training videos I had to watch just to do this job? You owe me, querida,' she growls, and it thrills me. I place my forehead against hers.

'Still think twenty-one is too old for you?' she asks.

'For you, I'll make an exception.'

In the ambulette that Ananda borrowed from a friend that works at el Hospital

Britanico, Luz sits on a stretcher, a little shaken by her ordeal, but not harmed by the fall. Who doesn't love a well-placed bouncy house?

'Are you okay?' I ask Luz.

'I don't know. Should I go back? He might need me.' Firefighters and policía are starting to swarm the place. I see Anna, the waitress I watched the captain humiliate, the one who had disappeared, wandering, disoriented, through the milling crowd until a medic puts a blanket over her and leads her away.

'Not now, amor. Lots of stuff going on in there. Best to leave them to sort themselves out,' I say in my most level voice.

'What will happen to him?'

I shrug, like I don't want to stab him through the heart myself. 'I'm sure he'll be fine. But the firefighters have to check the entire building, even the rooms where the other, uh, members were kept. They'll get them out and back to their families.'

'You planned this whole thing by yourself?' My older-by-three-minutes sister asks, sounding so much like her usual self it makes me smile.

'Don't sound so surprised! Planning is like wondering, but with a pencil in your hand.' *And your heart in your throat*, I think. How I had the nerve to call the bomberos and police, tip off journalists from El País until they did the work of pestering the authorities – I barely recognise myself. I didn't know what I was capable of.

'I didn't do it alone. Ananda and Roosevelt and—' I pull Laura into the ambulette and close the doors. Ananda puts on the lights and begins to drive away, the police letting her pass unmolested.

'This is my novia, Laura. She's Roosevelt's niece.'

'Hola.' Laura waves sheepishly. 'Encantada – or is that weird to say?'

'It's a weird night,' Ananda calls back from the driver's seat.

My sister rubs at her tired face, gold glitter eyeliner smudging on her cheeks. 'I didn't know if you'd come. Then I didn't want you to come. When I saw you, I was so happy and so angry.' She shakes her head. 'I think I'm glad you came. Only, I'm worried about him …' she trails off.

I have so many words I want to say, most of them muy malas, but none of that would help Luz. This is only the beginning of getting her back. The rest won't be as easy as a sequined gown and a bouncy house. 'Let's focus on you now, then we can see about the rest, okay, Sapo?'

'Don't patronise me, Rana,' she says with a tired smirk. She lies down, curling on her side and closes her eyes.

'Has she lost her mind talking about frogs? Should I worry?' Laura whispers.

'No. It's just a thing we used to say when we were little.' It would take too long to explain the intricacies of *Frog and Toad* in two languages.

I'm quiet, because I know that despite the elation of the moment and all we've accomplished, this experience will cast long shadows.

'Maybe we can go to Rocha,' Laura says, naming a beach many kilometres away from this one. 'Tío has a little house there. And I can teach you all to surf?'

I lean against Laura's chest, but hold tight to Luz's hand. That sounds like a perfect beginning after this end.

THE CHERRY BLOSSOM QUEEN

MAGGIE TOKUDA-HALL

Before we start, you need to know: the dog does not survive. This is the way of fairy tales sometimes, and life as well. For that I am sorry.

This all happened so long ago now that no one remembers when or where. The details don't matter; perhaps it was in the Fukui Prefecture or the Kyoto Prefecture, or maybe it was in Nagoya. The Edo period, or the Meiji period. History has a way of clarifying context and obfuscating magic. But this story is not true without its magic. And so I will tell you only about that which matters most to this story, so that you will better understand it.

On a narrow, winding road, there lived two households who were neighbours but not friends. Some say the road led through a forest, others through a valley. I am partial to the notion that it was on a hill, terraced for farming, humid with rice paddies. This does not matter, but I like to imagine the air hot and heavy around these households, as though the air itself waited for their decisions with bated breath. You can imagine it whichever way pleases you, I do not mind. What is most important to know is that these two households, so different, stood so close together.

In one home, grand and splendid, lived a husband and wife and three sons. They had all the money they would ever need. In the other, was just a father and his son; the mother had died when the boy was just a babe, and now the father did his best to raise his son, mourn his wife and tend to his farm. On many days, it felt he only had time to mourn.

The Poor Man had loved his wife with his whole heart, and when she died, he found he did not know how to live, not like he had before with happiness and pleasure. And so he took all of her things — her best kimono and her obi and her combs and even her simple summer yukata — and he buried them in her great tansu on his land. He could not bear to live with these items in his home, though it made his wife's ghost sad to see it. And so his son grew from a babe to a child to a young man without ever once having seen a single object that had belonged to his mother.

The Rich Man did not love his wife, which was fine because she did not love him, either. Theirs was a marriage of mutual convenience. She bore him sons, which was all he wanted of her, and he kept them rich, which was all she wanted of him. It was, in its way, a happy marriage, though their sons grew from babes, to children, to young men without ever once having seen the gentle kiss of true love pass between their parents. And so as they each came of age they struck off with their father's coin and their mother's advice.

The Poor Man's son remained on his father's land. He did not know what would become of his father should he leave; would he remember to eat? The son feared not. And so he stayed in the haunted house with the haunted man, always wondering what it might be like to live in a house that did not echo with grief.

One day, the Poor Man's son was out tending to the fields when he heard the plaintive cry of an injured animal. Curious and concerned, the son struck out and followed the sounds of pain until he found the source: a filthy dog, ribs jutting and fur matted, that had become stuck in the fence between the two properties. The Rich Man had built the fence himself, such that his neighbours would never benefit from even an inch of his land. And now, the poor beast was entangled in it, and if he had not found it, it may easily have perished. The son pulled the oni-giri that was meant to be his lunch from his pocket and offered it to the starving dog such that it would trust him. The dog sniffed the rice, then in two gentle bites swallowed it down. The dog could have bitten his hand in its mirth, and the son would have understood. But it didn't. The son felt a swell of affection for the animal.

'Shh,' said the son. He held out his empty hand, and the dog sniffed it. 'I want to help you.' The dog let him pet its head, and as he did the son saw that the dog had a gash on its back leg, not from the fence. Clearly, the animal had been chased off the neighbour's property in a cruel manner. The son swallowed his anger, and gently helped the dog free of the fence. It was not easy; the poor animal was well entwined. But the son had kind hands and a kinder heart, and soon the dog was free.

The dog trusted the son now, and let the young man pick it up. The son carried the beast all the way home, though it was a long and strenuous walk even with arms free. He did not mind. He put a blanket on the floor, and let the dog rest as he boiled water so he could bathe the filthy creature, and tend to its many wounds. The gash on its back leg would leave a scar, but the rest just needed cleaning. As he cleaned the dog, he told it stories. Of how the rabbit lost his tail. Of the little one-inch boy. And of the fairy tales he alone had grown up with, of his mother and his father and the perfect sunny day when they met in town. Of her beauty and her kindness, though he could recall neither. And the dog listened.

By the time the Poor Man returned from the fields, the son had managed to wash all the grit and soil from the animal. And though its fur was still patchy, and its wounds still fresh, it more resembled a dog, with white fur and pointed ears and a tail that curled in on itself.

At once the Poor Man's heart broke for the dog, and he hastened to boil some rice which he served to the animal with salted fish. The dog wagged its tail, and the Poor Man smiled, and his son smiled, too. He could not think of the last time he had seen his father smile. There is a version of this story in which the son had never seen his father smile at all; but I do not believe that a child raised with love would never have witnessed a smile, and it is important to know that this son was very loved, and knew that he was loved. And so in this version, it had just been some time.

'It's another mouth to feed,' said the son. 'But I think that we can manage it.'

'Of course we can,' said the Poor Man. And he scratched the dog between its pointed ears. The dog smiled, too.

So the dog became a member of the family. Each morning it would leave for the fields with the Poor Man, and each evening it would keep the son company as he cooked dinner for them all. It slept in a circle at the foot of the Poor Man's futon. As the weeks passed into months, the dog filled out, its ribs no longer visible and the great gash on its leg healed into a jagged scar. It had been nearly a year when the son realised that his father had not mentioned his grief in months. He still spoke of his late love, but when he did, he smiled.

One day, the Poor Man was out in the fields when the dog started to dig. Not idly, not curiously, but with determined intent, dirt flying in great clumps behind it as it dug.

'What are you doing?' the Poor Man protested. He worried for his crops; already it had been a miserable harvest, and he was already so poor. But the dog, who usually listened, did not listen. It just kept on digging, deep, deep into the damp earth. And then, quite suddenly, it arrested its frenzied work and let out a bark.

The Poor Man looked down into the hole and saw a small trunk. Though it hurt his back, he pulled it from the hole, and examined it. It was old, but unlocked. He opened it. For a moment, he could not comprehend what he saw. Gleaming like the moon were more silver coins than the Poor Man had ever seen in his life. He blinked at them, confused. But then he looked at the lid of the box, and saw the engraved crest of his late wife's family. The coins were his.

In a daze, he wandered home with the trunk tucked under his arm. The dog trotted happily beside him, occasionally loping ahead and then hanging back, waiting for the Poor Man. When he got home, he showed his son what the dog had found. Bewildered, the two counted the coins together as the dog lolled between them, chewing on the marrow bone the son had held back from their dinner's stew just for it.

It took more than an hour to count the coins, but when they finished the two stared at each other in astonishment.

'But Father,' the son said. 'This is just what we need to get through this spring. Almost exactly.'

'How did she know?' the Poor Man asked. 'That this was precisely what we need?'

They both looked at the dog. The dog lifted her leg and licked thoughtfully at her privates.

'It couldn't have known,' the Poor Man said.

'No,' said the son. 'Just a lucky coincidence.'

'Very lucky,' the Poor Man agreed. And father and son pet their lucky dog and whispered kind things in her ears for the rest of the night. Lucky or not, she was a very good dog.

That spring passed for the little family peacefully and more comfortably than it had in years, maybe ever. Curious why his neighbours did not seem as perpetually uncomfortable, the Rich Man asked the Poor Man what had happened. The Poor Man told him the truth.

'Bah,' said the Rich Man. 'If you don't want to tell me the source of your good fortune, that's fine.' And he would not listen to the Poor Man any longer. The Poor Man shrugged. He was accustomed to the Rich Man's rudeness. So he went about his day, planting cabbages for the summer harvest.

As the crisp spring heated into a punishing summer, the Poor Man's son felt a strange melancholy fall over him. He was more comfortable than he had ever been in his life, that was true. And his father was happier, and they had a very good dog. But there was something missing, something in his heart, that he had never once had time to address in his entire life. There had always been something else to worry about – dinner for that evening, coin for rice, a leak in the roof.

But now. Now there was finally time to feel the missing thing in his heart the way he could feel a stone in his shoe. Uncomfortable and perpetually painful. And he could not think of how to fix it.

'What is wrong, my son?' the Poor Man asked. 'It is summer, your favourite season. The sun is bright, and the rains are heavy and delicious. We have more than we have ever had. So why do I see such sadness in your eyes?'

His son did not know, and he could not answer, not completely. So he said instead, 'Something is missing in my life.'

'What is it? You know I will do whatever I can to help you find it.'

'I know,' the son said. 'But alas, I do not know what it is.'

And so his melancholy persisted.

Then, once again, the Poor Man was in the fields with the dog on a seemingly normal day. The sun was high and hot, and the humidity made him sweat with effort. He was minding his own business entirely when a clump of dirt hit the side of his face. Bewildered, he turned, and saw that the dog was furiously digging once more. This time, the Poor Man said nothing, and instead, went to help the dog. And so together in the punishing heat, they dug and they dug until they surfaced a great tansu in the damp soil.

This time, the Poor Man recognised it right away. It had been his wife's tansu, the one he himself had buried so many years before. Tears sprung to his eyes. He had not seen the tansu in so long, and a relic from his late love's life felt too portentous to bear. It was as if she were standing next to him. So, trusting his wife and trusting the dog, he pulled it from the earth, and opened it.

Inside were the kimono and obis she had worn on their wedding day, along with the lacquered comb she had worn in her hair. The Poor Man sank to his knees and wept.

His heart was full of grief and happiness, mingled in the way only conjured by love and love lost. He did not understand how the dog had found these things, so long lost to him and his son, but it didn't matter. In some versions of this story, he wonders if it were witchcraft, but all that truly matters is that it was inexplicable, as all the greatest miracles are. And so he tied the miraculous tansu to the dog, and to his own waist, and together, they pulled the treasure home.

When they got home, the son looked at the kimono with wide eyes. He had never seen anything so beautiful. He ran a finger over the obi gently.

'Father,' he said. 'This is the finest thing that has ever been in our home.'

'Yes,' the Poor Man said. 'Your mother was the most beautiful bride.' And he wept anew, as he watched his beloved son lovingly unfold the kimono that had once belonged to his beloved bride.

'I think,' the son said, 'this is what has been missing.' His eyes glittered with tears as well. He held his father's gaze, the kimono clutched in his soft hands. 'Can I put it on, Father? Please?'

The Poor Man smiled, and wiped the tears from his eyes. 'If it will make you happy,' he said. For the only thing that mattered to the Poor Man was his son's happiness. And he could see the shine in his son's eyes that had been too long missing as he held the precious silks that had once been his mother's.

After some false starts and many mistakes, the son dressed in his mother's wedding clothes. The Poor Man did not know how to fasten the many knots, nor did he know how to comb his son's hair into the nihongami his wife had worn on that day, but he helped as best he could. It took more than a couple of hours, but eventually, the son looked at himself in the clouded looking glass and gasped.

'This is me,' he said. 'Finally.'

'You have never looked more beautiful,' the Poor Man said. And it was true. He could see his son's happiness bubbling forth, unstoppable. It made his heart ache with pride. He looked so much like his mother, and yet so much like himself. In him, the Poor Man could see the best of his wife – her gentle hands and her easy smile that belied her great kindness – and he could see the best of his son – brave and beautiful and so much himself.

'Go to town and find the washerwoman. She is not a gentle lady, but she is the one who taught your mother to dance. You should learn, too.'

'But what of money?' the son asked. Already the coins the dog had found in the spring had dwindled, and though they were comfortable it hardly meant they had the means for extravagance. But the Poor Man would not let money stand in the way of his son's new-found happiness. He would simply work harder.

'There will be enough,' he assured his son.

There was not enough. But the Poor Man did his best to hide that from his son, who was flourishing. Each day, father watched son practising his dancing. Each day, that father knew he must do whatever he needed to protect that son, so that he might hold that happiness close to his chest for as long as he could. And so the Poor Man worked doubly hard, his back aching and his hands raw.

He was in the fields when, once again, the dog started furiously digging. But this time, before he could go to help, he heard his neighbour's voice calling to him. He did not wish for his neighbour to witness whatever it was the dog was doing; the Rich Man was quick with cruel words. But he also did not want to be rude.

'Why do you let your beast make such a mess of your fields?' the Rich Man called. 'You should beat it so it knows never to do it again!'

The Poor Man explained to his neighbour once again that when his dog dug, miracles happened. The Rich Man scoffed, but also did not leave.

'Come then,' he crowed. 'Show me this miracle dog.'

The Poor Man shrugged, and then went to help his dog, who was digging further down than usual. Hours passed, but the dog did not tire, though the Rich Man did. He sat down on the soil and watched, with crossed arms, as the Poor Man and his dog dug down, down, down into the cold, wet earth. Finally, just before the sun dipped below the horizon, the dog barked merrily, and the Poor Man pulled open the top to a large, heavy chest.

Perhaps it was the bleeding rays of the sunset, or perhaps it was simply that the golden coins were so plentiful and clean; they shone like the sun had been buried in the Poor Man's fields. With a shaking hand, the Poor Man picked up one of the coins, and turned it over in his fingers. Just that one coin could settle his debt for the season's seeds. And the chest was packed all the way full.

The Rich Man watched on in fury and envy. There, in the ground, was nearly as much money as his whole life was worth — and his hapless neighbour had come upon it all at once! One lucky day! The injustice of it rankled him. Why should his neighbour, witless, guileless, earnest, be bestowed this great fortune when he, the Rich Man, had been making the money he inherited from his father into more money by being clever, shrewd and remorseless? He watched as the Poor Man hugged his dog, tears falling down his stupid face.

The Rich Man needed that dog.

And so, the Rich Man helped the Poor Man pull the chest from the ground without giving voice to the titanic resentment that screeched in his heart. He pocketed a coin that fell from the chest, but the Poor Man didn't even notice, hadn't even thought to count the coins as soon as he found them, all the more proof he was a fool who did not deserve this great fortune.

The Rich Man helped the Poor Man carry the chest home. His arms would ache for days, he knew, but it was a small price. He congratulated his neighbour, and then asked as politely as he could:

'That is indeed a miracle dog you have there. My family could use a miracle these days, too. My wife, she has been so sad.' (He did not say why.) 'Would you be so benevolent and generous as to lend us your dog?'

The Poor Man's son's eyes flashed with concern. He remembered the day he found the dog, beaten and cut by this Rich Man's cruelty. 'I don't think that's such a good idea.'

But his father had always been a trusting, selfless man, so he said: 'Don't be silly, my son. Only the cruel hoard their good fortune. We have been so overly blessed by this kind animal. It is time someone else reaps some reward.' And he packed some dried fish and rice cakes for the dog, and kissed her between her pointed ears.

'You be a good dog,' he said. 'Do for them what you have done for us.'

And so the Rich Man left with the dog, and the Poor Man remained with his hope for the future, and his son with his fear.

The dog found the Rich Man's home to be very different than the Poor Man's. Upon their arrival, the Rich Man tied the dog to a post outside and left her there. He left the food her master had packed, but did not unwrap it for her, and so she was left to tear it open on her own. And when it started to rain in the night, he left her there. It was as if her life with her new family had never happened; she was back in the cold and the wet, shivering and alone. She did her best to imagine her sleeping spot at the feet of her master's futon, the sound of his gentle snores and the warmth of his fire.

There are versions of this story in which the dog is just a normal dog, and the things she found were just the work of luck and circumstance. But I do not agree, and so that is not the version of this story that I will tell you.

To me, the dog was a miracle, a creature of sentience and understanding and empathy. And so, the next morning, she did her best to remember what her master had told her: to do as she had done for him.

She was a good dog, and so she did exactly that.

When the Rich Man took her out into his fields, she found a spot that smelled right, just as he demanded. And just as she had done for the Poor Man and his son, she dug until she unearthed precisely what the Rich Man deserved. For that was all she had done for the Poor Man and his son. However, where she had found riches and solace and safety for her found family, she unearthed something else entirely for the Rich Man.

His initial delight was extinguished immediately when the smell hit his nose. He peered down into the hole, and saw the remains of the cat that had once belonged to his family, but which had starved. A servant had been ordered to bury him, and buried he was, though in a shallow grave. Ragged fur clung to the skeleton, and though most of the flesh was gone, the stench of the corpse was powerful. The Rich Man covered his nose with his sleeve, but still he could smell it. He cursed, and kicked the dog, who yelped in pain.

'Do it again!' he shrieked. 'But this time do better!'

The dog sniffed through the fields once again, trying her best to find something the Rich Man deserved. In the afternoon, she wagged her tail. A scent befitting him filled her nose, and she began to dig. Great clumps of dirt and soil flew behind her. She was a good dog. She did as she was told.

This time, the Rich Man did not even need to peer into the hole to know that the dog had once again not unearthed treasure. His nostrils pinched at the odour, cloying and sick. Decay. Rot. A cursory glance told him that she had found an old refuse pit, full of unspeakable, unnamable things. Fury coursed through his whole body. He had never felt anything like it before, as if he was burning from within. He fetched the gardener's spade.

I will not force you to watch this. I will not force myself to say it. But in every version of this story, the dog does not survive. In some versions, the Rich Man delivers the body back to the Poor Man with no apology. In others, the Poor Man finds the dog himself, when he comes to check on his pet. No matter which way the story is told, know that the Poor Man and his son's grief was expansive, terrible. No matter which way the story is told, know also that the Rich Man gets what he deserves.

The Poor Man and his son had the dog cremated, and they said their funeral rites over her. They grieved her and they missed her, and though I cannot say what happens when a life is ended, I can say this: the dead can hear us, more clearly than we realise.

That winter, the son, whose dance classes had been going beautifully, prepared for his first public performance. It was a particularly bleak winter, snowy and cold and heavy with sleet. But each day, the son practised, and each night, his father combed his growing hair until it shone in the lantern light. And on a particularly icy day, the son put on his mother's kimono, and tied his hair in the traditional way. He carefully applied the make-up he had purchased with the gold coins their good dog had found them. When he looked into the looking glass, he saw himself in his truest form looking back at him. And for the first time in months, both he and his father smiled. On impulse, as he headed into town to perform in the square, he grabbed the little box that contained his good dog's ashes.

Some who gathered to see him dance gathered in good faith, wanting to see something beautiful. A few collected out of curiosity, neither good nor bad. But the Rich Man and his wife attended out of spite. How strange, for a young man to dance for everyone, and for free! How bizarre. They laughed behind their hands at him. The Poor Man heard them, and for the first time in his life, he felt the urge to hit someone. He held his hand, but not his tongue.

'You terrible people,' he hissed. 'You killed our dog. You come to mock my son in his moment of truth. You should be ashamed of yourselves.'

The Rich Man held his hand to his chest, a gesture of mock offence. 'My good man!' he said, cajolingly. 'You must not tell tales, or our good neighbours will not realise you jest!'

'I—' the Poor Man started. But he was cut off by the swell of music that announced his son's debut. He would not miss this moment, and so he turned away from the Rich Man and his wife and their cruel laughter, and settled himself down in a spot where he could best appreciate his son's performance.

It was good fortune that he did, for he would not have wanted to miss it. The performance was beautiful — subtle and graceful, evocative both of the crushing grief of their shared losses, and the warmth of the love they shared. He was in that performance his truest self. And as he danced, the son threw the dog's ashes from the box and into the bare trees.

As the ashes touched the branches, a miraculous thing happened:

Cherry blossoms bloomed. In the dead of winter. In mere moments.

The crowd gasped and wept in awe.

Except for the Rich Man and his wife. For each of them inhaled a breath of those ashes. And after the ashes touched their throats, neither could tell a lie. For the rest of their days, both were forced to blurt their terrible truths aloud, announcing their sins and their embarrassments, and their petty thoughts. Indeed, even as they watched, the wife loudly proclaimed that she had passed gas. And the Rich Man shouted that he had killed the dog whose ashes caused this miracle. They were shunned, as they ought to have been, for revealing the cruelty of their truest selves.

The Poor Man and his son, on the other hand, were invited by the Emperor to come to the capital city, where the son performed regularly as The Cherry Blossom Queen. In some versions of this story, they both moved to the city, and lived in comfort and finery in the palace. But I like the version best where they lived in the same humble home they always had — just more comfortably than they had before. I suppose it doesn't matter. What's most important to understand is that, in the end, they got what they deserved. Respite from grief. Comfort. And, most importantly, each other.

LET DOWN YOUR H.A.I.R.

MEAGAN SPOONER &
AMIE KAUFMAN

Persinette Prince was not having a good H.A.I.R. day. The relay had been down all morning – or what she chose to call morning, suspended in the endless starry night of space – and the silence throughout the cockpit left her on edge for reasons she didn't care to explore. The relative silence, anyway. There was always the occasional beep and readout from her instruments. The hum of the engine. That unidentifiable rattle that had plagued her ship since she left Verona, and which she'd tried for a week and a half to track down, practically disassembling the *Friesian* from the inside out while in transit.

But the voice from the relay was gone – and it made her antsy. She'd gotten used to the company, after so long alone.

The star system she'd been heading toward for the last three months loomed in the viewscreen, distorted slightly by the faint waves of hyperspace breaking against the bow of the ship. The better part of a day away still, she could feel the light of Gorgyra Theta through the front viewscreen, warm on her skin even at this distance – pale, golden, a little alien.

Nice, though.

A screeching sound rent the quiet and sent Prince jolting upright out of her seat, moving before she'd even processed what she was hearing. She lurched through the tiny passageway leading back toward the engine room, half-falling down the ladder and ricocheting off the bundles of exposed cables leading down from the cockpit.

The sight of the engine room always made her heart contract a little. She didn't mind the chaotic jumble of outdated junk and badly organised wiring. The ache came because she had barely a memory of her dad where he wasn't here, or on the *Andalusian* or the *Thessalion*, up to his elbows in those messy wires.

She shoved those memories away and threw herself down on the floor beneath the hyperspace module, where the screech – identifiable now as the wail of metal vibrating against metal at some ultra-high frequency – was coming from.

'Damn damn damn, not now.' Prince grabbed for her gloves, insulated against the high-powered conduits beneath the module casing, and pried open the housing, unleashing a blast of searing heat against her face. Less than a day away from the planet she'd been trying to find for the last *five years*, and her ship was threatening to blow itself up and scatter her atoms across a lightyear.

She couldn't tell which of the conduits was coming loose, so she started going through them one by one, praying she had enough strength to shove the cables back in live. The whole galaxy knew what a mistake it was to get torn out of hyperspace unexpectedly.

If she had to make an emergency landing, would the H.A.I.R. let her in? Was its A.I. designed to emulate human empathy?

'Come on, sweetheart,' Prince whispered to the cocoon of steel and carbon fibre protecting her from the vacuum of space all around. 'Keep it together for just a few more hours.'

Finally something clicked under her hands, the vibrations echoing through her skull ceasing so abruptly her ears rang. She let her head fall back, ignoring the heat still pouring out of the hyperspace module against her body, and took a long, shaking breath.

'Well, that didn't sound good.'

The voice, which often chose oddly inopportune moments to reach out, no longer startled Prince. Now, all she felt was a strangely intense rush of relief that it was still around, after an entire morning without it.

She sat up so quickly that she slammed her forehead into the housing just above her, hard enough to make her see stars swimming and sparking in her vision.

'Oof, and that sounded even worse. You okay, Charming?'

Prince wriggled out from beneath the hyperspace module, her eyes going to the speaker in the corner of the room. She'd rigged the communications relay through the ship's intercom system so she could talk to the H.A.I.R. while she went about her daily routines and ship's maintenance – but she hadn't realised she'd left the channel open earlier when she'd been trying to reach out.

'Fine. Fine. I guess you don't know what it's like to bang your head on something, do you?' Prince rubbed at the spot just on the edge of her hairline.

'There are whole libraries of human literature devoted to the subject of pain,' the voice answered. 'I have a hypernet connection, and a good imagination.'

Prince felt a flicker of unease travel through her. Did computers have imaginations? But at this point, she was so used to being unnerved by the artificial intelligence protecting the planet that this was just a tiny blip on the radar.

'Where have you been?' Prince heard the edge in her voice and swallowed, taking a deep breath. What use was there in being annoyed at a machine? 'I mean – I thought maybe something was wrong when I couldn't raise you all morning.'

'I was busy, Charming.' The reply was somewhat sharper than usual. 'I can't be here every hour of the day, telling you to turn your ship around. I do have a life, you know.'

There was another problem. Since when were artificial intelligences programmed to have a sense of humour? The relay's nickname for her – given as soon as she introduced herself as Percy Prince – was another of those jokes that made her as uncomfortable as they did amuse her. That's how it was with the H.A.I.R. – a constant tug of war between Prince's wariness and the desire, as soon as their conversations ended, to find a reason to reach out to it again.

'Well …' Prince paused by the ladder leading back out of the engine room, dwelling for a moment in the strangeness of the words she was about to say. 'I missed you, is all.'

Even stranger, the reply that came back after a long, long pause: 'I missed you too, Charming.'

The fifth planet in orbit around Gorgyra Theta glowed like a jewel beneath the viewscreen in the galley. Its lush blues and greens, partially obscured by swirls of cloud, looked as inviting as an oasis in a desert – but Prince couldn't shake the uneasy feeling that she was staring at a mirage.

The surface was just a hop, skip, and a jump away, and yet she might as well still be on the other side of the stellar system for all she could do about it. The H.A.I.R. was mostly invisible, except the occasional flash of gold as bits of space dust and debris collided with the defence grid. Prince was reminded somewhat uncomfortably of a bug zapper on her aunt's porch, and couldn't help imagining the *Friesian*, and her inside it, as nothing more to the H.A.I.R. than a mosquito, one among hundreds.

The edge of night crept over the surface of the planet as the ship orbited above, and Prince leaned forward, practically pressing her face against the viewscreen like a kid at a candy shop. Her eyes scanned the shadowy darkness, searching for anything, for a single light, to tell her there was life down there.

The reward that had brought her here was for information – but the rescue of survivors would more than triple her take.

Plus, obviously, it'd be nice to save some folks.

The darkness below was absolute. Still, that didn't mean no one was down there. The original colony was comprised of only about two hundred and fifty people, and unless they'd gone on an absolute spree of city-building when they got there – which would've been a bizarre use of resources to say the least – the settlement wouldn't be visible from space by night.

Still, the shadows were inviting.

There were plenty of rumours about what had happened to the lost colony of Gorgyra Theta-L. One of dozens of colonies set up along the outer rim of settled space, everything went fine for the first ten years or so. Until one fateful day when a transport ship carrying supplies and inspectors from the company terraforming the planet suddenly found itself without coordinates in its navigation database.

Lost in the middle of the vastness of space, they contacted headquarters and got routed back to civilisation. But what they didn't know – what no one knew until it got leaked on the hypernet – is that it wasn't just a blip of their navigational system.

The coordinates of Gorgyra Theta-L had vanished from every system in the galaxy, every reference, every map, every database, simultaneously. It was as if it had deleted itself from history.

At any other time, this would have caused the entire galaxy to erupt in speculation and confusion and fascination. But it happened to occur smack dab in the middle of the *Daedalus* wreck on Corinth, the biggest disaster in galactic history. The mystery of the lost colony of GoTh-L, vanished without a trace only a generation after it was established, was lost amid the madness of those few months of tragedy and uncertainty.

But not for Percy Prince.

The rest of the galaxy was fixated on the crash, but she couldn't stop thinking about those two hundred and fifty people lost to the vastness of space. Nor was she the only one. There was a dark, dank little corner of the hypernet – amid threads covering ghost hunters and others claiming to investigate psychic abilities – devoted to people theorising about the lost colony of GoTh-L.

Prince knew all of them. And they weren't exactly her friends – most of them were too paranoid to let anyone close – but they were company. And any one of them would lose their minds if they knew where she was, and who – what, rather – she was talking to. A part of her wished, with an almost wistful pang, that she could tell them.

They all had different ideas about the fate of GoTh-L.

Some said aliens got them. The colony was situated toward the edge of colonised space, and proponents of this theory argued that it was at least as delusional to claim there definitely *weren't* aliens out there bent on stealing our planets or harvesting our carbon-based bodies for resources. It had to be aliens, because what human technology could have possibly deleted every reference in the entire galaxy to GoTh-L and its location all at once?

Others said it was a corporate cover-up. That LaRoux Industries, the corporation responsible for the terraforming of the planet, had discovered something about it – that it was made of gold, or something similarly nonsensical – that they had to hide from the public. *It was an inside job* was always a favourite among the conspiracy theorists.

Prince wasn't a huge fan of that one – after all, it was that same corporation's CEO who was offering a massive reward from her own personal funds for any information on the colony's location or well-being. Proponents of the cover-up theory pointed out that offering a reward just made her *look* innocent.

But this was the same CEO who, after taking over from her corrupt father, cancelled all the debts of the colonies her company was responsible for, while maintaining aid and support on her company's end. It wouldn't make sense for her to vanish a whole colony.

Then there was the H.A.I.R. theory. Meant to protect the planet, the Human and Artificial Intelligence Relay was a powerful machine overseen by human colonists. Some said that the A.I. part had gone rogue and destroyed its human masters – that it had somehow killed everyone on the planet's surface and was now destroying any ships that came near. That this was why the lost colony had stayed hidden all these years: no one who got close lived to tell about it.

Prince had started out thinking that theory was as stupid as the others. After all, it was just a defence system, a machine in place to shield the planet from the continuous rain of meteorite impacts it suffered. It was the meteorites that had made GoTh-L such an unattractive colony to most corporations – the bombardment was constant, and erecting the defence grid cost money.

Even so, its artificial intelligence was so simple it could barely be called an intelligence – it was just there to determine the difference between rocks to be vaporised and ships to be allowed through. That was why it needed human overseers. It was a stretch to believe it was even capable of such a mutiny, let alone that it could have happened.

And then the *Friesian* had come into range of the H.A.I.R.'s sensors, and a single voice had hailed her out of the darkness.

'You're being awfully quiet.'

Prince jumped, suppressing a shiver as she glanced up at the speakers in the ceiling of the galley. There was no video feed – no way for the A.I. to 'see' her – and yet she felt somehow observed nonetheless. As if the thing knew what Prince had been thinking about.

'Just thinking.'

'Penny for your thoughts?' The artificial intelligence had been given a pleasant, human-like voice that sounded like a young woman. It didn't *sound* artificial at all, though these days that wasn't hard to pull off. What was difficult, what made these machines fail time and time again to pass tests of sentience and consciousness, was a distinct sense of personality that was consistent from encounter to encounter.

This A.I. had a tendency to use antiquated phrases like you'd hear in old Earth movies. There hadn't been any pennies in centuries.

It made what Prince was almost certain were jokes.

She felt like she … liked it. Except *it* was just a computer. There was nothing – no one – there to like.

'Just looking down at that planet,' she replied, avoiding the question. 'You know my ship's half falling apart, right? Just a little bit of salvage from that colony would fix me up for a few years. You say there's no one down there anymore?'

'Correct.'

'And you still won't tell me what happened to all the colonists.'

'Nope.' The A.I. actually sounded a little amused.

'So why not let down the H.A.I.R. just for a few hours and let me look around?'

'It is my function to protect this place. That is what I intend to do.'

'But who are you protecting?' Prince insisted, feeling her throat constricting with frustration, raising the pitch of her voice. 'If there's no one down there anymore, what is there left to protect? Can't you just let me in?'

There was a pause from the speakers, long enough for Prince to sigh and go around to the other side of the galley and fetch a mug and press the tap for hot water. She threw a tea bag into the mug and poked at it until it absorbed enough water to sink, scalding the tips of her fingers a little in the process.

'If I am to answer your questions,' came the voice finally, 'perhaps you could return the favour and answer a few of mine. Why do you want so badly to land on this planet? You told me that you've spent five years uncovering its location – my location – and months travelling to reach it. There's nothing you could find here worth enough for that kind of time spent.'

Prince stared down into the mug as the water coloured, first a pale gold, then a light brown, and eventually a mahogany dark enough to rival the moonless night of the planet below. 'I don't know,' she said slowly. And that, she'd been realising more and more, was the honest truth.

'You must have a theory.'

Prince let out a slow breath, watching the steam above her tea dance on the air currents it created. 'My dad and I used to try to figure out what had happened to the lost colony of GoTh-L before he died. Every weekend we'd go down to the basement and pull out the files and pore over every scrap of evidence we could find. He was really into it, and I … I liked to be where he was. I mean, I'll take the reward money. But I guess I just … need to know. It's all I have. I have to know the story. What happened. How it ended.'

'You said you had the location three years ago. Why didn't you come here then?'

Prince curled her hands around her mug, though it was hot enough to spread a wave of warning pain through her palms. 'Dad didn't want to go,' she murmured, shrugging one shoulder even though the A.I. couldn't see her. 'He always said the story was more fun than the ending.'

There was a tiny sound on the other end of the conversation – a sound that suddenly made all the hairs stand up on the back of Prince's neck.

Was that the tiniest huff of a breath?

'Well, perhaps that's it, then,' said the A.I. quietly, evidently unaware of the effect of that tiny sound on the girl it was talking to. 'Perhaps by keeping you from your ending, I am protecting the story.'

Machines don't have lungs.

The tiny constellation of doubts and clues that had been swirling around inside Prince's mind ever since she first heard the voice of the A.I. suddenly coalesced into a dense, hotly burning core of molten stone. She caught her breath, fingers tightening around the handle of her mug.

'You ... you're not an A.I., are you?' she whispered, staring at the speaker as though it might somehow yield up more answers. 'You're a person. You have to be a person. You're too real.'

A startled silence came from the other end. At least, Prince imagined it was startled. Her heart pounded as she waited. *Anticipation,* she told herself.

'Um—' said the Human/Artificial Intelligence Relay.

And then a massive shudder tore through the *Friesian,* knocking Prince hard against the galley cabinets. Tea splashed upward as she hit the grid floor – she never saw it splash back down.

'Prince?' The voice swam through the inky, fuzzy darkness surrounding her. No more aloof amusement in the voice, either – its tone was frantic, shaking. 'Prince, answer me! What happened? Are you okay? I heard a crash. Prince? Prince!'

Prince groaned, and the movement of her face against the metal grid floor felt like diamond-grit sandpaper. She was going to look like half a waffle for a week. 'I'm – I'm okay,' she managed, pushing herself up on her hands. The galley looked the same – except for the tea dripping down the cabinet in front of her face – but she could hear the tinny shrill of an alarm somewhere. The cockpit.

'What happened?'

With another groan, Prince managed to get to her feet. 'I don't know.' Her voice was gravelly, and shaking even worse than the H.A.I.R.'s. A distant, remote part of her pointed out, *Machines don't have adrenaline to make their voices shake when they're scared.* 'I think something hit the ship.'

'I TOLD YOU THIS WASN'T A SAFE PLACE TO HANG AROUND IN ORBIT.' The H.A.I.R's voice was still quick with concern, practically babbling. 'METEORS, REMEMBER? WE'RE RIGHT ON THE EDGE OF AN ASTEROID BELT, IT'S A BAD PLACE TO BE IN A SPACESHIP. ARE YOU OKAY? IS THERE ANY DAMAGE?'

Prince had some trouble with the ladder leading up to the cockpit, her limbs shaky and weak with the adrenaline from the impact still coursing through her. 'I'm checking now.' Her eyes first went to the viewscreen itself, half expecting to see cracks in the glass spiderwebbing out from an impact site. She could almost picture it, like in a movie, each crack splitting and spreading bit by bit, with a horrifying tick-tick-tick of time running out.

But everything looked fine, except for the series of indicator lights flashing red. She dropped into her chair with a little moan as pain jolted through her hip – she was going to have a hell of a bruise right on her butt, where she'd hit a handle in the galley on her way down. Somehow in the movies the heroes never had embarrassing wounds, just impressive ones: a thin, artistically placed cut that emphasised the cheekbone, or a gash on one arm that tore the uniform just enough to reveal a perfectly formed bicep.

She gritted her teeth, reminding herself to focus. She must've hit her head to black out – she probably had some degree of concussion.

The alarm lights for the engine were dark, and those for life support too. Prince's lungs gave a shuddering heave of relief, as if she'd been trying not to breathe too deep – as if she could've survived without an oxygen scrubber. Thrusters were fine. Power generator was fine. Her eyes slid across the panel, arranged from the most critical systems to least, until they lit upon the ones that were flashing.

'Oh – no. God, no.'

'PRINCE? WHAT IS IT?'

But this time, not even the sweet voice from the speakers could distract her.

Prince lurched out of her seat again, hauling herself up into the tiny little crawlspace that granted the pilot access to the wiring and housing of some of the ship's computers and sensor arrays. She couldn't get all the way to the back wires anymore because the exterior of the ship had been stoved in – not enough to crack the composite forming the skin of the craft, or else she'd be breathing space right now, but enough to prevent access to the whole ship.

And enough to confirm what the alarm indicators were telling her.

She wriggled back out and dropped down into her seat, forcing her shaking hands to reach for the navigational display. She flipped the switch. The screen flickered once and came on, giving her a momentary rush of relief – and then her heart sank again when she saw what was on the screen.

`Error. No navigational array detected.`

She flipped the switch off and then on again, off and then on again, until the tears of panic in her eyes made it impossible to see the screen. She didn't need to see it – the message was burned into her brain.

'Talk to me, Charming!'

Prince lifted her head, clenching those shaking fingers into fists. 'The navigational array is gone. The impact must have done it – I have no coordinates anymore, nothing to show me where I am or how to get back.'

'You mean …'

'I'm completely blind.'

Sweat rolled down Prince's temples, sogging up her hair. The small of her back was sweaty, too, where it was pressed against the floor, and she knew she was going to have underboob sweat showing through her shirt once she got out of here. But there was no one around to see – the H.A.I.R. could only hear her, after all. Thankfully. This was not the image she'd want the other girl – for Prince was pretty certain she was talking to a person – to have in her mind.

She'd found she could just reach the cable junctions for the navigational array if she extended her arms overhead, exhaled all the air out of her lungs, and shoved against the ship's frame with her feet, cramming her body into the tiny space formed by the dent in the outer hull. Navigating with her fingertips, she disconnected and reconnected each cable with painstaking care, every single movement jabbing bits of ship and machinery into her ribs. She could only sip at the air, body so compressed she couldn't take even half a breath.

Maybe, just *maybe*, the array was still there. Maybe the impact had just jarred loose its connection to the ship's computer.

She inched the final cable back into its port, pressing until it clicked under her fingers, and then steeled herself to crawl back out. She was forced to wriggle, with no leverage against the ship to get herself out the way she'd gotten in. Despite having stripped down to her undershirt and shorts, bits of her clothing threatened to trap her, snagging on protruding pieces of the ship's frame or other vital wires jutting out from their ports.

She longed to take a deep breath to combat the panic threatening to rob her of her senses. All she could do was point out to herself that she had all the time in the world to work on getting back out of the crawlspace. She wasn't going anywhere.

The worst part was that there were no speakers up here. She couldn't talk to the … what? Calling a person 'the H.A.I.R.' seemed ridiculous. But she had nothing else to call her. Prince occupied her mind as she worked her way free trying to imagine the perfect name for the girl she'd slowly been getting to know the last few weeks as she approached GoTh-L.

The girl who made sly jokes when she thought nobody would notice.

The girl who pretended to be aloof, but whose voice shook with worry when she heard a crash.

And then, all at once, Prince found she could take a full breath again. For a moment she just lay there, half on her side, gulping breaths of recycled air and trying not to weep with relief. Slowly, she inched her way over the edge of the crawlspace floor and lowered herself back down into the cockpit.

Her eyes were resting on the blinking red lights for the navigational system for a good minute before her brain registered the import of the fact that they were still blinking red.

'Are you there?' she said, her voice sounding small and very scared.

'I'M HERE.'

Relief washed through her. She'd spent weeks in space alone with nothing but movies and books for company. She'd spent nearly two years before that, after her father was gone, with nobody around who'd wonder where she went if she disappeared. But now … Prince took a breath, trying to stop her thoughts from spinning away from her.

'I'M GUESSING, FROM THE LACK OF CHEERING, THAT IT DIDN'T WORK.'

Prince tipped her head back, thunking the base of her skull against the headrest and closing her eyes. At least there was ventilation down here, unlike in the crawlspace. The dry, recycled air was slowly erasing that damp and swampy feeling from her body. 'Nope. I'm still blind.'

There was no answer from the other side, only the faint white noise of the open channel when neither of them were speaking.

Prince lifted her head and reached out to switch off the indicator lights – the flashing red was giving her a headache – and gazed out the viewscreen at the planet. It appeared above her in the window, a strange sight even after a lifetime spent half in space on this errand or that with her dad's shuttle company. Humans weren't wired to feel comfortable floating in a sea of stars with a planet for a ceiling. Maybe it was the concussion, but the vertigo gave her a touch of nausea, making her swallow hard.

'You've got to let me land, even if it means I can't leave again. You know that if you don't let down the H.A.I.R. now, I'm going to die out here.'

A long silence. Then: 'THAT THOUGHT HAD OCCURRED TO ME, YES.' The panic that had sounded so human before had receded – now she was back to sounding every-so-slightly mechanical again. A remoteness that brought Prince no comfort whatsoever.

'Well?'

'CAN'T YOU FIX THE ARRAY?'

'Even to get a look at it, I'd need a spacesuit, which I don't have, and training in spacewalking, which I never got. Plus, given the meteor situation, I'd be a sitting duck out there for any pebble-sized bit of debris that wanted to shoot itself into me like a damned space bullet.'

A flicker of irritation coloured Prince's voice, and she didn't bother to hide it.

Another silence. Machines definitely didn't require a moment to gather their thoughts.

'I CAN SEE FINE WITH MY SENSORS. I COULD TRY TO ESTABLISH A REMOTE LINK WITH YOUR SHIP AND GUIDE YOU BACK OUT TO MORE POPULATED SPACE, THEN SEND A DISTRESS SIGNAL, GET YOU PICKED UP BY SOMEONE PASSING THROUGH.'

Prince pressed her fingers to her temple, massaging a circle and wishing she didn't have to try to think through the massive headache that had blossomed from the base of her skull.

'You know,' she said slowly, 'I had plenty of time to myself to think while I was trying to reach those cables. I was trying to figure out what possible reason there would be for some girl to pass herself off as an artificial intelligence hiding a ghost colony from the galaxy. I came up with a pretty compelling story – you like stories, right?'

Silence from the speaker.

Prince put her feet up on the edge of the dash and leaned her chair back. 'This was five years ago when GoTh-L fell off the map, yeah? Back then, the corporation terraforming the planet was still hella corrupt. Exploiting colonists and essentially making them into indentured labourers with no rights and no freedoms. It strikes me that if one colony managed to find a jackpot of a planet that would let them be self-sufficient right off the bat, they might not *want* the corporation to come back even to bring supplies. Does that sound right?'

More silence.

'The question is, how do you actually do that? Corporations put so much money and time and so many resources into terraforming these planets that there's no way they'll ever let go of that investment.' Prince stared out at the planet upside-down in the viewscreen – it offered nothing more than the speaker did, but she'd started to imagine a person down on the surface rather than a machine in the wiring. A person gazing back up at her. 'You'd have to move the colony away from the landing site. And you'd need someone capable of erasing the planet's location from the entire galaxy. And you'd need to pick a moment when they were all distracted enough not to investigate.'

'Maybe you should've been focusing on fixing your ship and not on a story to explain your own inability to remember I'm just a machine.'

'Mm, maybe, but machines don't get irritated.'

Silence again.

In spite of herself, her dire circumstances, her own annoyance, a smile tugged at Prince's lips. *Touché.*

'So colony spots are always competitive at first, only accepting the best of the best for the first wave. Smart people tend to have smart kids. Maybe even smart enough to have figured out a way, five years ago, to erase a specific set of numbers from every computer, everywhere, at the same time. Especially if, five years ago, some disaster happened to befall one of the most populated planets in the galaxy, and distract the corporation from chasing down this mystery.'

From the speaker came a long, soft sigh. Prince had never heard the H.A.I.R.'s voice do that before – a tiny, thrilling jolt of victory went threading down her spine.

'From there it'd just be a matter of moving the colony and leaving behind someone capable of keeping people away. With a hypernet connection, that someone could start planting whispers in the dark corners of conspiracy theory boards. Stories of a rogue A.I. smart enough to disable or even destroy any ships that come looking for the colony – stories about ships that never come back. And then, anyone who comes close enough to be detected? Well … just talk to them as the A.I. and scare them off. How many people have you managed to scare away?'

For a long stretch of heartbeats, Prince thought the voice wasn't going to answer. That maybe she'd just left – or the A.I. had severed their connection – and she'd never get an answer. And suddenly she needed that answer, even if she never survived to tell another soul.

Before, this had been her father's quest, carried on because she didn't want to let him go.

But now, it was something else. Now, there was some*one* else, and she *had* to know.

Just as she was about to try the line, check the connection, the voice spoke again, her tone quiet.

'You're the first to get this far. I knew someone would show up once LaRoux put up that reward, but I thought it would be easy to keep people away. You're a lot more stubborn than I expected.'

Prince smiled for that. 'I mean, it would've worked better if you weren't actually, you know, pretty great to talk to.'

'Um. I mean, sure. So are you.'

'Can you tell me this much? Are you alone down there?' Prince's heart gave a little twinge. She knew all about being on your own.

Silence. Then: 'Yes. I'm alone.'

'You don't get lonely?'

'I guess … I don't know. I didn't think I did. Now, I'm not so sure.'

Prince swallowed, her heart beating a touch more quickly. 'Then—'

'I can't let you in,' the voice interrupted her. 'I can't confirm or deny what you're saying.

You have to understand, *if* what you're saying is true, any information about the lost colony of GoTh-L that gets back to civilisation will bring every treasure hunter in the galaxy straight here. Not to mention the terraformers. Everyone wants to come rescue us – nobody ever asked us if we *wanted* to be rescued.'

'What if I'm asking that now?' Prince dropped her feet to the floor and sat up, leaning forward to get more of the planet in her line of sight. As if willing the girl on the planet before her to look back up, as if she could meet her gaze.

She could almost picture her beyond the glass, floating there in space, within reach but utterly untouchable. Her hair would be the same gold as GoTh-L's sun, the light streaming through it as it fanned out around her head in a halo.

Prince gazed out at where the girl would be. Her fingers flexed, as if to reach toward her, then made a fist. 'It's way too much, a whole colony depending on you sitting there, keeping everyone out. They shouldn't have done that. You deserve more. If you let me land and fix my ship, I could bring you with me when I leave. You could ... *we* could ...' But there her voice failed. Because what, actually, did she have to offer? Especially now that she didn't have someone else's obsession to chase anymore.

'I don't need rescuing.' Her voice was firm, but gentle. 'Do *you*?'

Prince's breath caught in her throat. Somehow, she knew the voice wasn't just talking about her current circumstances – the damaged ship, flying blind.

Nobody else had ever asked her that, either.

When she didn't answer, it was the voice's turn to address the silence crackling through their open channel.

'I could offer you an alternative story. The Human and Artificial Intelligence Relay was the first of its kind. What if, to improve the communication between human and machine, the colony protectors found a way to link their human minds with the artificial one? It's ingenious, perfect in a situation where threats need to be determined instantaneously and without computer error. The A.I. would have started out simple enough. But how long would it have remained that way, with access to the infinitely complex computers that are the minds of humans?'

Prince's skin prickled a little – the sweat was drying on her skin and giving her chills.

'Originally, the A.I. would have known only its function – protect the colony – and the best way to do that: shield it from the meteors raining down onto the planet's surface. But what if, as the A.I. grew, and learned, and digested the wisdoms and truths and stories of the people feeding it, it eventually realised there was a better way to protect this story? What if the colonists themselves – their emotions, their flaws, their loneliness – were the threat they needed protection from? What would the A.I. do then, if the colonists changed their minds about staying isolated?'

Prince wished she hadn't left her jacket down below. 'This is all very well and good, but—'

'I imagine the A.I. would have found a way to keep them quiet.'

Prince could no longer deny the shiver winding its way through her body, so she let it have free rein for a moment. 'That's a pretty good story,' she admitted. 'The perfect story, in fact, to keep people out.'

'You can't know it's not true. You can't prove either ending is real.'

Prince considered this, her eyes tracking a ripple of gold across the mostly invisible grid surrounding the planet as it vaporised an incoming bit of rubble. 'I suppose I can't. But either way, it's still you, right? Still the person – or the computer – I've been talking to the last three weeks. I kind of don't mind either way.'

'Um, you'd still want me to let down the H.A.I.R. knowing there's a chance I'm an evil A.I. just waiting to eat you like some sort of science fiction mind-spider?'

A burst of laughter startled Prince – it had been quite a while since she'd laughed so freely, so truly. 'Whether you're a girl left behind by her people to maintain this defence grid or an A.I. lonely and bored with the people she's been stuck with the last five years, you're still you.'

Silence greeted her. Prince could imagine the solitary control tower below, wreathed in vines, a prison for the girl within. She could imagine that girl, too, gazing at her own speaker, clutching her hands or biting her nails or pacing back and forth, trying to make a decision. She had more trouble imagining the other thing – what did a computer do when it was unsure? But that wasn't what was actually happening – she'd heard those breaths, those pauses, a sigh, an indecision, and a longing so human-like it couldn't possibly have come from a machine, no matter how nuanced it had become.

Could it?

Prince took a long, slow breath, and as she spoke, she willed the girl on the other end of the speaker to hear her. To really, truly, *listen* to her.

'I think you've been in charge of identifying threats and keeping them away for a long, long time. I think the responsibility is so huge that at some point you stopped being able to identify what was a meteor and what was a ship – you had to just vaporise everything. You had to just push *everything*, *everyone*, away.' Prince's own heart was squeezing. Who had she ever let in, herself, since her dad died? Obsession with a mysterious lost colony was as good as a defence grid when it came to keeping everyone out.

Prince's eyes burned a little, but she managed to keep her voice gentle as she added, 'Whether you're a lighthouse warning me away or a siren luring me in, I don't care.'

'I – I said I don't need to be rescued, Charming.'

'I heard you. But I'm pretty sure I *do*. So long as you're the one doing the rescuing.'

No answer came. The silence stretched on, the white noise of the open channel seeming to rise and rise in volume until it eclipsed all the other noises on the ship – that little rattle from the engine room, the beeps from the control panels, the cycling of the air scrubbers. Prince's heart was pounding so hard she thought she might scream from the waiting. She kept her eyes on the planet's surface, staring so hard her eyes were watering, as if she might somehow be able to see down through the vast distance and zoom in on that lonely little tower and the girl inside it.

She couldn't imagine going home anymore – there wasn't really a 'home' to go to, after all. Somehow, she'd never really thought past finding the lost colony of GoTh-L. She had vague ideas of collecting the reward and maybe having a few minutes of fame on some talk shows about how she'd found it, and then … what? Buying a house with the proceeds and sitting there by herself, reminiscing about when she used to be a space detective or treasure hunter?

She'd chased this thing all the way to the end, occasionally wondering if she was a fool, following her father's ghost, too scared, or stubborn, to try anything else in life.

But perhaps it was exactly what she'd been meant to do.

Prince closed her eyes.

Please. Let down your H.A.I.R. – let me in.

A swell of light against her closed lids made her eyes fly open again. Before her, against the blue-and-green backdrop of the planet half-lit by the rising sun, a ring of golden light was dilating outward like the iris of an eye. In its centre, the planet itself, unshielded.

A doorway.

Prince's throat closed, and it took her a moment to move – but when she did, her fingers flew over the controls, charting a course by sight alone through the opening.

'I'll see you soon,' she whispered to the speaker overhead. 'I can't wait to meet you.'

In the vast darkness of space, something flew toward the dark shadow of the planet – little more than another meteor, a bit of space debris. Just as it crossed the edge of the sphere, a golden light flashed – like a bug zapper on a porch.

But then, the sun was just clearing the rim of the planet, throwing its clouds into relief, spreading white-gold reflections across its oceans, illuminating the edges of the atmosphere.

Perhaps – probably, in fact – the flash was nothing more than a trick of the light.

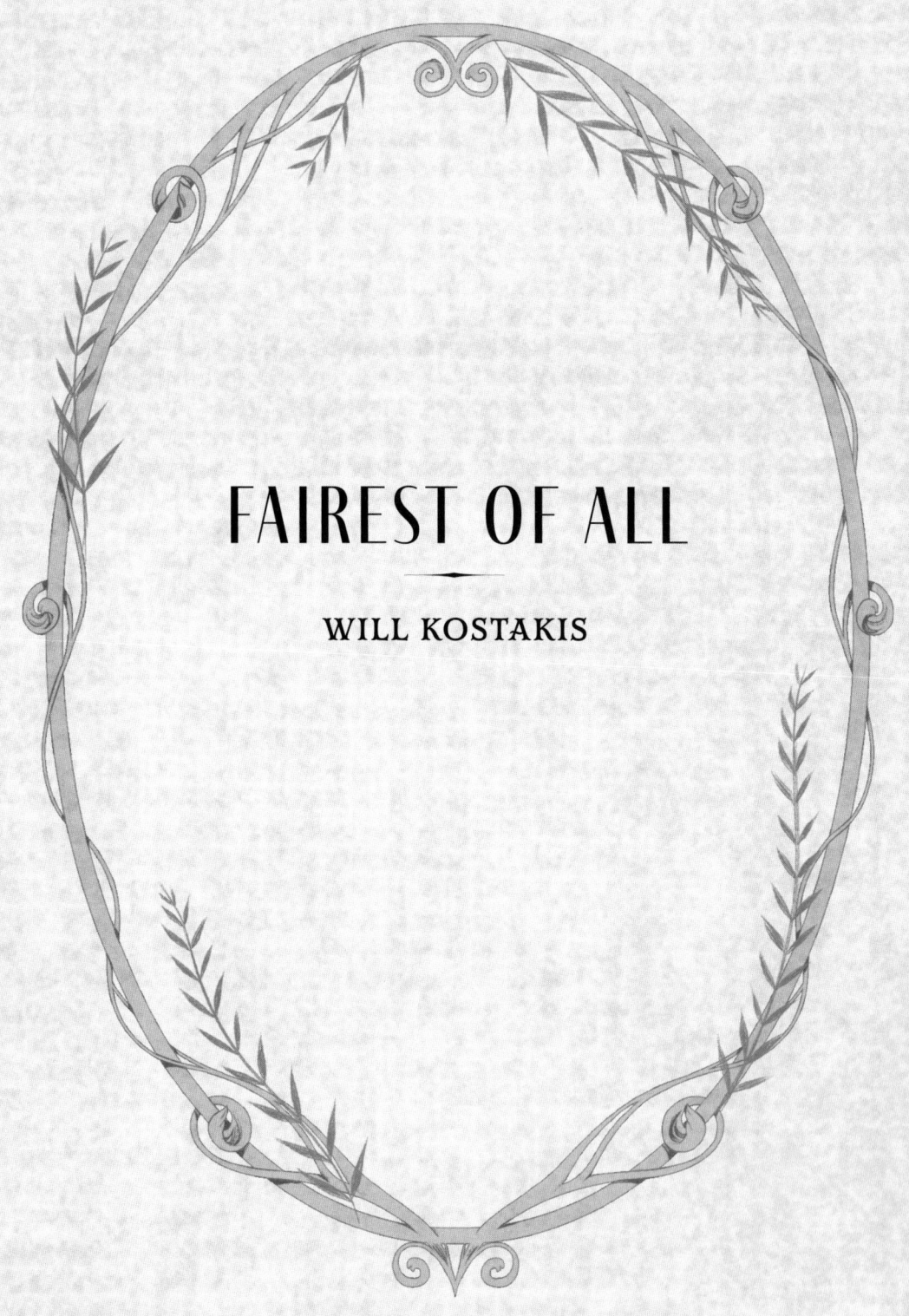

FAIREST OF ALL

WILL KOSTAKIS

The morning breeze has a sharpness to it. Eve's bouncing on the spot, teeth chattering. I'm standing still and my stoicism alarms her. She asks if I'm cold.

'Freezing, actually.'

We're on the edge of the oval, metres away from the nearest hole-ridden target. I'm rarely at school early enough to see the archery team in action. I can't say I'm particularly keen on the idea of catching a stray arrow. But desperate times, desperate measures.

'Can we head inside?' Eve pleads.

'You can.'

She pouts, but she doesn't go anywhere.

I'm here for Omar, school archery champion. He has the cheekbones of a fairy-tale prince and the arms of somebody who's stuffed potatoes up both sleeves. He's the reason guys at Canada Bay Secondary know they're gay. Unfortunately, he's hetero.

He adjusts his crotch, adjusts his stance. Both hands on the bow, he raises his arms above his shoulders. He draws back and aims at his target. His face is all concentration. Truly, a sight to behold. He releases the string. Bullseye. His expression softens. He turns and shares a laugh with a mate, then he turns the other way and notices me watching.

I give him a little wave.

Omar is more than eye candy. The guy is also, confusingly, the biggest gossip the school has ever known. He's a huntsman, and if he has your reputation in his sights, good luck to you.

He palms his bow off to his mate and saunters towards us.

'Great,' Eve mutters. 'Walk in slow-motion, dude. Nobody's dying of hypothermia or anything.'

I shush her, but Omar's close enough to hear. His smile is crooked. 'Jake,' he says, 'what's goss?'

I swoop in before Eve can say something sarcastic about feeling like she's burning alive. 'Remember that time you copied huge chunks of my English essay and said if I ever needed anything, you owed me?'

Omar laughs. 'Faintly.'

'I need you to take somebody down. My younger brother.'

He screws up his face like I've just asked for Will's lungs and liver in a box. He's an older brother, too. Very different dynamic, though. They eat lunch together sometimes. It's unnerving.

Omar glances at Eve. 'Why would you wanna do that?'

'Don't look at me,' she says. 'This is all him.'

I was expecting this to be purely transactional, a 'You plagiarised my bomb-ass *Hag-Seed* analysis, so you do what I say' situation. I reach into my pocket. I tap the screen with my frostbitten fingers. It doesn't recognise my face the first time but works the second.

'Hey, Mira,' I say.

Two notes chime, and then a familiar robotic voice responds, 'Hello there.'

No student has taken credit for building Mira. One day, we were a school with below-average NAPLAN results, and the next, we were a school with below-average NAPLAN results and our own voice assistant. Think Siri or Cortana, but personalised for the students at Canada Bay Secondary. On top of the usual search-engine trawling, she can respond to questions about the school and its staff. What are today's cafeteria specials? Where is my second-period Geography class? There were a chaotic few days early in Mira's life where you could ask her to rank the teachers, or enquire about the numerous scandals that have been bleached from the school's Wikipedia page. That capability was nerfed when it got the higher-ups' noses out of joint and they threatened to track down and expel Mira's creator. Now if you lob her anything remotely spicy, she just says she doesn't understand.

I raise the phone closer to my lips. 'Mira, who's the fairest of all?' I ask.

Mira takes a moment to think.

'You are fair; it is true. But *Will Cameron* is a thousand times fairer than you.'

Omar's eyebrows inch upwards. I can tell he's resisting the urge to encourage me to be a supportive older brother. I should be happy for Will, blah, blah. No. I built myself. I put in the work. I started early, Year Seven, back when somebody's worth was tied to how good their choreo was to a song or viral soundbite. I was the king of that shit. A handful of dance routines, the occasional confessional video. The tide turned in Year Nine. It became about lifting, counting macros, flexing in the changeroom after PE and copying whatever haircut was trendy on Oxford Street. I had it down to an art. *Have* it down to an art. So long as I'm at Canada Bay Secondary, *I'm* the fairest Cameron brother.

'How does Mira even decide?' Omar asks.

I say, 'There must be an algorithm,' but honestly, I have no clue. I thought it was based on our socials, but Will's account is private. He only has three hundred followers and he rarely posts. Twice a month, he'll review an apple.

Granny Smith. Bit bruised. Too tart. 6/10.

Red Delicious. It's in the name. 9.5/10.

It's bleak. Not even the slightest attempt to attract thirst.

'I think it's the mullet,' Eve chimes in. 'The black curls make his skin glow and his lips pop cherry-red.'

I toss her a death stare.

'What? It's true.' She's shifting her weight from foot to foot. 'Girls love a healthy mullet. Even though he's not ... They just wanna touch it.'

I give Omar my full attention. 'I'm not asking for much,' I insist. 'One rumour. A tiny one. His reputation doesn't need to be destroyed. I dunno. Tell everyone he hates puppies and you don't like his vibe. Whatever. People just need reminding he's not as fair as me.'

Omar seems more okay with committing mild character assassination. But he does try to tug at my heartstrings. He says Will's my brother, like I don't already know. 'Mira's just a random voice assistant,' he adds. 'Who even cares who she thinks is fairest?'

'Not the point.' I refuse to be talked out of this. 'And me. I care.'

Grabbing hot chocolates is Eve's idea. So's me paying for them. Penance for making her wait out in the cold.

We walk our drinks around the packed cafeteria. Dev sees us on our second lap and clears their bags onto the floor to make room.

'Cheers,' I say, sliding onto the stool beside theirs.

Dev nods and continues to shovel noodles into their mouth. 'No biggie.'

It's difficult to dislike Dev. I reckon if they dethroned me as fairest of all, I'd probably accept it. Yes, I'd be bitter. Yes, I'd question if somebody who slurped instant noodles at eight in the morning really was fairer than me. But I'd *get* it. Since they barrelled into their first homeroom in Year Eight, bold and fully formed, they have committed themselves to cultivating a following. Their brand is pranks and spectacles.

Will's brand is ... apples.

'Didn't wanna sit with your bro?' Dev asks.

'Huh?'

Dev points their nose past Eve, at the throng of guffawing Year Tens.

Eve twists around. 'Yes, why *didn't* we sit with your bro?'

She's taking the piss, but the honest answer is, I hadn't noticed Will. I mean, I know he's here now and I can only *just* make out his curly mane. The Year Tens have no sense of personal space. They're crowded around something, a phone maybe. What's got their attention? Footy highlights? Somebody's feed? Mira? I feel something harden near my heart. It sprouts vines and darkens what it touches ...

'He hates puppies, you know,' I spit, all venom.

Dev's not sure what to do with that information.

Eve turns away from the Years Tens, her brow furrowed. 'Maybe leave it to the professional,' she coos, reaching for a takeaway cup. She sips, shrieks and, with a flick of her wrist, sends the cup flying, noodles spilling out across the table.

Dev's laughing, and it takes me a second to piece it all together. The cup of hot chocolate that's still in front of her, Dev's noodles, the phone propped up on the next table, positioned to capture the prank and/or spectacle.

It's funny.

'It's not funny,' Eve stresses.

I can't help cackling. She peels a stray noodle off her jumper and glares at me. I've known her long enough that I can tell what she's thinking. It won't be so funny when somebody pranks me.

As if I'm the sort of guy who gets pranked.

When I'm stuck for something to post, the.one.and.oli is my go-to guy for inspo. He lives in some flashy apartment in the city. He has almost six hundred posts and five times as many followers. I scroll through his grid until inspiration strikes: him by a public pool in tie-dyed speedos.

I commandeer the bathroom. I prop my phone between the basin and the mirror. My shirt comes off. I study Oli's pose. He isn't just tensing his abs, he's twisting his torso so he seems impossibly thin. I exhale deeply, tense and twist. I glance between Oli's pic and the mirror. It takes some practice to look impossibly lean without the strain showing on my face.

I open the camera. I take three shots and upload the best one.

The pic scores a hundred likes before dinner.

This is my first time ordering a mild character assassination, so I don't know how long it's meant to take. I give Omar two days. That seems reasonable. On Thursday morning, I zip into the kitchen half-dressed – one leg in my pants, shirt unbuttoned. I'm early. The timer on the safe says I still have sixty seconds, fifty-nine, fifty-eight …

Mum clears her throat. She's by the sink, working through a bowl of bircher muesli.

I say, 'Good morning,' but my heart isn't really in it. I'm staring at the safe.

Forty-five, forty-four …

When you think of a safe, you think of a hulking grey contraption. Ours is more of a Tupperware container with an attitude problem. Mum bought it to lock away the good cookies during the horror week she went keto. There was an airbrushed family on the box, wide-eyed and smiling while they surrendered their smartphones. Mum said that seemed like a good idea. I brushed it off, then Mum brushed off keto, and suddenly, Will and I were going phone-free seven till seven, no discussion, no complaints.

The digital display counts down the final seconds. When it hits zero, the internal mechanism whirs. I pop the top and scoop out my phone. In an instant, Mira's open and I'm asking her who's the fairest of all.

'Oh, not this again,' Mum groans.

I shush her. Mira confirms that Will is still the fairest of all Canada Bay Secondary students.

'The shit?'

'I'm sorry, I didn't catch that,' Mira says. 'Could you repeat your question?'

Mum sighs like she's about to impart wisdom. Oh no. She sets down her bowl and approaches. Oh no. It's too late to escape. She lays a reassuring hand on my shoulder and says, 'Jake, sweetie.'

She reheats an old favourite. The tale of her five-month stint as McDonald's Employee of the Month. If you're one of the three people alive she hasn't told it to, Mum was gunning for an uninterrupted half-year as her outlet's finest employee when newbie Cara Bayley poured a soft serve without blowing up the place. They made her October's Employee of the Month. Mum lost it and quit.

'But you know what I've learnt since then?' she asks.

'What?'

'There's always someone younger nipping at your heels,' she says. 'There comes a time when what you do isn't special anymore. It's just what people expect. That's unfair, but it's the way it is. And as lousy as losing made me feel, the win probably gave Cara that little confidence boost she needed.'

I'm supposed to feel better, like it's the natural order of things for the Mums of the world to be shoved aside for the Cara Bayleys. Stuff that. The Cara Bayleys don't deserve squat.

Will stomps down the hall. Mum gives my shoulder a final squeeze. My usurper saunters into the room. He lobs us a casual hey, snatches an apple from the fruit bowl and heads out again.

I go to speak. Mum shakes her head.

'Let your baby brother have his moment,' she says. 'Be happy for him.'

'What the fuck, Omar?' I howl, hurling my bag into the changeroom wall, just inches from his face.

He stammers. He's all apologies. I didn't realise there were so many words for sorry, and none of them work.

'Couldn't bring myself to do it,' Omar says. 'It felt mean.'

'Says the guy who told the world when Melissa sharted on camp.'

'But she did! And everyone saw it!'

I remind him that he owes me.

'Man, I figured you'd get over it, what with Will being your brother and all.'

The rest of the PE class is filing in. I tell Omar he's weak as piss and leave it at that.

Huntsman, my arse.

In line at the cafeteria, I ask Mira the question. She tells me Will Cameron is still a thousand times fairer. Walking to fourth period, I ask the question. Wheeling the rubbish to the kerb, I ask the question. Washing my hands, I ask the question. Will Cameron. Will Cameron. Will Cameron.

I have no clue how Mira decides who's fairest. There's no qualitative difference between my days now and my days before. My posts get similar likes. My jokes in class? Similar laughs. I mean, I can lock eyes with Hunter in second-period English, flash a smile and know he'll be up for a pash in the middle cubicle of the L-Block toilets at recess. Nothing has changed, but the way I see everything has. There's a tinge. Even though everything's good – nah, *great* – I'm not the fairest of all. And that sucks. And that hard something in my chest? I feel it every time I so much as think of Mira.

I'm the best I've ever been, but that's not good enough.

I'm supposed to let my baby brother have his moment. I'm supposed to be happy for him. But I can't. That's not who we are.

Will and I aren't close. We never have been. Okay, I guess we bonded a bit when that crap with Dad went down and we've had good times since, but nobody's nominating us for Brothers of the Year. With only eighteen months between us, there's always been a rivalry. Wanting what the other has is in our DNA. I mean, he used to complain when Mum bought me a present on my birthday. He would scream bloody murder. She had to introduce the concept of brother-birthdays just so he had his own present to unwrap. He gets something every year.

He doesn't get to have this, too. Fairest of all is mine and I want it back.

It's all I'm thinking about at the dinner table while Will yammers on about how his mate Alicia smuggled the smoke bomb for her unborn sibling's gender-reveal party into Science today. She let it off during an experiment and Mrs Clayton cracked the shits. She was a nervous wreck when I had her in Year Eight, so I can picture her flailing around the lab like a muppet, enveloped by blue plumes. I'd laugh, if every word he spoke didn't remind me he's fairest and I'm not …

Mum laughs, then she catches herself and forces a stern look. She makes Will swear that he won't get himself in trouble.

'It was Alicia, not me.'

'Mmm. Just don't get any ideas.'

He waits for Mum to focus on her steak before his eyes find mine. He pinches the air and mouths, 'A few ideas.'

He expects a reaction I don't give him. He blinks but doesn't say anything. Not until after dinner, after he's brushed his teeth, after he's already said good night and walked past my room. He comes back. He stands at the door and asks if I'm okay.

'I haven't done anything to piss you off, have I?' he asks.

Eve doesn't answer my texts before first period, which means she's in the library. For the better part of two years, she's been engaged in moderate flirtation with a whisper of a boy: library monitor Ethan. It involves her tinkering away on Python and occasionally looking up from her laptop to catch Ethan stealing a glance while he restocks a nearby bookshelf. Sometimes she doesn't even tear her eyes off her work – she just senses the heat of his gaze and tucks her stray blonde strands behind one ear. It's less 'Will they, won't they?' and more 'They won't, because the idea of talking to each other gives them hives'.

Eve's playing with her hair when I slide into the seat opposite, blocking Ethan's view. 'New day, new plan,' I announce.

'Jake, I'm—'

'I've come to terms with the fact that if I'm gonna be fairest of all again, I'm gonna be the one to make it happen.'

Eve deflates. She lowers her hand, lowers the laptop screen. I have her full attention. 'Right.'

I shift in my seat. 'My strategy is two-pronged: stun and sabotage. The first is self-explanatory. Keep the jokes coming in class. Keep the photos coming. I've got some speedos in my bag, we can duck past the pool on the way home and you can take some fresh pics for my feed.'

'It's five degrees,' she deadpans.

'Sabotage is trickier.' I'm thinking out loud at this point. 'Without any inkling how Mira makes her decisions, I have to attack Will on all fronts.'

Eve doesn't give me the chance to elaborate. She sighs, goes to ask something, then stops herself. She asks if I've done the Maths homework instead.

Mum collects our phones at the start of dinner. God forbid anyone be distracted while Will updates us on the Mrs Clayton situation over chicken tenders. She put on the waterworks for his Science class, apparently. Anyone else would wear it as a badge of honour, conspire to escalate things, aim for the super-elusive leave of absence and a two-week stint with a substitute, but Will's had a crisis of conscience because, his words, 'as a teacher, Mrs Clayton goes all right'.

He has convinced his class to get shirts made with her face printed on them.

'We're going to prank her,' he says.

That winds Mum up.

'Nah, not like that,' Will pre-empts. 'No one else's mum is preggers and into cringey gender reveals. It'll be a normal class to start, then one at a time, we'll peel off our jumpers to reveal shirts with her face on it. She'll laugh.'

Mum relaxes. 'That's cute.'

Will looks so proud of himself. Unjustifiably. I get that I'm annoyed at him, so everything he says is annoying to me, but I reckon even without the fairest-of-all business, this would still irk me.

'Is that really a prank?' I ask.

His smile slips. 'It'll make her laugh.'

'Yeah, but isn't the point of a prank to be bit cruel? Like, it's supposed to be funny for *you*, not Mrs Clayton.'

Mum clicks her tongue. 'Well, *I* think it counts as a prank.'

Enabler.

I'm inspired to commit my first act of sabotage when I spot the soft package waiting on our doorstep. I don't have to open it to know what it is: a shirt with Mrs Clayton's face on it. I'm inquisitive at dinner. I ask about the big reveal. Specifically, I ask *when* it's going ahead.

I fake gastro the day before and spend the morning in the laundry.

He had her face printed on a silk shirt, which feels like somebody meant to order cotton but selected the wrong box at checkout. I've never shrunk silk before, but Ms Google comes through with the goods. I soak the shirt in hot water then chuck it in the wash at the highest temperature. After a tumble in the dryer, it's two sizes smaller – two sizes too small for Will.

I picture him struggling to get into it before class, gasping because it's so tight, giving up, rocking up to Science without his Mrs Clayton merch, his social standing diminishing as everybody else reveals her face stretched across their chests …

I've recovered from fake gastro by morning. Nobody bats an eyelid. Mum does ask why I have a spring in my step, though. I assure her there's no spring, but there is. I'm practically bouncing until the bus home. Will boards just as the doors are closing. He comes down the aisle in the too-small Mrs Clayton top he's cut into a cropped tank. He looks like he's had one hell of a growth spurt. It's … kinda goofy and endearing.

Fuck.

Some guy in his year high-fives him. 'Mullet Man!'

The hardness in my chest grows.

I stay up late. I find a letter from the school about the careers expo and scan it onto my computer. I keep the letterhead and footer, but I change the text. *The Canada Bay Secondary grooming guidelines clearly state that a boy's hair must not scratch the collar of his shirt …* When it's printed, it looks legit, a warning from the Deputy to Will's parent and/or guardian about the state of his mane. I add the doctored letter to a stack of legit ones on the kitchen island. Will doesn't notice it when he fetches his morning apple.

Mum does.

She goes a bit feral at him for not telling her he's been cautioned about his hair. He's clueless. She tells him she's booking an appointment with her hairdresser. He tries to negotiate a trim, a mini mullet. Nope. By dinner, it's all gone. Buzz cut.

He's all eyebrows. Nobody's high-fiving that.

It's too early for the buzz cut to have changed anything, but I ask Mira the question when I'm brushing my teeth the next morning. She apologises. 'I didn't catch that,' she says. 'Could you repeat your question?'

I spit out the toothpaste and take extra care to enunciate.

'I'm sorry, I didn't catch that. Could you repeat your question?'

'Fairest,' I bark. 'Who is fairest?'

'Did you mean *Mrs Forrest?*' Mira asks.

'No, I'm not asking about my Year Eight Geography teacher.'

The voice assistant starts rattling off keywords. At first, I think she's busted, then I contemplate the unthinkable …

I plonk down opposite Eve, interrupting a steamy round of doing absolutely nothing with Ethan. She seems put out, but this is important. 'I need to know who coded Mira,' I say.

She's *really* put out. Flustered. She stammers a bit and eventually lands on: 'Why?'

'They've made a change. I've asked the question all morning, no response.' I whip out my phone and demonstrate.

Mira doesn't catch the question. She politely asks me to repeat it.

I lock my phone. 'Whoever's in charge nerfed the feature.'

Eve doesn't seem shocked. She goes into reassuring-friend mode. 'Maybe it's a good thing?'

'What? Not having an answer?'

'Not focusing on what Mira says.'

I swallow hard. 'How can that be a good thing?'

Eve reaches out and lays a hand over mine. Her touch is warm. 'It was a nice ego boost,' she says. 'Remember how you were a bit down on how you looked and then Mira appeared and you felt good?'

I clear my throat forcefully. It becomes a laugh. 'That isn't how it went.'

Her lips purse. She doesn't break eye contact for one, two … She blinks. 'You're right. I must've got it wrong.'

'Yeah.' I clear my throat again. 'So, can you do it?'

'What?'

'Find out who codes her. You're good with …' I twinkle my fingers over an invisible keyboard.

Eve shakes her head.

'You sure?' The pleading note in my voice is embarrassing.

'I've watched you tear yourself up over this, you think I haven't tried?'

Makes sense.

'You were bound to lose the title at some point,' Eve adds. 'Say, hypothetically, I coded Mira—'

'Sure.'

'Say I did,' she insists. 'Say, as your best friend, I thought up the gentlest way for you to lose the title and not feel hurt ... I reckon it'd look like this, you passing the baton on to your younger brother, not some random.'

I never expected to be fairest of all forever. I mean, who's top dog of their high school in their thirties? No, I was certain I would reign until I graduated. I wouldn't have access to Mira after that. I wouldn't know who replaced me and I wouldn't care. I would focus on making a name for myself at uni, outside uni ... I know Eve thinks being fairest of all doesn't mean anything, and it probably doesn't in the grand scheme of things, but it hurts, losing it so close to the end of school.

'Why did I have to lose it before I left?' I ask. 'Why aren't I enough for people?'

'Why aren't you enough for you?'

I keep asking Mira the question, on the off chance she reconsiders. In the toilets at recess. On the bus home. Before dinner. Before breakfast. I'm halfway through my protein oats when I hear Will stomping down the hall. I always found his inability to walk softly irritating, but since he robbed me of my last few weeks as Canada Bay Secondary's fairest of all, the irritation has been off the charts. I feign an intense interest in my breakfast when he enters. He says hey. I don't respond. He asks where Mum is. She's at yoga, but I don't tell him. The most he gets out of me is a shrug.

He doesn't pluck up an apple and piss off, as is his custom. This morning, he's particularly fussy about his choice, moving fruit around the bowl like he's not the only one in the house who enjoys apples. Whatever he doesn't eat today, he'll have by the end of the week, so what does it matter?

I keep my eyes on my oats.

Will settles on a Pink Lady eventually. For the first time in ages, he sits at the table to have his breakfast. Great. Awesome.

I consume my oats at double-speed.

He bites into the apple. The crunch is intense. And he moans like all apples don't taste the fucking same. And then, another sound. I furrow my brow. I focus on the oats. They have all of my attention. Most of my attention.

There's that sound again. Something like a gasp. A struggle for air. I look up. Will's staring at me, mouth open. He points at his neck. He's choking.

I drop my spoon, push myself up off my seat and ... pause.

His eyes widen, as if to ask what's taking me so long. He taps the table. He wants me to perform the Heimlich manoeuvre. Urgently.

I hover over my seat.

He took fairest of all from me. He didn't apologise. He never even mentioned it. Like it meant nothing.

Will flails, points at his neck again.

I know Mira isn't keeping track, but he's still fairest of all by her measure. And he can't be fairest of all *and* dead, can he?

My heart thumps. I tell myself it's vindication, excitement at the universe correcting itself, and not fear, the precursor to regret ...

My younger brother is choking in front of me and I'm doing nothing. The same younger brother who would climb into my bed when we were kids, who hid behind me when Dad ...

Another gasp, more strained. Will slams the table, all his strength escaping in one movement.

It'll play well on social media, me having a dead brother. And wherever I go, I'll have everybody's sympathy. 'Yeah, my brother passed away in front of me,' I'll say, and they'll look at me with tortured expressions and when I'm out of earshot, they'll tell each other how strong I am to keep going in the face of it. Forget being Canada Bay Secondary's fairest of all, I'll be something bigger ... This is the sort of origin story that launches somebody into the stratosphere.

I feel my heartbeat in my ears. It's all I can do not to smile.

Will's eyes dart to the fruit bowl. His brand is apples. I bet he feels betrayed.

To be honest, he eats so many, if he was gonna choke, a poorly masticated Pink Lady was odds-on favourite.

My gaze follows his. He's watching the mountain of waxy Pink Ladies. It takes me a second to clock the phone jutting out, its camera trained on us. Will wasn't fussing over his choice of apple before, he was …

My stomach drops. Shit.

I can't stare at it forever. I turn back to my younger brother. He's sitting with a slight hunch. Only hurt in his eyes.

'You were going to let me choke,' he says.

'I …' I struggle to find the words. 'I was in shock.'

'You were angry at me, so I thought I'd prank you.' His voice cracks. 'You said pranks were supposed to be a bit cruel. I figured making you believe I was dying was cruel enough … and you just watched me.'

And he recorded it all.

I can delete the video. It'll be Will's word against mine.

I scramble towards the fruit bowl. I snatch the phone, apples spilling onto the island.

I turn it round.

He wasn't just recording, he was livestreaming.

My hand trembles. I—

It's okay. This is Will's account. There are only six viewers watching live. No damage done.

My hand steadies. I—

A comment crawls up the screen. A single angry-face emoji from OmarTheArcher.

I find Eve in the library. She's by the circulation desk, surprisingly close to Ethan, who's sorting the returned books into manageable piles. If I didn't know any better, I'd think they were about to talk to each other. I sidle up to her and she almost jumps out of her skin.

'Reckon you can hack Omar's socials?'

She looks from me to Ethan. 'Huh?'

'He might spread some shit about me. We need to discredit him.'

'I'll just …' It's a voice I haven't heard outside of Year Nine Economics. Ethan's. He isn't finished sorting, but he scoops up a stack of books and walks out from behind the circulation desk. Eve watches him head towards the fiction shelves.

Good. He's out of her hair. I press on. 'I can get you Omar's email address, if that helps.' She's still looking at Ethan. 'Hello? Eve?'

Word spreads quickly. I hear my name murmured in the corridors. I lock eyes with Hunter in second-period English and he looks away. I shed followers. Every time I check, in the changeroom, on the bus, the number's shrunk a little more …

I need to stem the bleeding.

I search the trendiest audio clips. I find the most popular. I listen to it over and over until I feel the vague shape of a routine forming in my mind. I prop the phone up in my bookcase, start recording and step back. The beat kicks in and I move, light on my feet like I'm dancing on burning coals.

I'll do whatever it takes for as long as it takes. Forever if need be.

I will win everybody back.

They'll tell me I'm the fairest of all.

ALDA, AYSEL & THE EDISTO RIVER

AMBER MCBRIDE

GRIOT

It's mischievous how much a tale tilts
when the grit of it is chewed & passed on.

The moral is double underlined in red
(don't love girls, don't be Black, don't dream vast)
or Death might undertow you. Might claim you early.

& the bones & the sticks
& the stones & the bullet & lies
& the noose of it
are cut out, shrunk down.
The villains change robes.

But dear reader, remember myths can't recite
their own stories. So, how true are the Fairy Tales?

A good story is feast that must be eaten whole
even when stuffed.
This one has been morphed,
bones stuck in the lines & is undercooked in places.

By the time it was written down
it started with a girl, Mary-Belle,
& a Mermaid in some snaking southern blackwater river.
It ended with a gunshot.

Their real names were Alda & Aysel.
Alda whose name means great wave

        & Aysel whose name means waves called forward
                by the moon.

                Two Black girls
    (both born with webs between their fingers)
& red clay beneath their nails & memories of ancestors
            tied tightly in their locs.

~~~~~~~~~~~~~~~~~~~~~~~ **ALDA** ~~~~~~~~~~~~~~~~~~~~~~~
(5 Years Old)

On the night my Mama died, I was five & the sky magicked a cold.
    It coughed & sneezed rumbling thunder.
So, I held tight to Mama's strong hand which was unlike other hands.
    Mama's fingers had translucent webbing like cellophane between them.

When I looked through the webbing the world was blurry
    like gazing up from the bottom of a lazy river.

During this storm Dad was away
    (but he was always away).
        Dad claimed he was busy negotiating with soil,
            (asking it to sprout). Except when he did come home
                he smelt like smoke & beer & perfume.

Still, I held tight to Mama's webbed hand – me, Alda, a tiny boat trying to keep
    Mama's breath afloat as the rain's soft petals kissed our house goodnight.
Mama smiled & whispered softer than mist kissing the valley at dawn,
        Listen, June. Listen, child.
        Do you hear the song like a psalm?

I strained my ears to hear what Mama heard, but I did not understand

  the language of the storm. Instead, I worried that the swampy water
from the Edisto River might rise up, stroll toward us
    & swallow Mama & me whole.

That night the Edisto rose
as the storm wailed
& Mama lost her breath.
  Mama, I wailed!
    Mama, I screamed.

Finally, the storm corked itself.
Which was good because my tears
were swamping the house
& oceaning the front yard.

& Mama was gone when Dad stumbled up the porch stairs.
He stood over my Mama & pulled a small knife from his pocket.
He held Mama's hand in his & sliced the flimsy
webbed skin that connected her fingers.

As he cut, I heard it, a hymn from the direction of the river.
  A song heavy with waves & a swirling tsunami.

Dad kept cutting & as he cut I felt my fingers tingle & burn.
Gazing down I found flimsy cellophane-skin between my own fingers.
  Like Mama's magic seeped into the floorboards
    & rose up strong in me.

Dad finished & said, *Now you can call the Pastor*,
  before he left through the front door
passing a fallen tree whose green branches sprawled

on the ground resembled the tail of a dying mermaid.

ALDA
(7 Years Later)

My name is Alda & my hair is black (except for one green patch
that rivers in the front) & my nails are painted black & at school
I sit in the back folded in my desk
hiding my webbed hands in my shallow pockets.

My name is Alda & my Dad died (from drinking) & Mama died (during the storm)
& a Pastor with pale skin & 10 children adopted me when I was eight.

That means I wash clothes for 12 people (10 kids & two adults).
That means I cook meals for 12 people (10 demons & two angels of death).
That means (if life is a school of fish) I have dropped out. I have no one.

The Pastor writes my behaviour down in his snake-skinned journal:
Alda stayed in the sun too long (got even darker).
Alda dropped a vase again (stupid girl).
Alda thought she was equal again (she was punished).
Alda spent too much time at the river again (we must drought her).

AYSEL
(Always Watching)

The girl with black hair (except for the one green patch
that rivers in the front) & the nails that are painted black
works in the dirt near the Edisto River, my river, until her nails spilt.

She places offerings for her ancestors on white plates
& when she leaves & the move waves over the river
I pull myself from the still water (nicking myself on the rocks)

& feast on the offering. I leave a shell behind every time.

Each offering shrinks my tail & 10 tiny toes slowly sprout
like brown coral. The girl always has rivers racing
from her eyes. She asks her ancestors for a miracle.

& something tugs, like a red string, me to the offering
& I think I'll grow legs by summer.
I hope I'll grow legs by summer.

On a slab of stone, at the bottom of my river,
I leave fishbones & red coral from the ocean
for my ancestors. Asking them for a miracle too.

Some nights (when everyone is sleeping)
I sing a strange psalm
my Mama, Jane, taught me –
it sounds like a tsunami
trying to reach the moon.

& I know the girl has heard my song in her dreams
because she often sings the hymn at the water's edge.

& her voice is spring sun through stained-glass water
& her hands are sea-turtles wise
& her eyes
her eyes
her eyes.

ALDA
(Summer Break)

In the summer I wake up early (moments before the sun)
     & stretch like a moon-rise across the floor. I tend to the garden
& clean the house before I make breakfast for 12.

I like to read stories the Pastor would not approve
on the small back porch (I am not allowed on the front one).
     Stories with girls with loc'ed hair & big brown eyes.
     I write the stories in my green journal & try to dream myself away.
& I make believe I am one of the talking trees.

I sip my tea & raise my hand. I study the sun
through my webbed fingers.

Before dinner I walk down to the Edisto River which is a weaving vine

that crawls all the way to the coast of South Carolina where it empties
into the great Atlantic. So, the Edisto never ends – it connects me to ancestors.

I trust water & rain & the river. I tell the river all my secrets.
I tell the water sometimes I think I am magic, I ask plants to grow
& they sprout overnight. I whisper to crows & they gift me marbles.

I tell that river I feel at home on its banks.
I tell the river I find the curve of a hip a prayer.
I tell the Edisto they call me a witch –
      for practising Hoodoo (like Mama)
      for my webbed fingers (like Mama).

The Pastor says, *Your Mama practiced Hoodoo, that's why your hands are cursed*
      & perhaps you can work your way out of your sin-filled birth.

Because Mama is gone, I had to walk five miles to the small home
of a Black woman who lives near the river to learn about Hoodoo.
      I tiptoed out at night. Until she died (now I am all the way alone).

I've been asking the ancestors for something to make me smile
& I leave offerings & get gifted seashells & I wonder where they come from
& I string them into my hair & hope & dream.

~~~~~~~~~ **ALDA** ~~~~~~~~~
(Hoodoo Gril)

Hoodoo is when you talk with the leaves, the trees, the herbs
      & the soil beneath your feet. Hoodoo is when you leave offerings
for ancestors to help protect you. I leave lots of offerings for Mama.

When I make breakfast, I put a slice of toast on a white plate for Mama

   & take it to the river. When I sip tea, I pour a little of mine
in a teacup for her. I even leave space in my bed in case Mama's spirit visits.

I think maybe Mama will get tired of flying high in the sky.
   Maybe she will want to come & rest a while at night
beside me. *At night when anything is possible,* Mama always said.

I tell the river secrets, like how in school my eyes trace the faces
   of girls not boys. If the Pastor knew he would be furious.
I've heard him say, *That ain't natural. God thinks those people are sin-stuffed.*

It's strange because Mama always said, *Love is love.*
   It ebbs & flows. It heals & hurts.
You gotta love who you love fiercely, Alda.

I know the Pastor knows the stories about my Mama:
   that her Mama & Pops made her get married
after they found her kissing her best friend, Jane.

Sometimes, before Mama went to the sky, she told me stories about Jane
   & her entire face would change like she was talking
about the softness of the moon.

But the town took Mama's story & realigned the facts.
They said Jane poisoned her (& that's how Mama died).
& Jane disappeared in the river one day.

That is not how it happened. I was there.
Mama heard a hymn like a psalm on the wind
& her spirit was tired of earth & floated to the river.

But people don't listen to true stories.
They like to make up the facts.

AYSEL
(Knees & Toes)

The rocks press hard on the bottoms of my new feet.
My thighs feel like jellyfish tentacles & the moon shines.

My knees bend & my toes wiggle & the trees kiss
their leaves together & the water laps at the shore.

Then I hear a shout, *get back here Black girl!*
I hear a crashing in the woods
I see her
& I freeze.

ALDA
(Trouble)

I should have known there would be trouble
because the sky was cloudy when the Pastor arrived
     & a sharp rain started. It was like the rain wanted
to slice the Pastor in two. It was like an omen.

The Pastor shoved open the door to my closet
of a room tucked tightly under the stairs.
What is this, he yelled, waving my journal
in front of my face. *It's filled with filth.*

                              It's mine! That's private!
                  I wailed & the storm screamed louder.

The Pastor tugged me
by my hair to the kitchen.
I can't have you here around my 10 girls.
You are an abomination. Liking girls!
      Black & gay!

                                                     What's wrong with loving??
                                         I scream. *Why does it matter who?*

The Pastor pulled me out
the front door & down the stairs.
I am going to fix you.
I am taking you to The Camp!

My heart tightened on itself
        (I knew about The Camp).
Where they beat & burned 'sin' out of you.

Black & gay,
the Pastor repeated again
sounding disgusted.

Lightning flashed & I bit the Pastor's hand
& I broke free scrambled to the woods
& tore through the woods to the river.

& I saw her with green hair except for a stripe of black.

~~~~~~~~~~~~~~~ **ALDA & AYSEL** ~~~~~~~~~~~~~~~
(Help!)

Alda (breathing hard): *Hi.*
Aysel (wobbly with eyes wide): *Hi.*

Alda (watching the woods): *They are coming for me.*
Aysel (eyes wider): *Who is coming for you?*

Alda (stepping closer): *The Pastor & his men.*
Aysel (gripping my arm with webbed fingers): *Quickly, we have to hide.*

                                                Aysel led me to the water's edge.

Alda (toeing the water): *How will I breathe?*
Aysel (smiling): *Ask the ancestors. I won't let you drown. They won't let you drown.*

Alda (hearing heavy stomps): *Did the ancestors send you?*
Aysel (eyes smiling): *I was going to ask you the same thing.*

Alda (eyes smiling): *I left offerings. I sang songs.*
Aysel (voice singing): *I gave you seashells. I sang you songs in the dark.*

GRIOT
(Moon & Waves)

On the day the Mermaid sprouted legs
& blossomed from the Edisto River
        Alda needed saving from a mob of men.

On the day Alda tore through the woods
& found a girl with skinny brown legs on the shore
        Aysel needed saving from the sadness in her mind.

Aysel, with brown eyes the color of tree sap,
made Alda's heart ball-change in her ribcage.

Aysel stepped into the water holding hands with Alda.

They were underwater & they could both breathe easily.
      Alda's hand felt like spring in Aysel's hand.
Like magic. Like hope.
Like love sprouting
a red string through the water.

〜〜〜〜〜〜〜〜 **ALDA & AYSEL** 〜〜〜〜〜〜〜〜
(Runaway)

Holding hands under the water Alda could breathe
& they ventured 200 miles to the end of the river
surfaced & looked out over the horizon.

Aysel (stretching her arms wide):
We can swim all the way to Africa.
Alda (eyes wide): *Is it dangerous?*

Aysel (studying Alda's face): *All journeys have danger.*
Alda (watching Aysel): *My Mama is buried here.*

Aysel (touches a seashell in Alda's hair): *So is mine,
but the ancestors are everywhere, so is your Mama.*
Alda (touches a scale on Aysel's arm): *I don't think I can swim that far.
I'd need a flourishing tail like yours.*

Aysel (watching the moon rise):
*Do you ever
blame the southern dirt?*

Alda (frowning): *Land is not evil.
The people living on it are.
Do you blame the water?*

Aysel (nodding slowly):
The water has nothing to do with the flood,
nothing to do with boats carrying brown bodies.
Alda (watching the moon): *Exactly.*

Aysel (softly): *Will you hold my hand.*
Alda (softer): *Will you never let go?*

Aysel (quietly): *Did you hear my psalm?*
Alda (quieter): *Every night.*

Aysel (moving close): *Our hands match.*
Alda (moving closer): *So do our lips.*

~~~~~~~~~~ **GRIOT** ~~~~~~~~~~
(Alda & Aysel)

The river knows nothing of time.
It knows the curve of the bank
& the hope of the fish
& the tumbling of stones
& how meaningless seconds
are to something so ancient.

Alda & Aysel
swim & laugh
& the Pastor searched
& searched but the river
hid them.

They only surfaced to collect berries
& cook fish over the fire.

Alda's lungs grew strong
& Aysel's heart grew full.

Alda (hearing something): *Someone is coming.*
Aysel (pouring water on the fire): *Run.*
The Pastor & all his men (crashing through the forest):
If you don't come back I'll kill you
& no one will care.

Alda's legs are weak from swimming instead of walking
& Aysel's legs are weak from never running

& they don't scramble fast enough
before they are on them
at the edge of the Edisto River
that empties into the Atlantic
& that kisses the shores of Africa.

The Pastor's nails dig like nails into Alda's skin
while Aysel holds tight to her hand.

The other men shove Aysel away
she tumbles backward into the river
& her tail flourishes
& the men gawk
& scream
& a shot resonates in the river.

~~~~~~~~ **ALDA & AYSEL** ~~~~~~~~
(*Gun*)

The gun waterfalls to nothing

in the Pastor's hand
& the bullet falls like a giant teardrop
& Alda breaks free & runs to the river.
Her toes kiss the tip of the shore
& a tail as blue as a whale
flourishes.

& the girls begin to sing their psalm
& the river rises & rises
& gallops to devour the Pastor
& all his men.

The ancestors made it this way.

GRIOT

They say Alda & Aysel were never seen again –
except their story is told on West African soil,
& near southern rivers.
It is like they opened their mouths
created a flood with their kiss
& the bullet drowned
& the men drowned.

Love lived
they lived
(Alda & Aysel)
flourished tails
& followed the river
to everywhere
together.

They tell it wrong because that day
two Black Mermaids
Loved
& sang the ancestors' psalm
& they got free.

SEEING COLOUR

JES LAYTON

Dear Great-Aunt Edward Hayes,

*Anne Seiler-Day and Marsey Moore
invite you to share in joyous celebration
as they begin their new life together on
Saturday, June 15th, 5pm at
Marsey, Anne and Eb's place. RSVP for addy!*

Ebony bikes through the dishwater-grey light of early morning, tearing across footpaths and bitumen. After a full weekend of delivering invitations, this final one burns a hole in his pocket, promising freedom from the slow rain that seeps into his jeans and hoodie.

At least until the next ridiculous task. No matter how hard Ebony pedals, he can't outrun Marsey's bridezilla fever, or her assumption that just because Ebony's finished his holiday reading, he's free for her to boss around.

On either side of the road, rain-slick houses cast bruise-blue shadows on themselves, and at the end of it stands an imposing chain-link fence barely holding back wild, overgrown hedges.

Ebony skids to a stop in front of the fence and nudges the gate open with a toe to reveal the near-perfect picture of a haunted house. Grotesque, carved human faces grin down at Ebony from the gutters. He can see that the faces would once have spat out runoff, but now rain slushes through the rusty holes in the gutter instead. The effect is still pretty cool.

'Anything interesting?' asks a deep voice.

Ebony jumps. 'Jesus Christ!'

'Not quite. More the opposite, really.'

There's a stranger standing in the open doorway. They're tall, with slightly stooping shoulders and wisps of dark-grey hair trapped under a netted wig cap. They're wearing a

pair of stiff blue jeans and what Ebony assumes from all the dropped stitches is a hand-knitted cardigan. Classic grandparent-core, except for the sharp-black eyeliner, red lipstick and half a dozen bangles glittering on their thin wrists.

'Uh, hey,' Ebony says, stepping under the verandah and out of the rain. The open doorway before him is dark and shadowy, but when Ebony moves towards it he can feel an inviting swath of warmth. Surprising, since he was kind of expecting the screech of bats or the wail of a ghost.

Ebony thumbs the invitation in his pocket. 'Are you … Edward Hayes?'

'You got something for me?' they, no, *he* asks, tightening his cardigan around himself. Anne uses he/him for Aunt Teddy, so Ebony adjusts accordingly.

'If you're Anne's aunt, yeah,' he starts, then stops, confused. 'Great-aunt? Or—'

'I am. And Teddy's fine,' Teddy says, looking Ebony over. 'You're Marsey's kid.' It's not a question.

'Brother. Marsey's brother,' Ebony corrects, eyes darting again to the stone faces staring down at him. 'Nice … gargoyles?'

'Thank you. I modelled a few of them after myself.' Teddy takes in Ebony's soggy appearance before nodding up to the carved faces. 'You can come in until this all clears up. They're not fans of being stared at for long.'

Ebony doesn't normally follow sort-of strangers into their definitely-haunted houses but he makes an exception for almost-relatives who carve their own face into stone and offer him tea when it's raining.

The house's inside is completely at odds with its outside. Once past the entryway, everything is a riot of colour. Intricately decorated masks, landscape-painted billy cans and jewelled animal skulls hang on peeling, aged walls, and tall, lit candles line the hallway. In one room, they pass two bonsai grown so large they've stopped being bonsai, their roots wrist-thick and cracking their small bowls. Across one open window, a line of neon-orange pill bottles all stand at attention. Pasted, hung and nailed to almost every wall are photos of people smiling and laughing in places Ebony can't identify.

Ebony's eyes widen as he follows Teddy into the kitchen. 'Marsey would never let me paint my bedroom …' Ebony struggles to find the word he's looking for. 'Pee-yellow,' he settles on, then immediately flushes with embarrassment.

'Xanthic,' Teddy corrects, but not without a slight smile that Ebony catches and flushes at further. 'The name comes from the word xantho, meaning yellow or golden in Ancient Greek. I think of this place as more of a studio than a house.'

Ebony runs his fingers across the xanthic wall before him as Teddy shuffles around and flicks the kettle on with knobbly fingers. He looks up when Teddy pauses, turning back to him and holding out a hand. 'May I?'

It takes Ebony a second to realise what he's asking for. 'Oh, um, yeah.' He passes the invitation over. It's a little crumpled in the corner. A little damp. 'It's an invite to—'

'My great-niece's wedding. I imagine Anne has about driven herself half mad. Obsessed with pageantry, just like my sister. Her grandmother.' Teddy's fingers tighten on the envelope. 'At least, she was as a child.' He sits the unopened invitation down on the kitchen table, then reaches up for two mugs. 'You been roped into that whole clown show yet?'

Clown show. Ebony has to smile. 'Yeah, I mean,' he gestures to the pink envelope, stark against the wildly coloured kitchen. 'They've both been flipping out about getting all these delivered in time.'

Teddy's painted lips purse into a judgmental moue. 'Makes you wonder why an email wouldn't do.'

'Right?' Ebony says. He stops and squints at Teddy. The guy must be at least eighty. 'Wait. Do you even have email?'

'Of course,' Teddy answers. 'Now, a computer, that's a different matter.'

Ebony laughs loudly, and it surprises him and Teddy both, judging by the way Teddy smiles with one half of his mouth. He hands Ebony a spotted white mug and leaves the kitchen with his own in hand. After a moment, unsure of what else to do, Ebony follows.

'It's weird, right?' he says, wanting to widen Teddy's smile to a full grin. 'People owning each other? Legally being one …'

Ebony stops still. The painting in the hall before him isn't overly large. On the canvas, nonsense shapes a deep purple-red in colour are broken apart by streaks and splashes of white and grey. Parts of the canvas have been left completely untouched, with others drowning in globules of paint. Oil, Ebony guesses. The paint is so thick in places, it has dimension.

He realises he's been motionless a while and shouldn't be a weirdo who follows sort-of strangers into their houses and stares at their stuff – but he can't bring himself to look away.

'Do you paint?' Teddy asks.

Ebony shrugs and pulls his gaze from the canvas to meet Teddy's. He swallows. 'Always wanted to try it.' He has asked for his own oil paints before, but the only ones Marsey can afford have been dull and watery.

Teddy's fingers tap the rim of his mug. 'Feel free to stop by if you want to paint on canvas. You'll be family at the end of all this wedding nonsense, after all.'

That evening, it takes a concerted effort for Ebony not to bolt into the lounge room and interrogate Anne about Teddy the moment he gets home. He forces himself to change out of his wet clothes and binder first, then shower.

Anne and Marsey are snuggled up on the couch. Ebony hopes he sounds about as bland and uninterested as he does any other day when he asks, 'Anne?'

'What'd you do?' It's Marsey who answers instead, not even looking up from the seating chart she's arranging. Or *rearranging*, rather, given the heading that reads *Draft 5*.

Ebony doesn't even know why he bothers. Asking Anne anything while Marsey's around or vice versa is like trying to talk to an echo. It hadn't always been like this, the both of them so impossibly *together* that Ebony ends up feeling like a third wheel in his own home. Before the engagement and Anne moving in, Ebony felt like he had both of them. Now he has neither.

Anne looks away from the laptop and over the back of the couch at him. 'You alright, Eb?'

'Teddy – Edward Hayes. He's your great-aunt, right?'

Anne cuts her gaze to Marsey. 'You invited Aunt Teddy?'

'Probably? You have a big family, babe,' says Marsey. 'And the invite list your mum gave me's a thousand people long.'

'I didn't think she'd mean Aunt Teddy. How is—'

'Why?' Ebony interrupts. 'He a murderer or something?'

Marsey looks up then. 'Eb! Don't be a shit.'

'No, it's fine,' Anne insists. She presses a sloppy kiss to the side of Marsey's face before telling Ebony, 'Not a murderer or anything. It's just, I don't want him to feel … awkward?'

'Awkward?' Ebony asks. 'Why would he feel awkward?'

'He's eighty-something,' Anne explains. 'And he's never been able to find someone, you know?' She chews hard on her bottom lip. 'I can't remember him ever having a relationship with anyone, not even when I was a kid. I don't want him to come to our wedding and feel … left out? God, and the way my mum and Nan just *needle* him about not having anyone to take care of him? It's so awkward.'

Ebony grips the bannister tightly. 'Dunno what the big deal is. He seemed fine.'

But it's like Marsey and Anne don't hear him. Marsey is pulling Anne back into her side, and Anne is looking up at her with big, brown cow-eyes.

'It must be hard,' Ebony hears Anne say, and he feels a part of himself float away, leaving what's left on the stairs grey and empty. She keeps talking. 'I think of him in that big house all alone. God knows I could never do it.'

'You won't have to, babe,' Marsey assures, kissing the top of her head. 'You got me forever, amiright?'

Wordlessly, Ebony heads back upstairs.

After a long week of fielding RSVPs; stacking, unstacking, then re-stacking guest chairs; and offering unheard opinions on catering, Ebony finds himself back under the twisted faces guarding Teddy's verandah.

'Paint,' he explains to the older man standing in the doorway. 'If— if I still can, I'd like some paint. And some brushes. Uh, please?'

Teddy regards Ebony over the rim of a different, chipped mug. He's wearing a wig today, which is piled up into a messy bun with little butterfly clips. 'You ever worked with oils before?'

Ebony shakes his head.

'Prepared a canvas?'

Ebony frowns.

'I would rather you work here until you know how to properly use the tools,' Teddy tells him after a sip. 'If you've never used gesso—'

'Okay,' says Ebony. 'I'm happy to do it. I want to learn.'

Teddy, with a nod and maybe something of a smile, steps aside to let him in.

The easels in Teddy's lounge are bisque-coloured and old.

The medium he hands Ebony is a glossy chartreuse.

Pink. Purple. Red. Blue. Lighter, warmer, redder, duller.

Yellow ochre paint splatters Teddy up to his forearms, while alizarin crimson stains his jeans.

'Weddings are oppressive,' Ebony tells Teddy after a horrendous morning of flower arrangements followed by a somehow even more horrendous shopping trip. Marsey may dress like she just escaped a Vinnies by the skin of her teeth, but apparently now she's all about buttoned cuffs, matching socks and 'slacks', as though they are British royalty or something.

'My shirt's, like, mouldy-pea-vomit-green,' Ebony insists as he picks at a globule of canary-yellow that's threatening to run into the baby-pink he set down earlier.

'Mouldy-pea-vomit-green,' Teddy says. They're both working on canvas today, side-by-side. There are paints and brushes and all sorts of tools between them, as well as a few of Teddy's bright neon-orange medicine bottles. 'Is that a new shade from Sennelier?'

Ebony rolls his eyes but can't help laughing.

What he likes best about Teddy is the easy way he talks to him, as though the two of them are on the same side. He laughs at Ebony's jokes and tells him stories of living and studying in Rome and climbing to Machu Picchu in drag. But that was a long time ago, Ebony thinks, as he watches Teddy step back from his work and carefully take hold of his cuppa with fingers too swollen to fit through the handle.

Ebony holds his bottom lip between his teeth for a moment. When he finally speaks, he hates the way his voice cracks. 'Anne's worried.'

Teddy eyes him over the rim of his mug. 'Hmm?'

'About you. About you living alone.'

Teddy's eyes slide from him like water from a duck. 'Dramatic, again. Just like her grandmother.'

'Don't you hate it though?' Ebony asks. 'People, hell, *family* talking about you like that? Looking at you, and at all this' – he gestures around them, hoping to encompass Teddy's kaleidoscopic house, the figurines and achievements and photos, a lifetime's worth of living – 'and thinking, nah, actually, all this is worth jack 'cause you're not spooning some random every night who probably snores in their sleep?'

The touch of Teddy's hand to his wrist brings Ebony out of his head. It holds a tenderness he remembers from when he'd scrape his knees as a kid and Marsey would kiss him better. Ebony drinks in the gesture for a moment before Teddy speaks.

'Everyone feels lonely sometimes, even those who sleep next to snoring randoms.' His thin, stubbled lips twitch upward at that, and Ebony can't stop his own mouth from cracking a little. 'And while I've lived my life on my own, I've never been alone,' Teddy says. He looks at Ebony thoughtfully before turning to face Ebony's canvas. Ebony feels Teddy's hand trembling as he reaches out and covers Ebony's hand with his own, giving it a shaky squeeze. 'Now, your brush is too dry for the little details. Here. Try this.'

'Never saw the point of a higher education in the arts,' Teddy says. It's Thursday, late afternoon, and the two of them are in the kitchen. Ebony, watching as his first pigment attempt is rinsed down the sink, drinks in Teddy's guidance like a pot plant does water.

'New York, Toronto, London, Germany,' Teddy rattles off just a handful of the places that Ebony has seen in photos spread throughout the house. 'For an artist, the world is your best classroom.'

'Still got a bit until school's back and they start pestering me about doing VCE or VCAL,' Ebony says as he passes Teddy the lint-free cloth he's been twisting in his hands. 'Marsey says there's some good arts courses up in Melbourne.'

'I'm sure there are,' Teddy allows. 'It is good you have your sister's support. But do yourself a favour and don't think too much about it for now. You don't have to start right away. Here.' He gestures for Ebony to take up the washed palette, cloth and some solvent.

Ebony works a dollop of solvent onto the palette and scrubs, mesmerised by the way the oil paint breaks down and drips off the tempered glass.

'Anne did that,' Ebony finds himself saying after some time. He sets the palette aside to dry.

Teddy pauses and turns to look at him. 'Pardon?'

'Packed a swag and towel, went off on a whole gap year thing before uni.'

'Where?'

Ebony has to think for a moment. 'Oh, uh, Italy? Think it was there. Her and Marsey wanna go back again for their honeymoon.'

'Honeymoon. She was a child when I—' Teddy stops and shakes his head. 'For the future, you should mix with your palette knife, not your brush,' he scolds Ebony gently, taking said brushes and running them under warm water. 'A painter's brush should last them their whole life if taken proper care of.'

Teddy isn't sad, like Anne seems to think. He's not senile, like Marsey supposes. Teddy just *is*. What he *isn't* is what everyone thinks he should be. From what Anne said, maybe Teddy's aromantic and just doesn't know it. Or maybe not. He's lived his life alone for years and years, but he's happy, Ebony thinks. Until now he hadn't truly believed that people, that *he*, could have that too. Emotion gathers at the base of his throat.

He swallows and nods, aware of how they're standing shoulder to shoulder, so close they could touch if he moved just a little.

Teddy nods back, a light press against Ebony's side before he's moving them on.

It's after midnight when Ebony finds Anne sitting out on the front steps alone with a bottle of burgundy wine. The posts of the verandah frame her like a painting. The outside light perfectly captures the copper notes in her hair, her darker roots. She's in one of Marsey's oversized hoodies and somehow looks more vulnerable for it.

'Anne?' Ebony asks, careful not to slip in his socks.

She doesn't flinch, only waves him off. 'I'm fine. Couldn't sleep.' Coming to sit beside her, Ebony can see more tense furrows in her forehead than he knows what to do with right now. He watches her take one long pull from the bottle.

'What's he like?' asks Anne after a few moments of nothing but the bugs zipping around them. 'Aunt Teddy? Like as an actual person?'

Ebony blinks. 'Teddy? He can be kind of … odd? He's an artist, y'know? A mixed-media one, so he's got all this weird shit. His house is *awesome*.'

'I remember it being pretty cool. Massive.'

'It is,' Ebony agrees. 'Every room's a totally different colour. He's got this library, and there's stuff everywhere. He likes music. And he bakes sometimes.'

The expression on Anne's face is unreadable. 'I grew up with everyone worrying about him. It's, like, ingrained in me at this point, I think,' she says.

'Because he's old,' Ebony says, his voice firm.

'Because he's *alone*,' Anne replies. 'It's really good of you to spend time with him. It's really kind.' She smiles, as though going around to Teddy's place is some kind of charity. As though her words don't cut at something deep in Ebony's chest.

'I just wish he had someone, you know?' she continues. 'So he wouldn't be so lonely.'

Ebony stands, unable to stop his words from dripping like turpentine. 'Did you ever think maybe he's happy with how his life has turned out? That maybe not everyone wants to live with someone else like that?'

'Eb—'

He cuts her off with a snarl. 'Maybe you wouldn't be sitting here worrying if he's happy if you actually got off your ass and went and asked him yourself.'

Marsey's lipstick-pout over their cluttered kitchen table is ivory.

The sunken skin beneath Anne's eyes is glaucous.

Her pancake apology to Ebony is gold.

'Okay, so, Aunt Teddy's place is definitely haunted,' Anne says, kicking shut the car door behind her.

Ebony shrugs. 'Probably.' He hops the steps to the front door two at a time and turns the handle.

Anne rushes to him. 'You're just walking in?' she hisses.

Ebony steps into the familiar warmth of Teddy's cluttered hallway and beams back at her. 'It's fine. Seriously.' He trusts Anne to follow once she's had her fill of the foyer. She's a big girl. 'Teddy?'

Rounding into Teddy's studio, Ebony sees him. Black earbuds, face partially turned away from the two of them, a silvery-grey wig reaching midway down his back. Teddy stands there in paint-splattered jeans, busy at work, mouth moving wordlessly along to whatever's pumping through his earbuds. Ebony watches him paint a cloud of white across the wall in front of him with his bare hand.

Feeling himself grin, Ebony steps forward. 'TED—Oh!'

Standing in a deep-orchid robe in the corner of the studio is another person. Their hair sits on top of their head like a stick of silver fairy floss. They turn towards him and Anne, removing earbuds from their own ears with a friendly nod, and call out in a surprisingly firm voice, 'Doll! You've got visitors!'

Teddy starts as though woken from a dream. He turns towards the person before noticing Anne and Ebony. He plucks the buds from his ears with paint-drenched fingers.

'Anne,' he says, emotion clear in his voice. He grabs a rag and tries to wipe the paint from his shaking hands. 'Wh—It's lovely to see you.'

'Hey, Aunty,' Anne says, stepping forward for a hug. She folds into him easily, and the two stand there a moment before pulling away.

'I'm sorry, we should have knocked—'

'Wouldn't have heard you, and Adine's as deaf as a post.'

'Rude,' Adine says. They step forward to clasp hands with Anne before greeting Ebony with, 'And you must be the protégé.'

'Ebony,' Teddy agrees, while Ebony struggles to keep the heat from his cheeks. *Protégé.* 'And this is my great-niece, Anne.'

Anne beams up at him, looking younger than she has in months.

At this, Adine seems to consider Anne anew. '*Blellow,*' they say. 'Your aura, it's a mix between blue and yellow. Blellow.'

'They mean green,' Teddy corrects with affection.

'No, green is green. Blellow is blue and yellow, the two both existing at the same time without mixing into one another.'

Anne blinks. 'I'm not sure that's a real thing.'

Adine snorts. 'Maybe. But neither is magenta. Our brains see what we think is magenta, but it's not.'

Before Adine can go on, Teddy claps his hands together. 'Well, if you're hanging about you can make yourselves useful. Grab a tin and brush. Been wanting to redo the second bedroom for a while.'

Ebony's hands leave splotches of egg-white paint as he smears them along the wall.

Working on the opposite wall with brushes, Anne flicks her wrist in delicate flourishes. Her hair is held back by one of Teddy's old wig caps, but that hasn't stopped her from getting little splatters of white in some of the strands.

Ebony drags one finger through the still-wet paint on the wall before him, scraping in the bridge of a nose, eyes. He can feel the weight of Anne's stare before she says, 'You're a really good artist, Eb.'

Ebony wants to gather those words up and tuck them into his chest. 'Thanks.'

The moment breaks when Anne's phone chirps. She grabs a rag to pick it up. The smile on her face is flecked with white.

'That Marsey?' asks Ebony.

'Yeah, she's at a tasting right now. My parents' choice, of course. Says hi.'

'Hi back,' Ebony says. 'You guys still wanna go with the, uh, three courses?'

But Anne's not listening. She smiles at her phone as she taps out a reply.

Ultimately, Ebony figures it's just basic sums. If the world is comprised of pairs, then he is the remainder.

It's not that he wants someone to be with. He just …

'Hey, Anne?'

Something must be different in the tone of his voice. She looks up this time. 'Yeah?'

Ebony swallows. He isn't entirely sure where the words are coming from. He's never voiced any of this. 'You know what Adine said? About magenta?' Anne nods. 'Well, I think I'm the magenta of people. Like, I'm not sure I really exist?' he tries to explain in a rush. 'Not in the way I'm meant to. I look at you and Marsey and I don't get it? Love.' He glances at Anne, unsurprised to see she looks completely baffled. 'It all gets sort of mashed together and confusing for me; family and friends and—' He stops for a second. There's no way he's talking to Anne about sex. 'For me, love's like putting lots of flavours of ice cream together in a smoothie. Except romantic love. That's not even an ice cream flavour for me. It's a whole different thing. It's … cereal.'

Anne stares at him. 'You hate cereal.'

'Exactly,' says Ebony, heart in his throat. 'And I don't need it, right? Don't even want it. I've got my smoothie. With all the other, I dunno, flavours of love inside it.'

'Flavours of love,' Anne echoes, then smirks at him. 'That's such a shitty band name.'

'So crappy.' Ebony laughs, though there's a little edge of heaviness still in it. 'Smoothies and magenta – sorry, I got mixed up somewhere there. But honestly, being aromantic, it can be confusing. But aromantic, that's me – that's what I am.'

He's grateful Anne doesn't immediately jump into questions and assurances. He's thankful she's taking the time to digest his words honestly.

It doesn't help the pounding of his heart any.

'I think you're right,' she says, after a while. 'You kind of are magenta.'

Ebony's stomach twists. 'Okay, ouch.'

'No, no, listen. You know about mantis shrimp, right? That they have a ridiculous amount of colour receptors in their eyes, while we only have three? Meaning they can see hundreds of colours we can't even imagine, probably including magenta. So, it's not that magenta doesn't exist, it's that it's something our minds can't fully comprehend. It only exists for special people. Or special mantis shrimp who like cereal-less smoothies.'

Ebony's heart is still racing. His vision is strangely clear. He's full of confusion and relief and joy. 'You … you're a dork. You know that?'

'It's been said.' Anne has a smear of white paint over her right eyebrow. 'C'mon,' she says, nudging Ebony in his side. 'I think—'

There's the harsh sound of glass breaking.

Adine's voice ricochets from down the hall. 'Ted. Teddy?'

Anne dashes out of the room, and Ebony follows after her, a moment before Anne's shriek rips through his ears.

'TEDDY!'

Ebony and Anne sit together on stiff, ugly chairs. He hasn't managed to rinse all of the paint from his hands, and he knows he's probably leaving white prints on the hospital seat. Maybe, Ebony thinks numbly, some paint might make the geometric design something actually approaching tolerable.

Enough time passes for the paint on Ebony's hands to dry before he catches sight of Adine shuffling down the corridor towards them.

Anne's standing before the words are out of Adine's mouth. 'Can I—'

'Head on in, doll.' Adine wraps their silk robe more tightly around themself. Anne stumbles forward, but Adine stops her, leaning in close to say something Ebony can't hear. Something that leaves Anne looking sick.

She sniffs, withdraws, and without a backwards glance, heads off to Teddy.

Ebony picks at the dried paint around his fingernails as Adine takes Anne's seat and sighs.

'Place is gonna be packed soon.' They absently thumb at a worn tear in the chair's fabric, but after a greasy from a passing nurse, fold their hands into each other instead. 'Your sister's on her way.'

Adine's nails are paint-free, surprisingly. Long, too, and tapered to pale-pink points. Ebony stares at them as he tries to speak. 'I can stay—'

'He doesn't want it,' Adine cuts in.

Ebony baulks. 'What?'

'For you to see him die, lovey,' Adine says gently. 'He doesn't want that for you.'

The need comes with Adine's words. The need to be destructive. To *wreck*. To pitch a fit like a kid and shout out 'it's not fair' because it isn't – Teddy was fine. He was old, but he was *fine*, and Ebony had only just found him and Anne had only just maybe started to understand and now he's gone.

When Marsey arrives, he's not sure how long it has been.

'Eb!'

Arms wrap around Ebony. Hands touch his face. Warm hands. 'Ebby,' Marsey says, her big, brown eyes already wet. 'Ebby, I'm so sorry.'

Teddy's funeral is on a Wednesday.

It's sunny.

Mid-afternoon.

Beautiful.

His casket is black.

The flower arrangements are yellow.

The hundreds of eyes packed inside the old RSL are red.

'Doll!'

Packed in the crowded RSL, Ebony, pressed close to Marsey, hears Adine calling to him and tries to turn around.

'A—Adine?'

Their fairy floss hair bounces through the crowd. Ebony can't properly see them until they're right up on Marsey.

'Mauve,' Adine says to themself, looking Marsey over before drawing her into a giant hug. 'You must be the other bride-to-be.'

Always a hugger, Marsey relaxes into it. 'I am so sorry this is how we're properly meeting.' She draws back from Adine with a wobbly smile. 'Anne's with her parents outside. They couldn't find a park.'

'Mustn't have thought our Teddy's final hoorah would be a sold-out event,' Adine teases gently.

Ebony hiccups or laughs – even he can't tell. 'There are so many people who love him.'

Adine nods. 'All the best people do. Speaking of, doll, here—'

The first thing Adine hands him is a pair of house keys.

The second thing they give him is a note.

> *Finish it for me. The spare room at the end of the hall, beside the fireplace.*
> *Bring a couple of bags with you, take any of the supplies you can carry.*
> *Your perspective is something unique, Ebony. Trust it.*
> *Consider me your first collaborator.*
> *Gratefully,*
> *Teddy*

Ebony slips the most ornate key he's ever held into Teddy's front door, all the while being stared down by the carved stone faces above him. Once inside, Ebony's struck by how surreal it is, looking around and not seeing Teddy shuffling about. Ebony's fingers curl around Teddy's note as he heads for the room at the end of the main hall and flicks on a light. Inside there's a simple array of shelving, supplies and a work-table. On the far side of the room is the boarded-up fireplace, and next to it, like Teddy said, is what Ebony's looking for.

Ebony sits down in front of the unfinished canvas. He stares at the expanse of white, marked only with a few sketches in grey lead, for ten minutes. Twenty. Grey lead sketches, a bit of medium. It's waiting for paint. Teddy has left that up to him.

Earbuds in, Ebony gathers what he needs from the rest of the house. A head-sized wooden palette, several ice cream tubs filled with tubes of paint, a handful of brushes stuffed into the back pocket of his jeans.

Ebony doesn't bother with underpainting; he simply dips a brush into a deep well of cerise and begins. The paints do what he wants, when he wants, and even without Teddy's encouragement, Ebony knows now he's good at this. Music crescendos in his ears, reverberating like church bells, as he loses himself painting in the sketches Teddy left him.

The house is decked out in red and gold. Little fairy lights are strung around the whole back garden, over tables and through the archway Ebony only just finished painting last night. Everyone is lined up to greet the brides, and Ebony can see them both: Anne in her pistachio-green dress, Marsey in black slacks and a now-unbuttoned shirt not unlike Ebony's own. *Happy.*

He's happy they're happy.

The actual ceremony was a short affair. Ebony had been in his front-row seat for less than forty-five minutes before Marsey and Anne were married. Legally, for all of eternity. Ebony even got to sign the certificate as a witness while Marsey snapped pic after pic on her phone.

It's not *entirely* nauseating.

'Hey,' Ebony says as he approaches his now two sisters. They are huddled on the front verandah, stealing a moment together away from the rest of the reception. They both look up at his approach, cheeks pink and smiles dopey.

'Good to see marriage hasn't changed either of you,' he teases, noticing a few lipstick stains beneath his sister's shirt collar. 'Anne, you got a sec?'

Marsey squints at him. 'You gonna murder her?'

Anne swats at her. 'Shut up, Marsey, *god*.'

'I wanna show you something,' Ebony says. 'But it can—'

'No, god, please. *Save me.*' Anne jerks to her feet with only the slightest of wobbles. 'Swear, if I have to fumble through another interrogation about "When are you having kids? Mrs Blah-Blah swears by IVF", I'm gonna *scream* and maybe break someone.'

'Something,' Marsey amends.

'Nah, love. Some*one*.'

'Now you know how I feel, when you both go on about all that stuff,' Ebony says.

'I'm sorry, Eb,' Marsey says while Anne pulls him into her side, her dress so thin Ebony knows it's only the champagne and rush of everything keeping her warm. 'Honestly, next time either of us make you feel crap with stuff like that, you have full permission to punch me.'

Anne shakes her head. 'There won't *be* a next time, Eb.'

'We'll try,' Marsey promises, looking up at him in a way that makes Ebony feel as though the long list of differences between them doesn't exist. 'We'll learn.'

Ebony laughs. 'Just *a* punch?'

Anne tugs on him. 'No, no punching!'

Marsey cackles. 'You say that now, but just you wait. Little brothers are the worst.'

It's only after a few close calls and half a dozen promises of 'I'll be there in a moment' from Anne that they finally make it to the privacy of upstairs. Outside of his bedroom door, hand on the knob, Ebony feels the tips of his fingers tingle with nerves.

'It's not much,' he says before letting Anne in behind him. 'But happy Signed Piece of Paper Day or whatever.'

Anne looks ready to roll her eyes at him until she steps into his bedroom and sees the canvas propped against Ebony's bed.

'Oh. Oh, Eb.'

Cast in hues of magenta, blush-bronze and gold, two women sit under a winding expressionist-style tree surrounded by layers of pale-yellow, pink and orange smoke. The tree's roots reach up like mangroves, morphing into paint drips and winding around the two women. They're both facing away from the viewer, pressed in close to one another, thigh to shoulder.

'Teddy was working on it. A wedding gift,' Ebony explains, tugging at the edge of his binder nervously. His chest already felt tight, but now it's a little hard to breathe. 'I helped him finish it.'

'You *both* did this?' Anne whispers.

'Yeah, it was – oomph!'

Unable to speak through Anne's sudden spine-crushing, blackout-inducing hug, Ebony stands still for a moment before getting his head in the game and hugging her back. He rubs at her shoulders when they start to shake.

'Thank you,' she murmurs into his hair. She rests her chin against his temple. 'Thank you.'

Ebony's not sure how long they stay like that, but when she draws back he feels emotion build in his throat, coming out as words. 'Have I, uh, ever thanked you?'

Anne sniffs. 'For what?'

'Everything. For giving my sis a chance when you found out she had me to look after. For being the only other person in existence who loves her as much as I do.' He takes a breath, offering her a shaky smile. 'You are seriously the luckiest person in the world. Know that.'

Anne's grin starts in her eyes and builds up slowly until all at once it reaches her lips, causing tiny dimples to form at her cheeks. 'We both are,' she responds. After a moment, she says, 'It's kind of like he's here after all. In a way.'

'It's important, I think,' Ebony says, unsure if it's actually possible to ache with both joy and loss at the same time, in the same moment, the same breath. But he does. He steadies himself by reaching out to Anne. 'Th—that, y'know, he isn't forgotten.'

'He won't be,' Anne promises him and, without hesitation, reaches back.

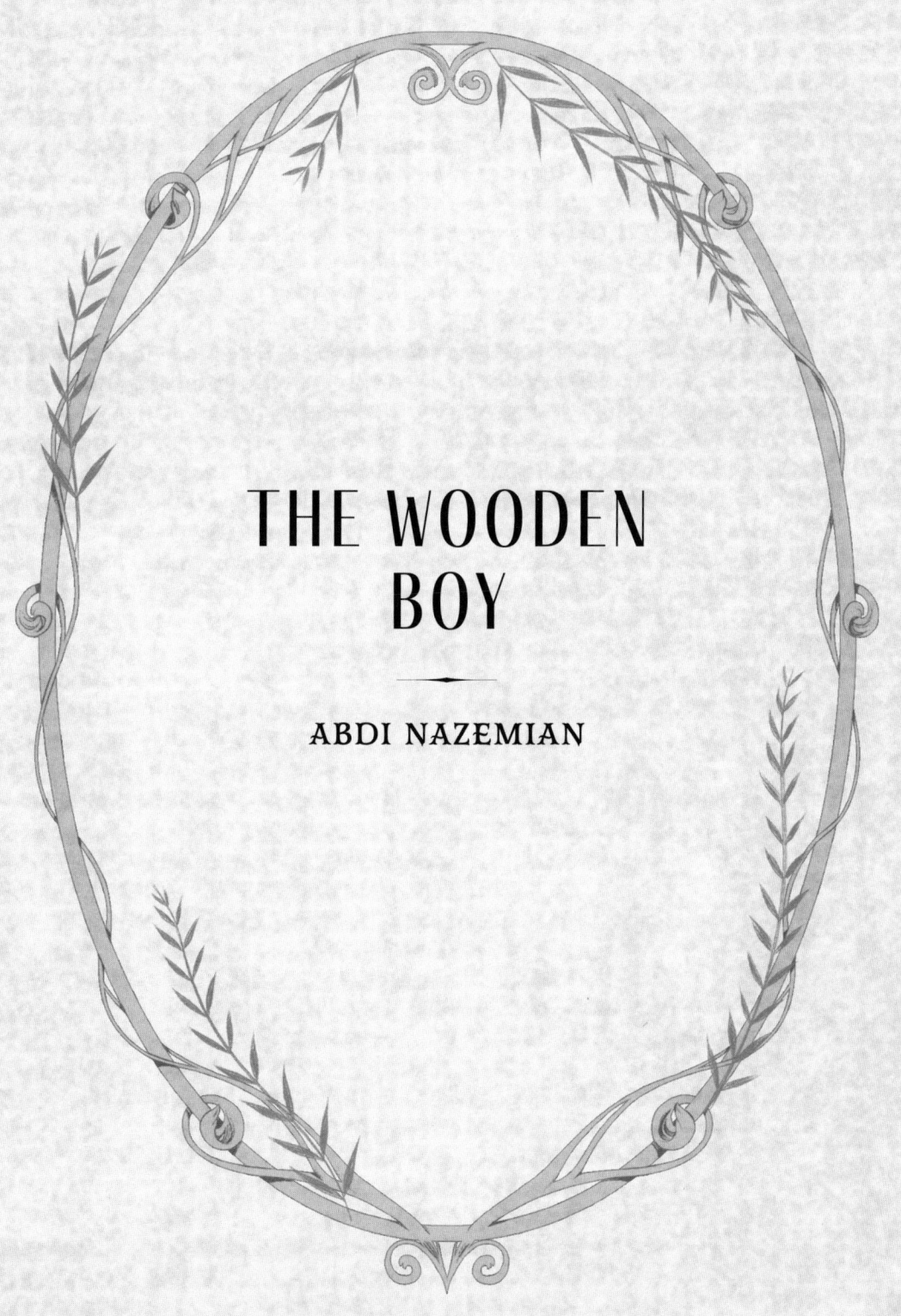

THE WOODEN BOY

ABDI NAZEMIAN

'Dad, can I talk to you about something?' I hand my father the crisp white pages I printed for him. I can't help but think that the paper in my hands is made from the same wood I was carved from. That's all I am. Paper.

I have no heart, just the desire for one.

No soul, just a silly wish that some day I'll have one.

And no freedom, just the deep and ever-present desire to explore the world.

I watch my dad closely as he scans the pages. 'Pino …' His eyes tell me everything on his mind. *You can't go on an in-person school trip to Rome. You've only known other kids virtually. Seventeen years of living and learning through the safe distance of technology.*

'I'm ready for this,' I say. 'And this is my last chance. I'm a senior. Next year I graduate and—'

'And then you'll begin working for me. We'll carve beautiful things together.' His eyes travel to the wood shop, where he creates armoires and tables and chairs and chests and where, seventeen years ago, he created me.

I feel my body stiffen. I know my dad is protecting me by keeping me here. But I want more than to spend my life stuck in this house. 'Please,' I beg. 'All the other boys in the class are going.'

'All the other boys are …' He doesn't finish the sentence.

'I want to see the world,' I plead, fighting back anger. 'It's a school trip. I'll be safe. Our teachers will all be there.'

'Your teachers don't know what you are. If they find out …'

I know what he's thinking because he's told me all this before. He's afraid that if they find out, they'll fear me, the way people are taught to fear those who are different. They'll hurt me. Hit me. Soak me in water, because wood warps when it's wet. Scorch me with fire, because wood burns. My father can't handle losing another family member. I'm all he has now.

'And besides,' he continues, 'those other boys should think twice about going, too. The virus could come back. A whole new generation of sons and daughters and mothers and …' He loses steam, adrift in sadness. I know he blames himself for not protecting his family, but it wasn't his fault. Millions lost their lives to the virus in our small country alone.

'I know you're scared. But I'm begging you. I have to know someone other than you someday. I want to know my classmates as more than a head in a box on a computer screen. I want to see buildings that aren't our home. A real city. Art. Stray cats. I want to meet *people who aren't my dad*.'

His eyes tell me, *You can't meet other people when you're not a person*. His words tell me, 'I just don't want you to get hurt.'

'I've been hurt before. Remember when I lost a finger and you carved me a new one?'

'That's not the kind of pain I'm talking about.'

'Remember when the kitchen pipe exploded and my cheek got wet? You had to—'

He sighs. 'I'm talking about heartbreak. The kind of heartbreak that makes a person …' He doesn't finish the sentence. I could finish it for him. I suppose that's what happens when you've only known one person your whole life. You know exactly what they're feeling, fearing and dreaming.

'It's your own heart you're worried about.' I put my hand on his heart. 'Because I don't have a heart, remember?' He nods sadly. 'That's one thing you weren't able to carve for me.'

He looks at me tenderly. 'I forget. When I look at you, sometimes, I can hear your heartbeat.'

I was created from my father's loss. From the loneliness he felt when the virus took his family from him. His wife, his parents, his sister, his nieces and nephews – all gone quickly. Every cousin, too. And every aunt and uncle. But somehow, he survived it. Scared of being next, he bunkered himself away in our small Tuscan village with his carving tools. For months, it was just him and his spoon knives and hook knives and whittling knives and carving knives. Knives have the potential to harm, but he chose to create with one instead. He created me. Pino, born from wood and loneliness.

'Maybe …' I hesitate, but I have to say it. 'Maybe it's time for you to get out there, too.' I take a beat to gauge his reaction, but he turns away from me. 'Maybe while I'm in Rome, you could go somewhere nice. Meet new people. The virus is gone.'

He doesn't look at me as he says, 'For now.' My dad never told me about losing his whole family in a matter of days. A tsunami of loss. I only know because I once overheard him on a video call with an old friend who lives in a place called Portland now. The friend said to

him through the computer, 'Gepetto, leave Italy. Come to America. The food may not be as good here, but the ghosts are strangers. They can't haunt you when they never knew you.'

I hold my father's gaze. 'I promise I won't tell any of the other boys our secret. I promise they won't find out.'

'You can't promise that. They'll expect you to shower like they do. They won't understand that you can't get wet. They might tackle you. You don't know how violent boys can be. If they touch you, they'll know what you are.'

'I promise I won't let anyone—'

'The answer is no, Pino.' I hate that the word no is in my name, like negativity is a core part of my identity. 'I'm sorry. If you're lonely, maybe I can work on carving a companion for you. A girl for you to love.'

I've never hated him more than right now. He thinks he can just carve more wooden people and gift them language and desire, but he can't. I know because I've seen him try. It never works. I'm one-of-a-kind. Magic.

And I hate him for assuming I want a girl, for assuming I'm just like him, made in his image.

I hate him for keeping me trapped.

'I wish you'd never created me!' I shout in his face. I want him to blame himself for thinking he could carve a good boy to keep him company. I'm not a good boy. I'm a bad, spiteful block of wood. That's all I am.

It's my turn to choose the movie. Every night, we alternate who chooses the film we watch. I choose one of his favorites, *La Dolce Vita*, from the days when our country was still *his* Italy. We watch tensely, too upset with each other to relax, too committed to our tradition to skip a night. Anita Ekberg wades through the waters of the Trevi Fountain. All my life, he showed me images of the world outside. Did he think I wouldn't want to see Rome after seeing *La Dolce Vita*, wouldn't want to see France after seeing *The Umbrellas of Cherbourg*, wouldn't want to see London after watching *Notting Hill*? Didn't he notice the way I leaned in when we watched *Moonlight* and those two boys kissed? As my dad watches the images, I see his expression change. He looks over at me and offers me a smile. 'Rome is beautiful,' he says. 'You'll see.'

The Rome of our school trip is not the Rome of Anita Ekberg. It's not the city my dad once knew, when he still had a family. It's not a place of luxury and decadence and men who look like Marcello Mastroianni. The twelve of us stay in a cold monastery atop a hill. We're surrounded not by urbanity and speeding Vespas but by orange groves, public rose gardens and an endless sky. The classmates on my trip to Rome are nothing like I hoped they would be either. I've only known them as faces in boxes during class time. We've always been supervised. But here on our trip, they have bodies bursting with muscle and hate. They tease each other constantly. They tackle and give wedgies and headlock each other. But they save the worst teasing for me.

When we play soccer in the cold courtyard, Luca yells, 'Loosen up and run, Pino. You're stiffer than me when I'm watching porn,' and they all laugh.

When we sit down for dinner in the cold refectory, Tommaso says, 'Keep your eyes on the food, Pino. Those beady little things freak me out,' and they all laugh.

Maybe my dad was right. I should never have come on this trip with these confident kids with names like Luca and Tommaso and Francesco, who all seem to dress the same and talk the same and use the same limited vocabulary of cruelty.

When we go to the Spanish Steps, Luca and Tommaso whistle at the girls and women they see on the streets. And our teacher doesn't stop them because he seems just as enthralled. There's a lascivious smile on our teacher's face when Francesco eyes a woman old enough to be his mother and says, 'Mamma mia, the things she could teach me.'

Only Ankur is different from them. Quieter. Kinder. More beautiful. He's the only one who says good night and good morning to me, and then good night and good morning again. We've been on the trip for four days now, and those are the only kind words anyone has said to me. *Good night. Good morning.*

On our fourth night, I walk into the courtyard of the monastery and stare out at the sky. It's the same sky I've been staring at all my life. The same sky my father is staring at right now. I wonder why I came here in the first place. Nothing's changed. I've just spent four days being mocked and staring at ancient art that isn't as impressive in person as I hoped it would be. I thought maybe being around real-boys would turn me into one of them. I was wrong.

'Good night,' a voice whispers. I turn around and see Ankur standing behind me. He's

wearing shorts and a baggy T-shirt he bought from a seven-year-old selling souvenirs outside the Colosseum. The T-shirt is covered front and back in a silkscreen replica of the amphitheatre. It makes Ankur look like a work of art, like a piece of history.

'Good night,' I echo.

He doesn't walk away like he usually does when he says good night to me. He lingers. Pointing up at the sky, he says, 'That's me up there.'

I squint, confused. 'I don't get it.'

'Sorry, that was a bit weird.' He smiles. 'What I meant is … see that constellation up there …' I look at the stars up in the night sky. 'Pisces,' he says. 'It's my Zodiac sign. The fish. We're very sensitive. Creative. Imaginative. At least that's what my mom says. She loves astrology. I'm Leo Rising and Libra Moon. What time were you born?'

I avoid his eyes, which never looked at me with this much curiosity when he was a face on a screen. 'I don't know the exact time,' I say. The truth is I wasn't *born*, not the way he was. Not at a precise minute that was recorded on a birth certificate, timed to the placement of constellations that would give me my personality. I was carved over many months. If I had a star sign, I suppose it would be Taurus, Cancer, Leo and Virgo. My birth happened slowly, each piece of me a different astrological sign.

'You have to ask your mom,' he suggests. 'She'll know.'

Before I realise what I'm saying, I hear the words, 'I don't have a mum,' come out of my mouth.

He nods. 'Oh.' Then he asks, 'Gay dads?'

I shake my head. 'No, just one dad. Not …' I hesitate before I say the word, '… gay.' Because I know now it's what I am. Maybe I knew it before, when I watched *Moonlight*, but it feels different when the object of my affection is breathing this close to me. 'My dad did have a wife, before …'

Ankur closes his eyes and sighs. 'I'm so sorry. She's dead, and here I am asking … I'm so sorry. Was it … the virus?'

I want to keep talking to him, to keep his warmth close. But I can't tell him what I am. So I just nod and say, 'Yes, the virus. I never even knew her.' I can feel the lie taking up space inside me, like it's a physical thing.

He inches closer to me. 'I'm sorry you lost her, but I'm glad she didn't die before you could be born. The world needs more boys like you.'

'Boys like me?' I echo.

'You know, boys who aren't assholes.'

I laugh. If he knew I was lying to him, maybe he'd think I was an asshole, too. I want to tell him I didn't grow inside my father's wife. I grew in my dad's shop, one limb at a time. I want to be honest. But I just can't.

The night breeze blows his long, beautiful black hair away from his face. He touches my nose with his index finger. 'Hey, this is going to sound really strange, but I think your nose just grew.'

I cover my face with my hands, panicked. Once, a long time ago, my nose grew when I lied to my dad. I never lied to him again after that. 'It does that when it's cold out,' I quickly blurt out. Another lie. And I can feel my nose grow bigger under my hands. I turn away from him so he can't see my face.

'It's just me and my mom,' he whispers from behind me. Before I can ask, he says, 'My dad's not dead. He just isn't … with us. My mom moved us to Italy when I was a baby to escape him, I think. I don't know. She doesn't like to talk about the past.' The pain in his voice makes me wonder why I want so badly to have a heart. He takes a big breath of air. 'Isn't that the most incredible smell? When the breeze blows in our direction, you can smell all the oranges and all the roses.'

My nose has shrunk to its usual size. I turn back toward him, but I can't smell anything. I've never been able to smell anything in my life. But I can't let my nose grow again, especially by lying to Ankur, so I just say, 'The roses are so beautiful, but watch those thorns.'

He offers me a warm smile. 'The most beautiful things can hurt you. Roses. People.' He laughs. 'Maybe there's a reason for that. Maybe it's the universe telling us that if we don't risk getting hurt, we'll never experience true beauty.'

I nod. I've learned more from him in one conversation than from all those other boys in years. 'You should talk more in class,' I say.

He shrugs. 'Those guys would have a field day with me if I gave them the opportunity.'

'Well, then, just talk more to me.' I smile, and he smiles back. No one has ever talked to me like this, like they want to be my friend. I think of all the little things I've noticed

about Ankur over the last four days, things I could never have observed in a box on a screen. Things like how kind he is. One morning, I saw him tutoring Italian children in a small corner room. He was teaching them words in Hindi. He told them that his name, Ankur, means blossom, new life. One evening, when I went for a walk, I spied him bringing food and a blanket to the lady who lives around the corner from the monastery in an old Fiat with only three wheels. The car is always packed with stray cats, and the other boys mock her every day. But Ankur asked her if her cats had names and listened as she introduced him to each and every kitty.

'Are you enjoying the trip?' he asks.

'I think so,' I say.

'You don't know for sure?' He laughs.

I can't explain to him that I don't know if I've ever felt true joy, so I put the focus on him. 'Are you?'

'Like I said, the other boys are fucking assholes.' He giggles nervously. Maybe he's not used to swearing. 'But seeing Rome for the first time is cool. And meeting you.'

'Me?'

'Well, yeah, you're the most interesting person here. You're different.'

I bristle when I hear the word *different*, worried I've let him see too much of me. I can't be found out. 'I have to go, and I need a bathroom, too,' I blurt out too quickly. I feel my nose grow again. Of course, I never need a bathroom. When I go into a bathroom, I just sit there, pretending to use the toilet. And after enough time has passed, I flush to make the other boys think I'm like them.

'I'll be here a while if you wanna come back and talk more,' he says.

But I know I won't come back. I escape his beauty and his curiosity. Maybe what makes him so beautiful to me *is* his curiosity. He's the only one on this trip who seems interested in learning something about history, art, me. The very thing that makes him so attractive is the thing that makes him dangerous to me and my secrets.

After our final lesson the next afternoon, as all the other boys head back to the monastery, Ankur pulls me aside. 'Hey.'

I stop and smile. I like that we've moved from his formal *good morning* and *good night* to *hey*. It feels less ... wooden.

'Let's wander,' he suggests.

'Wander where?' I ask.

'Anywhere you want.'

What I want is for him to guide me into our next adventure. What I fear is him discovering just how *different* I am.

'The world belongs to us now,' he says. 'That's how it works. Each generation hands the world down to the next one. It's our turn. We have free access to anywhere and anything.' He points to a gated garden. 'What about that garden? Don't you want to smell its flowers?'

I can't risk my nose growing around him again, so I say, 'It has a huge gate around it.'

He rushes toward the gate and, like an Olympian, he throws himself over to the other side. I feel a rush of excitement as I watch his body leap and flex. He's the first person I've ever desired this way. Not as an image on a screen, but as someone standing in front of me. Someone whose skin I long to touch. 'Come on,' he commands with a smile.

'I can't. I'm not limber like you.' But he won't let me make excuses.

With his help and guidance, I climb gates all day. We find ourselves inside an ancient palazzo after it's been closed for the night.

We sneak into the Roman Forum as the sun sets, and he tells me we're walking in the footsteps of Caesar and Brutus, walking on the same dirt, under the same sky. 'Do you think we just turn into dirt when we die?' he asks.

I shrug. I don't know if I ever will die. I don't know what my future holds. There's no precedent for me. 'I don't know. Maybe we turn into stars,' I say.

He thinks about this for a long time. 'I like that better. I'd much rather be stardust than dirt.'

'Me too,' I whisper. What I'm thinking is that I'd rather be stardust than sawdust, which is realistically what I'll be one day. 'Should we head back to the monastery for dinner?' I ask.

'I'm not hungry,' he says. Then his eyes open wide with excitement when he says, 'Let's swim in the Trevi Fountain.'

'I think that's illegal,' I say, scared. I can't swim. My dad always kept me in the house

when it rained. He wouldn't even let me go into the courtyard to feel a single drop from the mysterious sky. He taught me how porous I am. He warned me that if I'm exposed to too much water, I'll start to rot and mould. When the kitchen pipe warped my cheek, it took him two weeks to fix me.

'Come on, don't be so scared of everything.' He puts a hand on my shoulder and squeezes. My coat is bulky enough that I don't think he feels the hard wood underneath.

'I'm not scared. I'm—'

'Follow me.' He starts to run, out of the Forum and toward the Trevi. I look up at the stars, wishing they'd tell me what to do. 'Hurry up!' Ankur calls out. I feel like I have no choice. Or maybe I just want to follow him.

When we get to the Trevi, there are tourists everywhere. Couples kissing. Families posing. Carabinieri standing guard, holding heavy guns.

'We need a plan,' he says.

'What kind of plan?'

'We can't just jump into the fountain. They'll arrest us. We have to make it look like an accident.' His brow furrows when he thinks. He bites his lip. 'Okay, here's what we'll do. We'll sit on the edge of the fountain and at the count of three, I'll scream like a bird is flying toward my face or something.'

'A bird?'

'It doesn't matter. I'll just make it look like I'm falling in. And you'll come in after me, to save your best friend.'

I feel my fingers stiffen under the gloves. 'I'm your best friend?'

'Isn't that obvious?' he asks. 'You know everyone we go to school with. You think one of those homophobes is my best friend?'

'No, I suppose not,' I say, and the gleam in his eye tells me something has changed between us. I know he's queer now. I wish I could tell him I think I am, too.

We sit at the edge of the fountain as planned. There are people from all over the world around us. Americans and Japanese and French. I hear different languages. Arabic and German and Portuguese. People drink from open containers. One man plays his guitar, and the people around him sing 'Una lacrima sul viso' as he strums. Children and their parents throw coins into the fountain, because the tradition says that if you throw a coin into the fountain, you will definitely come back to Rome. And I understand now, in this beautiful moment with Ankur, just how magical this place is.

'One, two, three,' Ankur whispers.

I wish I had a coin on me. I need my wishes to come true. That I come back to Rome some day. That I see Ankur again and again.

'What the hell is that!' Ankur screams, expertly ducking away from some imaginary flying object. I watch as he falls backward into the fountain. He's so convincing that even I think it's an accident. The crowds around us gasp. The carabinieri rush toward me.

This is my moment. I have to follow him into the water. When I leap into the fountain after him, he catches me in his arms. We're underwater together. He's not a real-boy anymore, and I'm not a wooden boy. We're two mermen, swimming side by side, floating toward love and understanding.

He pulls me up for a gasp of air. Time stops all around us. The guitarist doesn't play anymore. No one throws a coin. Everyone is frozen, staring at us.

Ankur pulls me back down. We keep our eyes open underwater. I know why my eyes don't burn from the chlorine, but Ankur's eyes don't seem to burn either. Or if they do, he's too exhilarated to care. Together, we stare at the ancient magical structure above us, illuminated by stars and moon, and by the sudden flash of cameras, because the people outside have become unfrozen and they all want a photo of these wild-boys swimming in the Trevi.

He pulls me up for another gasp of air. 'Once more!' he yells.

'Once more!' I echo.

And down we go again, down where there are no words, just energy. He grabs my hands underwater. I feel his surprise when he touches me. I see him realise he's holding wood. Wet and warped. *Pino*. He looks at me and smiles. I smile back. I feel him moving closer to me, so close his lips almost touch mine. I squeeze his hands and pull him closer, letting him know it's okay, letting him know he can kiss me if he wants to.

His soft lips press against my wooden lips. He knows what I am, and he still wants me. I close my eyes when he kisses me. That's what the stars always do in the films my father shows me. And now it's our turn. I feel his body against mine under the moonlight. I feel the power of the brilliant night sky above us, all those beautiful stars and constellations. I know what constellation I would be now. Not Taurus, Cancer, Leo and Virgo. No, I'd

be Chamaeleon because I have the power to transform. I don't need to open my eyes for confirmation. I feel it happening. My hands tingle. My feet feel cold. My nose smells the bleach. My heart soars. I'm turning into a real-boy, and I didn't need to throw a coin into the fountain and wish on it.

This time it's me who pulls us up for a gasp of air. 'Ankur …' I whisper as cameras flash outside, and the officers order us to get out of the fountain immediately.

'What is it?' he asks quietly.

'You know now …' I look into his eyes to see if he's disgusted by me. 'You know I used to be made of wood …'

'I don't care what you're made of,' he says. 'I care that you're kind. And curious. That's what makes you Pino, not whether you're made of wood or flesh.' Under the water, he holds my hand.

I glance at the crowd nervously, wondering what they're making of this moment.

'Let them look,' he says defiantly, like he can sense my fear. 'Let them try to stop us from loving each other with our bodies and our hearts.'

'I have a heart now,' I whisper.

'Maybe you didn't have a physical beating heart before,' he says. 'But you had a soul.'

'Did I?' I ask.

'I know it because I felt it.' He smiles. 'Maybe you just never knew how to see yourself the way I see you.' He pulls me underwater again. I know that someday, my heart will break like my father's did. I know what my future holds now. It holds pain and sadness and loneliness, but it also holds love and joy and lust and friendship.

I look up to the sky for answers. I want to know what made me transform. Was it his love, his kiss, his touch? Or was it the leap of faith I took by submerging my wooden body in water? Perhaps it is only by risking our life for what we want that we can ever get it. Just like Ankur said, I needed to risk getting hurt to experience true beauty.

And then I remember my father on one of his calls with his friend in Portland. My father wanted answers. He wanted to understand why God would take his whole family from him. And his friend said to him, 'Gepetto, you know I'm not a religious man, but I do have faith. And faith is about accepting that being human means we'll never have the answers to the biggest mysteries of life and death.'

The carabinieri get impatient. They grab hold of us and yank us out of the fountain. They tell us that they're going to have to arrest us, that they need our parents' numbers since we're clearly minors. I can't wait for them to call my dad. I want him to know who I am now.

I give them my dad's phone number, and I hear him say 'Pronto' through the officer's phone. I hear the officer tell my dad that his son was swimming in the Trevi, and I hear the panic in my dad's voice because his son *cannot* swim.

I grab the phone from the officer. I grip Ankur's fingers with my free hand. 'Dad …'

'How could you go swimming?' he yells. 'Don't you know water can warp you? And in the Trevi, with all that chlorine? And all those people?' I can hear him pacing, his footsteps fast and anxious. And then, it sounds like his voice is coming from two places. From the phone, and also from … right in front of me.

He's running toward me. He followed me to Rome. 'Are you okay? Do they know? Are they scared? Are *you* scared?' He rushes to my side. He puts the phone away.

I hand the carabinieri back his phone. Still holding Ankur's hand, I let my dad see the emotion on my face. Tears form in my dad's eyes when he places a hand on my soft cheek. I can't help but cry too. Tears can't warp me now. I close my eyes and remember the end of my dad's conversation with his friend in Portland. Before he hung up, his friend said, 'There's life, and there's death. We have no control over that. But in between life and death, there's love. The only thing that matters. All we can do is keep loving.'

I open my eyes. I love Ankur so much for gifting me bravery. I love my dad so much for gifting me life, and for following me to Rome to make sure I'm safe. I love this city. I love that the Trevi returns to its usual commotion. I love the people drinking from open containers again. Speaking in a multitude of languages. The guitarist playing 'Bella Ciao', the college students singing along, the coin throwers, I love them all. None of us are afraid of the virus anymore. We're not afraid of heartbreak either. Not anymore.

In the distance, I take in a gelato stand. I want to taste every one of their flavours, and I will. There's plenty of time to taste the world. To discover all the things I love. And I will love. I'll love everything this world offers me while I can.

I clutch Ankur's hand. I pull him closer.

'Dad,' I whisper. 'Can I talk to you about something?'

MORSEL

HELENA FOX

*Please note this story contains references to
implied sexual assault.*

We are crumbs. We are strewn on the path. We are scattered. We didn't know what was coming until there we were, left to our own devices, in the woods.

My brother was scared. I wasn't.

(Of course, the story begins before that. All stories do.)

Dad fell in love six months after Mum left.

He brought the woman home to have dinner. We sat and stared at her, me and Harry. I was twelve, tall and brittle. My brother was nine, small and tender, still having nightmares about Mum leaving. Dad's girlfriend didn't have the shape of Mum or the softness of her edges or the crinkles by her eyes. And she didn't look haunted like Mum did before she walked out. This woman looked … neat. Tucked in and efficient like a just-made bed. And she wasn't very spontaneous, which we discovered when Harry brought out his fart cushion to see if she'd laugh.

She moved in not long after. 'Call me Sue,' she said. That changed a year later to 'Call me Mum,' which we wouldn't do.

Sometimes, Sue would sit on the couch and look at her phone – her face sharp, eyebrows pointed down in a V – and Harry would say, 'Is she angry?'

'Maybe,' I'd say.

'Who with, though?'

'The world?'

Harry always wanted to know the answers to all the things. He'd ask Sue what she was mad about at dinner.

'Just someone being stupid on the internet,' Sue would tell us. Or an airline being stupid. A hotel. A client. Sue was a travel agent. She worked from home in the spare room that used to be Harry's until Sue moved in, and Harry moved in with me.

Dad wasn't usually home for dinner; he often worked late. Dad left us with our stepmother, like he could cut and paste Mum into another person's body and then leave us to each other.

'They're your kids, Malcolm,' I heard Sue say one night, in their bedroom. 'I can't be expected to look after them all the time.'

Through the shared wall, I heard Dad murmur his answer.

'That's not what I—' Sue said, loudly.

'Shhh,' said Dad.

So Sue shushed. And then they talked together, voices undulating like lowing cows. And then Sue laughed. And Dad did too. And then they were doing it.

I lay very still. Even with a pillow over my ears, I could hear their animal noises.

Mum used to threaten us with 'Consequences' when we were small. She never followed through. It was a joke: 'If you kids can't calm down,' she used to say, 'I'm going to dump you in a lake /in a park /in a mall /in a garbage can /in the woods.'

We'd laugh – me and Harry and Mum. Our funny joke! *Incorrigible, diabolical,* Mum would say, and she'd wave the pancake spoon at us. Then one day, she just … stopped. So Dad made pancakes for us on the weekend, sometimes – always burning or undercooking them, or both. Mum would come out of the bedroom and find us all in the kitchen. She'd blink and say, 'Pancakes?'

She always looked so sleepy.

A year after Mum left, Dad and Sue were driving us home from some grown-up's birthday party. Harry and I were bickering and kicking each other. Sue *scree-d* over to the side of the road.

'Too much fighting!' she said. 'Out!'

I didn't have my seatbelt on, so I slammed forward when Sue braked. My face hit the back of the front seat, but not so hard that I cried.

Sue didn't say sorry. 'The kids need to understand consequences, Malcom,' she said.

Dad just nodded, like he agreed. Or maybe his head always moved up and down when he needed to look like he agreed.

My brother and I had to walk the rest of the way home. It was a couple of kilometres, not too far, but Harry worried it was going to get dark. 'There might be bears!' he said. He was always imagining the worst.

'There aren't bears in Australia, dummy,' I said.

'Don't fight!' he said, eyes darting around. He broke into a run.

'They can't hear us,' I yelled after him, but he didn't stop.

I walked slowly. Harry ran so fast, he turned into a speck.

Then I was seventeen and Harry was fourteen, and our stepmother suggested we go on a walk. 'Aren't they doing Duke of Edinburgh at your school, Greta?'

'Yup,' I said, slurping up a long strand of spaghetti.

Sue frowned. 'Have you thought of doing a bushwalk?'

'A bushwalk?' I stared at her. That was like suggesting I grow wings and fly to the moon. I was a *sit-at-desk-with-computer* kind of girl. Harry and I had our desks side by side. We'd play games online even after Sue and Dad told us to go to sleep. One time, we saw the sun come up and Harry looked at me and said, wide-eyed, 'Oh, shit, Greta.' He thought Sue would kill us; I told him she would never. But when Sue found out, the house filled with cold. It was never like that when Mum was here.

Sue nodded. 'Well, yes. I already talked to your Year 12 coordinator, and she thought it would be really good for you. Harry could go along. Would you like that, Harry?'

Harry stared at Sue. 'Um?'

'Keep your sister company?'

'On a bushwalk?' he said. He was like me. We were inside animals. Peas in a pod.

'Yeah. I think you'll have a great time!' Our stepmother sprinkled *great* with glitter.

'I don't know—'

'It'll be great. Won't it be great, Malcolm?' Sue looked at Dad. He was looking at his phone.

'Malcolm?' She touched his hand.

'Oh?' Dad looked up. 'Yeah. Sure,' he said, and he sprinkled *sure* with some kind of enthusiasm.

My dad was like a magician – half here, always disappearing. When did it start, his fading out? Two years ago, three? Or was it before, with Mum? When was he last really with us?

'Perfect,' said Sue, clapping her hands together.

And it was decided.

Sue packed our backpacks, freshly bought from the camping shop. She also got headlamps, water filters, sleeping bags and sleeping mats, a tiny tent, weird-looking freeze-dried food and a little gas stove she showed us how to light. She actually seemed excited, like this whole thing had filled her with purpose. Work was slow, so Sue's days were filled with afternoon naps and cups of tea and going to the gym. Maybe this felt like forward motion in our house of inertia? Maybe she thought something good would come of it – like Dad would start noticing her, or at least, that something might be different from this.

Dad drove us to the train station. 'To the woods!' he said, sounding almost cheerful.

Harry and I stepped into the carriage, our packs heavy. We turned and stared at Dad, pausing in case he might reach in and pluck us out, take us on a random road trip somewhere, and not tell Sue.

'Good luck, kiddos.' Dad waved. The train doors clunked closed.

Harry and I looked at each other. He was too old to hold my hand, but I could feel him wanting to.

We got off the train in the mountains and walked to the beginning of the hike. The sun was in the middle of the sky. It wasn't too hot. It wasn't too cold. I texted my girlfriend, *Hey, we made it to the start*

She texted back, *Good! You're going to do great I can feel it in my bones*

Jordan and I were kind of new as girlfriend and girlfriend, but we'd known each other since Year 7. We both liked science. We always got As on our experiments. 'We have good chemistry,' she said after our first kiss. 'Get it?'

Jordan wasn't a fan of my stepmother. The two of them last spoke when we went out for Chinese food. It was my seventeenth birthday. Sue nibbled at the green tea dumplings, commented on the colour of the sweet-and-sour sauce. Looked around at the paintings on the walls and said, 'The décor here is … interesting.' Sue liked restaurants with white, European tablecloths and flavours she understood, like salt and pepper.

Afterwards, Jordan said, 'Gret, your stepmum is the *alone-est* person I've ever met.

Did you see her aura tonight? It was fucking iridescent. Like nuclear waste.'

Jordan had suggested she come for the bushwalk too. Sue said she wasn't sure whether Jordan would be up for it, but Jordan and I were both keen. When Harry fretted about maybe dying in the bush, Jordan said, 'Don't worry, Haz. I'll protect you.' And Harry looked at her like she was a goddess, sitting cross-legged on his bed in her Doc Martens and nose ring.

But then Jordan got the flu. Her temperature was a solid 39.5 °C.

I might be dead before morning, she wrote.

Hope not haha. I wish you could come with us

Jordan wrote back: *You'll be fine*

You think so?

    You think so?

Lol

    Lol

Stop it, dickhead

    hahahaha

On the bushwalk, it wasn't that we got lost so much as we couldn't find our way.

It started about half an hour in. There were two paths. One was labelled clearly, the other not at all.

I said, 'Let's take the left one.'

Harry said, 'But it doesn't have a sign.'

'The other path goes to the Lookout. We want to go to the Grotto. Remember what the map said?'

'Let's look at the map again.'

We looked in the pocket where Sue had packed the map. It wasn't there.

'Oh,' said Harry. 'Didn't you check everything was packed?'

'I thought Sue did it.'

'But you're the leader.'

'*Ha*. Definitely not.'

We tried our phones. There was no signal. We stared at each other.

Lookout? Grotto? Harry wanted to turn around and head home.

'Let's keep going,' I said. I didn't want to go back and hand Sue our failure. 'Let's flip this rock. Mossy side up is Lookout. The other way must be Grotto.'

We flipped. Mossy side down. We took the unmarked path.

And that was the first crumb.

Or was it? Was that really the beginning, or did it start earlier?

When Mum stopped wanting to be with us, she forgot to get out of bed. When she stopped loving us, she said things like, 'Please, kids, stop making so much noise.' When Mum ran off in the night, left us in our beds unawares and made a life without us, I felt like someone had taken me between their fingers and ground me into pieces.

When Harry moved in with me, he would wake up some nights all sweaty and weepy and say, 'I wish she'd taken us.'

I nodded, even though Harry couldn't see me in the dark.

I missed Mum. Missed her sleepy hugs in the morning. Jam sandwiches when she couldn't be bothered to cook. Stories she made up in the car, driving us randomly somewhere when she needed an adventure.

I think we both would have left with her, if she'd asked.

After Mum left, the rooms felt clunky and hollow. And I think Dad wanted to muffle the sound of all that nothing, so *quick-quick* he went on an online dating site, swiped right for Sue, and brought her home.

At first, Sue sang in the kitchen as she cooked for us.

'Sing with me, Harry!' she said. 'Come on, Greta!'

We didn't want to. She was a stranger at the stove, making lamb chops. Harry and I didn't eat meat, but Sue kept forgetting.

It didn't take long for silence to creep back into the house. My father stared at his phone, went back to his late meetings and trips away for work. Harry and I stayed in our room. Sue stopped singing.

Harry and I got quieter and smaller and more distant from Dad and Sue, and Dad and Sue got further away from each other. The four of us were like an electron cloud – atoms disconnected but stuck together. The rooms echoing with our silence, with no one asking or answering questions at dinner, no one filling in the gaps. And we watched Sue get smaller and smaller too, until she turned mean.

Misery can do that to you.

And maybe *that* was the first crumb.

Into the woods, we walked. Our feet crunched pebbles and leaves. A lyrebird scratched the undergrowth. I knew it was a lyrebird because Mum had pointed one out on a rainforest walk once, in another life. A whipbird's song flipped and cracked. Harry copied it. *Ooooowhit! Ooooowhit!*

'Shhh,' I said, for no good reason.

We walked up and around and over and through. We saw craggy rocks. We saw ferns nestled in the crooks of trees and eucalypts scraping the sky. We saw a rustling *Something* but never caught its eyes.

'How much further?' said Harry.

We had stopped because we were thirsty. I noticed we were almost out of water.

'Not much further,' I said, because that was the hopeful thing to say.

Then we were out of water.

Harry and I clomped through the forest, away from the path, searching for a stream. We went downhill because Harry swore he could hear something liquid moving. We mashed ferns with our stompy feet. I pushed through a brambly bush and it whipped back and hit Harry.

'Ouch!' he said, recoiling. He had a long, red welt on his cheek.

'Sorry.' I was so thirsty, my tongue clagged at the '*S*'.

We couldn't hear the creek, and then we could, and then we couldn't. And then we found it, but it was tiny. We crouched like cats and lapped at it. Because Sue had forgotten the filter for the water when she filled our packs.

Did she do it on purpose? Did she want to kill us? Or were we so irritating, so vacant and slumpy, that she just forgot what we needed?

There aren't many people who want to harm you on purpose.

The ones who just don't care that much about you are countless.

(Another crumb.)

The sun dropped like a song fading out.

We sat by the creek. There was nowhere to pitch our tent. No room for a fire, and anyway, I didn't know how to make one. We ate muesli bars and shivered in our sleeping bags. The ground was pocked and rocky. There was nowhere comfortable to rest.

We did not sleep that night. Every motion of the earth and all the tiny things on it made noises we didn't like.

Harry cried.

'Stop crying,' I said.

'I'm not,' he said. 'You always think I'm crying when I'm not.'

But I knew what I knew.

Next morning, we stumbled around trying to find our way back to the main path. We didn't find it. We couldn't find it.

In the meantime, I thought about things. What kind of things? All sorts. My mind was a bug, turning circles.

I was seventeen, about to finish school. I had a girlfriend, a real one. We'd said 'I love you' to each other. I had just been thinking about whether I loved Jordan enough to have sex with her. But the idea of having sex with someone made me feel …

I tried to describe it in my mind.

It felt scrambly, like these rocks we were trying to crawl over.

It felt sticky, like the heat rising around us.

It felt like this walk I hadn't wanted to go on.

A metaphor, I thought, foggily.

We moved on. We followed the creek as though it would bring us towards something good vs. further away. The day simmered and thickened. Our skin itched with bug bites and heat and bramble scrapes. We scratched at our skin, licked at the creekwater. We splashed it on us, trying to cool off, but there wasn't enough water around us or in us to make us feel better.

I thought about Mum, and how there wasn't any of her around us any more.

Our mother had vanished. Harry and I had looked her up over the years, tried texting her old phone number, tried calling, even tried googling. We'd asked Dad if he knew where she'd gone. He said she'd left a note, taken out all her money, left no trace of herself behind.

We asked him again. Over and over. Each time, he had nothing to offer.

'I'm so sorry, kids,' he said. As though 'sorry' might put a Band-Aid over a lost mother and heal us.

'I'm hot,' Harry said, his voice pinchy.

I nodded, too worn out to answer. 'I'm *itchy*,' Harry said. 'And I'm so *tired*.' He wanted to lie down, but I said to keep moving. I didn't want us to stop and die. If we kept moving, we were okay. We were still here.

I thought about our stepmother. I thought about how she had decided to kill us. I thought about how we'd watched her shrinking, half and half and half again. I thought about how alone she was, iridescent with it.

Was it loneliness that made people do cruel things? Was it loneliness that brought bodies together? Would I be that lonely one day? Was Sue having sex with Dad while we were gone? Were they dancing in the kitchen? Was Mum somewhere, making pancakes with someone she loved? Was everyone singing? Was everyone realising their full potential with us gone?

'I'm scared,' said Harry, in a whisper.

I nodded back.

We tilted towards nothing, drifted till we felt nothing.

Harry started to vomit.

'I'm sorry. I'm sorry,' he said.

I wanted to tell him: 'None of this is your fault.' I wanted to say: 'Everything is going to be okay.' But I couldn't find the words.

I wanted to find and grab and hold the words I needed to say.

I wanted the words I said to be true.

I just wanted our story to be happy.

(More crumbs.)

We reached a waterfall at the end of the day. Beside the waterfall, there was a cottage. It was tiny, with a gabled roof, a squat, smoking chimney and a red, red door.

We knocked.

The door opened wide, like a mouth.

A woman stood before us. She was beautiful. *Radiant*, I thought. *I'll tell Jordan about her when we get home.*

'Come in, children!' the woman beamed, her teeth bright white.

Inside the cottage was food, piled on the table. Piles of food. We ate pies and apples and banana bread and some falafels, and the woman made us pineapple juice with a little juicer plugged into the wall. We ate till our bellies stretched, and the woman looked at us like we were pineapples she wanted to juice.

At some point, Harry started vomiting again. A stream of chunky half-foods that hadn't turned into anything good.

'I'm sorry,' he said over and over, like he meant to mess up this beautiful cottage, this gabled roof, this woman.

'He's sick,' I said to the woman. 'Could you call someone?'

'Are you sure?' she said, peering at Harry.

'I'm sure,' I said. I looked at the floor, the vomit on it. Couldn't she see? 'Where's your phone?'

The woman did not have a phone. She'd moved here, next to a waterfall in the wilderness, to be at one with nature.

'But you have a juicer,' I said.

'Are you sure?' she said.

I looked around. The walls rippled. I saw a bare floor and a bench and a bucket and some tinned food on a shelf.

The cottage and the woman and the food on the table were all liars.

I lay on the bench. Walls bending, stretching. The woman's face loomed overhead, her teeth leering and pointed.

I felt her hands on me, like she was checking out my flesh for biting.

I thought of the boy I had been with the year before I started dating Jordan. Almost all the girls in our year were getting together with the boys in our year, and for a while I thought I wanted to be like those girls. I remembered how it felt to kiss the boy, his tongue roaming my mouth like it was looking for treasure. He wanted to have sex, like, straightaway. We were sixteen. I didn't want to have sex; I wasn't sure I ever wanted to have sex, but didn't know how to say no. I didn't think girls with boyfriends were supposed to say no. We were supposed to open our bodies like flowers, then talk about it at school afterwards.

The night my boyfriend touched me and kept saying we should have sex and kept touching me, I got stuck in time. I couldn't move. I couldn't speak. I felt disconnected, loose from my body. I held myself very still. If this was the kind of thing people did to stop being lonely, then why did I feel like the loneliest cloud in the universe?

I remember my boyfriend saying, 'Come on, Greta, don't be a tease.'

His hands moved over and over me.

I turned still and small and silent as a stone.

So still. So silent.

So, so small.

(Another crumb.)

The boyfriend broke up with me two days later, via text. *Ur too frigid G get over urself*

I tried to talk to my father about it. The words stuck in my throat. He said, 'What?' and 'What?' and 'You need to be louder, Greta.'

I didn't tell Sue. I didn't want her to say: 'What were you thinking?' or 'Are you sure anything actually happened? He just touched you, right?'

I told Jordan, who was my best friend before she was my girlfriend. Her eyes went wide. She cupped my cheeks and said, '*Shit.*' She shook her head. '*Piece of shit. Shit.*' Then she made a voodoo doll of the boy out of an old sock, and we stuck pins in it.

Being with Jordan was like being held in moonlight. We were two cherries on the one stem. We'd sit in the Macca's courtyard, sharing fries and dunking them into our chocolate shakes. We watched 70s horror movies. We dissected dead rats. We talked about winning the Nobel Prize for something 'sciencey'; we didn't know what.

Back when we were thirteen, Jordan said she didn't like boys in *that* way. I told her maybe I was the same? When I was fourteen, I had wanted to add, 'I don't think I like girls in *that* way either,' but didn't know how to say it. What I felt in my body didn't make sense because you had to like someone *that* way. At least, that's what the movies said.

What I felt in my body was a difference I couldn't explain. I didn't have words for any of who I was back then. But when Jordan and I got together, something clicked a little into place. We didn't go rabid with desire. She kissed me. I kissed her back. Her lips felt like home.

A week before we left for the bushwalking trip, Jordan said: 'Gret, listen. We don't have to do anything. If you don't want to have sex, we don't ever have to.'

'Really?'

'Really.' She nodded emphatically. 'We're made for each other. Nothing can tear us apart.' She paused. 'Call me a cheese ball.'

'You're a cheese ball,' I said.

And then we sat on the couch, our legs looped over each other. We watched a documentary on the insects of the world. We fell asleep holding hands.

Later that night, in her room, in her bed, she whispered into my ear: 'I'm sorry your ex was such a dickhead.'

'Thanks.'

'I won't ever hurt you like that. Never. Ever.'

'Thank you.' Could I believe her? When I was with her, I didn't feel small or alone. When I was with her, I made her laugh. Would it always be that way? I didn't know. I thought of the things I didn't want to do. What was it like, to feel desire like that? Did Jordan feel it? Would she miss it if I didn't give her what she wanted?

My thoughts got viney that night. Fear and loneliness – they can grow tendrils, make you do things. Like hurt people, or leave them.

Would everything be okay?

Jordan touched my side. 'Gret.'

'Mmm?' I said. I turned my head, seeking her out, as if she could save me from my undergrowth.

'Believe me.' She pulled my hand to her. Kissed it. Kissed it again. Pulled me close and wrapped my arm round her body.

And we slept like two bananas.

(Another crumb.)

Thwapthwapthwapthwap

A helicopter.

A helicopter?

I heard the *thwapping* outside my ears.

'We are a bit delirious,' I said to the walls, to my brother.

Harry didn't answer. He hadn't talked for a long time.

We flew up into the air, shedding molecules, shedding stories like those dandelion seeds.

'We are dandelion seeds!' I shouted, but I didn't make any sound.

The woman was in the helicopter with us.

No, she wasn't. I made that up. You can make things up in stories. But not the really true things.

The woman did come to visit us in hospital. She brought flowers.

The truth was, she explained, she was on a weeklong bushwalk and found us beside an almost dried-out creek near the edge of a cliff. Harry and I were tottering around, heat-stroked and vomiting. Harry told her he could hear the whipbird whipping. He kept whapping at his face trying to get the sound out. I was mumbling about love and bananas. I was turning circles.

The woman used some kind of walkie-talkie to get help.

And she saved us.

Dad and Sue stood by the bed in the hospital room.

Sue said she was so, so sorry. She had forgotten the water filter. She thought she'd packed the map. She wept by the bedside.

The woman from the not-cottage stared my stepmother up and down.

Dad and Sue were taken away by the police for questioning.

And that was the last we saw of Sue.

For months afterwards, I asked Dad what happened to her. Did she go to jail? Did Sue pack her things and leave, so sick and ashamed of what she'd done? Then I asked harder questions. Did Dad regret not being there? Was that why Mum left? Or was it because of me and Harry? Were we not enough? Too much? *Did anyone actually love us?*

Dad couldn't answer. Every time he tried to talk, he choked up. Just waved his hands and started to cry.

Sue didn't go to jail, but that's all I got out of him. In the end, Dad and I didn't have much to say to each other. He couldn't talk to me, and I got tired of trying to turn his silence into something real.

Jordan came to the hospital that first night. She sat by the bed and held my hand. 'Oh my god, Gret.'

I felt numb. Stuck in time. I wanted to talk to my brother. I sat up, my head woozy. 'Where's Harry?'

Then Jordan's face made shapes so loud, I had to close my eyes.

(So many crumbs.)

I carry my brother inside me.

Harry is the part of me I follow at night when I can't sleep. He's a lost morsel. He's the part of me I couldn't help, couldn't shelter, couldn't bring home.

We walked on a trail till we lost ourselves and then I was delirious and had thoughts while drinking juice that didn't exist, in a cottage that wasn't.

I had epiphanies, a whole row of them. And maybe that's what has made me? Maybe I'm made of pieces, maybe I'm made of visions. Maybe we are the crumbs we choose to keep.

In a perfect story, the answers would all come at once. 'I know who I am!' I'd shout at waterfalls. 'I know what happened to me!' and 'I know why she left!' and 'She can't be trusted!' and 'I have found the path!'

My answers have taken a while to gather.

Maybe I'll always be gathering?

We live together now, Jordan and I, in a different city from Dad. He is a day's drive up north. We are south.

We are twenty-one. We live in a cottage with a frangipani tree out front. The rent is low – wood is rotting in some cornices and the walls have mould patches. I try to spackle the holes. I spray the mould with vinegar.

Jordan and I spend nights watching movies on a laptop, legs intertwined. We talk about going to live in Paris like poets. 'But we aren't poets,' says Jordan. She works in a lab and is doing honours in molecular biology. I'm studying to be a pharmacist. We talk about how we are particles. We talk about what makes us and what disintegrates us and are we who we are if we don't know who we are yet?

Jordan sometimes reaches over and strokes my skin. She tells my brain to *Shhhhhhhhh*.

'I think that mould is turning sentient,' she says, pointing. Then she sees my face. Sees all the churning. She holds my hand. 'Feel this,' she says.

I feel the weight of her, made of flesh, bones, crumbs, love.

'Believe this,' she says, and squeezes.

The woman, the one who found us by the creek, comes over sometimes, to the little home I have made with my girlfriend.

We cook her green curry. We pour her red wine. We cut up pineapple and serve it with vanilla ice cream.

She leans back and says, 'This is delicious.' She pauses. 'It's so nice to see you, Greta.'

'You're welcome,' I say. I pause. 'Thank you for saving us.'

Her face changes then, because of course she only saved one.

The moment slows.

Time opens,

and I open,

and out comes ...

My pieces float around the room. The parts of me that had a brother, a mum, a dad, a Sue. The parts still forming, all the losses. And the big Loss, the biggest.

The woman leans forward. Touches my knee, catches my eyes. 'Talk to me, Gret,' she says. 'Tell me about him. Tell me anything.'

I open my mouth. Say a word, the edge of a word, the edge of an edge of a start of a beginning. My voice is like a spoon, scooping. It moves around the room, reaching, gathering, turning all these crumbs into something like a story.

THE KEYHOLE

Michael Earp

FRIDAY NIGHT

The *Keyhole* was busy in the way Rory loved: lights low, music loud and spirits high. Enough noise to drown out his traitorous brain. To overpower the voices that suggested he had nothing to offer. In a crowd, Rory became anonymous. Became someone with more self-esteem than in his quiet moments.

The club *felt* shoulder-to-shoulder, but Rory knew how to navigate his way through the crowd to the bar. He was here often enough he might as well be staff, if only management would hire anyone under twenty. He sidestepped a guy whose rainbow elastic harness peeked out from under his tank top and scanned the faces nearby. Where was Ollie? They were meant to meet him ten—

Rory was used to being distracted. Until he started taking meds, it was like every passing thought was its own carnival. But getting distracted had never been *this* attractive.

It was her dress that caught his eye first. An elegantly fitted slip, dazzling in its radiance. Sun-gold and covered in the smallest of diamond beads that snatched at the ceaselessly dancing lights. Her long, dark hair fell between the thin straps on her shoulders and stopped short of the folds of fabric gathered at the small of her back.

The space next to her at the bar became available and he stepped forward, not wanting to lose his chance in the roiling queue. Now he was next to her, Rory could see that her dress was only a small part of her beauty. Her familiar manner with the bartender, sharing some joke Rory couldn't hear, made her radiate a sunniness he'd happily bask in.

He usually felt like he talked too much, but he found himself scrambling for something to say. Anything, really. He leaned towards her slightly, enough to show an indication that he was about to speak but not so much to encroach on her personal space.

'Your outfit is on point!' he shouted over the noise.

She turned to look at him. 'What?' she shouted back, and he couldn't help but notice the way her eyes scanned him. He was glad he'd found his striped pants in the pile of clothes inside his wardrobe, but he couldn't work out what her verdict was.

'Your outfit!' He pointed at her dress, hoping she didn't think he was ogling her. Even if he was, just a little. 'Amazing!'

Her face lit up with a smile that almost looked coy. Almost.

She leaned closer to his ear and said, 'This old thing?'

The bartender was making her a drink with a pinkish tinge in a tall glass filled with ice. Rory felt impulsive and called to them, 'When you're done, I'll have the same, please.'

'You're game,' the sun-girl said. 'You don't even know what I've ordered.'

He felt his heart wrestle with the beat from the music. 'Sometimes you have to take a risk.'

Flirting like this felt like a risk. As if, suddenly, everything was at stake. She was the most beautiful girl in the club. He couldn't look away, and he was sure that he wasn't the only one. Would he capture her attention in return? Or would it get embarrassing? He didn't like to put people in *leagues*, but she felt elevated, somehow.

She didn't answer but picked up her drink and took a sip. Rory expected her to walk away, but she stood watching him, amused. His drink was ready. He took a sip. It was sweet – very sweet – with a sour bite to it. He'd been expecting a kick of some kind, but there was no alcohol, just a sugary hit. He raised his eyebrows and looked at the glass, trying to decipher what was in it.

She grinned as if she'd won some kind of game. Had he won, too? Her hand rested gently on his shoulder as she began to walk past him. Maybe not.

'It's cranberry lemonade. Have a wild night.' Then she stepped into the crowd with unfathomable ease. He almost went after her, but he heard his name.

'Rory!' It was Ollie. They were at their usual table – the best spot to see the drag shows that would start later. Sara was there, too, and her new girlfriend, called …

Names: the natural enemy of those blessed with ADHD.

Rory took a stool facing the dance floor. He wanted to keep an eye out for the girl in gold.

'What is that?' Sara said.

Rory followed her gaze to the drink in his hand.

'Cranberry lemonade, apparently.'

'Riiight,' she replied before she took a gulp from her beer.

He managed to clear the lovestruck fog in his head long enough to focus. 'Hey!' He waved to Sara's girlfriend.

'Hey,' she said back. 'Sugar high it is. I support your choices.'

He grinned at her, but the memory of that sunshine dress took over the reason for the smile. The sweetness smacked his tongue, his teeth.

Rory scanned the room, his attention back on the dance floor. This place felt like home *and* the frontier of social interaction at the same time. But where was the sun-girl?

SATURDAY MORNING

The morning wreaked havoc on Rory's head. Although, more accurately, it was the night before doing its dirty work. He hadn't seen the sun-girl again for the rest of the night, and he'd started ordering vodka sodas after the cranberry lemonade.

Ollie had one arm hanging over the side of the bed and was snoring up a storm. Ollie's place was so much easier to crash at than heading all the way home, but he could only do that when his friend hadn't found someone else to crash with them. Rory got up and went to the bathroom. The shower made him feel a bit better, even if he did have to dress in last night's clothes.

Before leaving, he picked up Ollie's phone, took a photo of the sleepy drool coming from their mouth and set it as the lock screen.

Out on the street, the light was vicious on Rory's pounding head. It was too early for this level of brightness. Eight o'clock looked like midday. There were even people out running errands like it was a normal thing to do. When a person pushing a pram went into the bakery on Smith Street, Rory did the same. A breakfast pie was just what he needed.

The smell of freshly baked bread and pastries hit him as he entered. His empty stomach rumbled in protest. When he saw there were no pies to be had, the cinnamon scrolls and sticky buns distracted him from his original goal.

Leaving with a larger-than-necessary brown paper bag filled with an assortment of bready treats, he crossed a side street and went down an alley. He had to cut through a couple of blocks to get to his tram. The terraced houses and apartment blocks of this suburb all seemed nestled together in a way that celebrated their different eras. Like a pot-luck street party.

On the corner of two streets was a park with a couple of benches and a small playground. Rory decided he may as well be civilised and sit to eat. Partially civilised, anyway.

It wasn't until he'd sat down that he noticed the guy sitting on the bench opposite him. Rory sensed he was being watched, so he pulled out a cinnamon scroll and held it up in a 'cheers' motion. 'Breakfast!'

The guy laughed. He was slight and attractive and looked like he was around Rory's own age. His hair was cropped short with a bit to feather on top, and his smile was bright.

'Big night was it, then?' the guy said in an approachable way.

Rory felt overdressed for this hour. His outfit didn't exactly transition easily from club to park. He finished chewing. 'You could say that.'

'More than an energy drink, then?' The guy had one in his hand and used it to mirror Rory's 'cheers'.

'More even than cranberry lemonade.' Rory laughed to himself.

Strangely, it made the boy grin wider. 'So, breakfast of champions, is it?' he asked.

Rory took another bite and nodded enthusiastically. Then he spoke around the food in his mouth. 'Although not as good as a breakfast pie.'

'Watch it.' Mock seriousness came over the boy's face. 'That's my baking you're insulting.'

Rory stopped chewing, his mouth still full, then looked into the bag at the sticky bun he had saved for dessert, then looked back at the boy.

'Looking for a family resemblance?' the boy asked with a playful smile.

Rory realised this guy didn't just like wearing all white and maroon – it was the bakery's uniform. 'I – oh, umm – I didn't mean.' He started worrying the corner of the paper bag.

The boy laughed again. 'I'm teasing.' He winked so casually Rory thought he might have imagined it. Are people really this at ease with strangers in the sober daylight?

'It's just that on mornings like this, I crave grease, not just bread.' Rory felt like he needed to explain himself thoroughly. Was that enough? Should he keep going? He didn't like offending people, especially ones he liked the look of so much. So many thoughts tumbled through his head. He really should leave some of his meds at Ollie's place.

'I'm Bo, by the way. I figured you should know my name, the way you're chowing down on my buns.'

Rory choked on the half-chewed cinnamon scroll. It had seriously lodged itself in his throat. Oh great, he was literally going to die of embarrassment in front of a cute baker who was talking – flirting? – with him.

Bo got up and ran over to join Rory on his bench, whacking him on the back. There was nothing do to but let the slimy wad of dough fly from his mouth and land in the dirt, along with his dignity.

'Gross,' he managed to say, wiping his watering eyes.

'Epic,' Bo said.

'Oh, I meant that,' Rory pointed to the projectile. 'Not your ... buns,' he finished pathetically, looking back into the bag.

'Seriously, do not stress about it.'

At that moment, a kookaburra swooped down and snatched the dirty mess from the ground mid-flight, then disappeared into the tree behind them.

'That,' said Bo, 'was gross.'

They looked at each other for a moment before they both laughed.

Rory's nerves settled. Bo's ability to roll with whatever put him at ease. Even regurgitation hadn't killed the mood. 'I'm Rory.'

'Nice to meet you, Rory,' Bo said. He extended a hand, and they shook. Rory liked the way Bo was unapologetically dainty, his slender fingers gentle, even with the hidden strength of a baker. 'But I need to get back to work. Break's over.'

'Sure thing,' Rory replied. 'I'm going to finish my breakfast.'

'Dine again sometime,' Bo said, like a cheesy maître d', but with a genuine invitation kneaded in.

The interaction had been so bizarre yet so friendly. Rory knew he'd be back, just to see what happened the next time they met.

Bo the baker sauntered back to work, and Rory knew he was in trouble when he found Bo's ill-fitting uniform adorable. Studying fashion didn't mean he thought there was a hierarchy of human-worth under whatever rags people had on. But so few uniforms had any style whatsoever. He made some slight alterations in his mind – to the uniform and to the conversation that had just taken place – and smiled to himself.

FRIDAY NIGHT

Ollie rolled their eyes. 'You are not still going on about this!'

'What?' Rory insisted. 'She's got to be the most beautiful girl I've ever seen.'

They were in line at *The Keyhole*. There was a slight breeze, and Rory felt goosebumps rise on his arms. His outfit – a tank top underneath pink overalls – would be worth it once they were inside. Ollie, in their singlet top, folded their arms across their chest.

'And she seems really nice,' Rory finished.

'Look, you've told me the story from beginning to end plenty of times this week. I do not think you had enough of an interaction to know one way or the other. You, dear sir, are lust-struck.'

'Fine, whatever. I'll just have to find her and talk to her some more.' Rory looked up and down the street. 'Oh, quick, before the others get here, what's Sara's girlfriend's name?'

'It's Riley.'

'Cool. Thanks.' Rory nodded.

Breaking their crossed arms long enough to tap Rory on the chest, Ollie said, 'What about this baker-boy? He sounded cute.'

'He was definitely cute.' Rory had been thinking about Bo a lot this week, too. The sun-girl and baker-boy orbiting in his mind. 'What about him?'

'Are you going to see him again? Maybe I should go buy some bread.'

Rory felt a flush of embarrassment at the memory of coughing up the scroll, followed by a warmer flush still at how okay Bo had made him feel about it. 'I really would like to see him again. But all's fair in love and war. So, you buy all the bread you want. Who knows, he might not like either of us.'

Sara was walking down the line with Riley.

'Hey,' Rory said and reached to give her a hug. 'Hi, Riley,' he said from over Sara's shoulder. If he said it enough, it might stick.

'Hey,' Riley said, hugging them both.

Ollie joined in; four sets of arms all tangled together.

After two rounds, they left their table for the dance floor. Rory, even with unrelenting searchlight attention, hadn't seen the girl from last week. He remembered the sparkle of her dress, the brightness of her smile. But there had been no shining sun drifting through the swarming galaxy of the club. Part of him even hoped to see Bo. He wasn't sure this was the kind of place Bo would come to. It was impossible to guess from the baker's uniform what kind of things he might enjoy on a Friday night. Especially if he had a Saturday morning shift.

The crowd was heaving. The four of them burrowed in as best they could and carved out a tiny nook in the bodies so they could dance together. Rory let himself go. He didn't let his constant thoughts of the sun-girl stop him from moving to the music, and from laughing with his friends. Sara and Riley would regularly catch each other's eye and then move in for a close dance, kissing briefly before breaking apart to dance with the group again. Rory noticed Ollie throwing flirty looks at nearby cute boys, but they didn't show signs of leaving the circle of friends so soon in the evening.

Rory knew that some people used the dance floor to find someone to make out with or whatever. That was a bonus, if it happened. His motto was: *the dance floor is for dancing.* He could even let go of wondering how other people thought about him when he was dancing.

Maybe fifteen minutes passed, perhaps an hour. Riley and Sara bought another round. Ollie was dancing with a boy who had sheepishly joined their circle.

Rory lost himself to the music, his neck and shoulders rolling in time with the beat. He did a spin. Mid-turn, he saw her.

She wasn't in yellow-gold this time, but a jumpsuit so blue that it could have been cut from the sky. The flared legs tapered in to hug her hips, and a cowl neckline hung from a strap behind her neck. She was dancing with one of the drag queens who performed here regularly. They were both bopping to the music in impossible heels.

Rory stared. It was a thing of myth for his mind to be blank, but right now it was like a cloudless sky – a jumpsuit shaped sky. It wasn't until she looked up and saw him that he realised he wasn't dancing. He started moving again, not wanting to seem awkwardly stationary in a mass of bodies. She grinned, and the recognition on her face was all the encouragement he needed. He stepped forward, edging between the bodies until he was close enough to dance beside her and her friend.

'Hey,' he shouted. 'I wondered if I was going to see you again.'

Her eyes glittered in the strobing lights. 'Wondered or hoped?' she called back.

He felt his face burn. 'Both?'

She pointed to her friend, who had been watching them. 'This is Judy.'

Judy leaned forward and kissed the air on either side of Rory's face. He returned the gesture. 'Judy Duty, right? I've seen you perform.' He nodded his head towards the stage at the other end of the club. 'You're awesome!'

'Thanks, doll! You can stay.'

'I'm Rory.' That time, all his attention was on the girl. His name was for her.

She tucked her long hair behind her ear. 'I'm Dym.'

They hadn't stopped moving to the beat, even as they'd been talking. Now they started dancing in earnest; Dym meeting Rory's eyes from time to time.

Lights flashed. Bodies moved. Occasionally, Dym's hips would brush against Rory's or their arms might touch briefly. Each time, a wave of sensation passed over him, radiating from that spot.

After some time, Judy leant in and said loudly, 'I've got to get ready.' She and Dym held hands for a moment.

'Go slay!' Dym said.

'Yeah,' Rory added weakly, stopping himself from saying good luck at the last second. Wasn't that bad luck for performers?

And then they were alone. Or they may as well have been. Rory and the girl who was a slice of a summer's day. It didn't matter that the club was packed or that people pressed in on them from all sides. All Rory's attention was on Dym.

She smiled at him as she started moving to the beat again, reaching out a hand to gently rest it on Rory's hip. He let his movements be guided by that hand, thrilled by the closeness of her.

In what felt like no time at all, their dancing was cut short by an announcement for the performance.

But before Rory could be disappointed, Dym took him by the hand and said into his ear, 'I've got to get to the front.' She led him through the crowd.

As they passed his friends, Ollie called out, 'There you are! Where have you been?' They glanced at who was holding Rory's hand and grinned, answering their own question.

Rory used his free hand to grab Ollie's. Ollie held onto Sara, who was already holding hands with Riley. The chain of them snaked through the crowd to stand right in front of the stage.

Dym looked surprised when she stopped and discovered the caravan of people gathering beside her.

Rory said, 'Dym, these are my friends. Friends, this is Dym.'

The music faded suddenly. Judy emerged on stage as the frenzied strings of the introduction to Judy Garland's 'The Trolley Song' began.

Judy's over-the-top make-up was lit up by the spotlight. Her eyes were wide and heavily shadowed blue to match her blazer, which had puffy sleeves and a large starched collar. Rory watched her lip-sync while her limbs whirled in camp choreography. At the end of one of the choruses, the song changed into Anita Ward's 'Ring My Bell'. Judy tore away her blazer and a copper sequined dress spilled out from underneath. The costume change was flawless, and Rory marvelled at what good sewing could achieve. Judy's dancing was now energetically disco.

'She's so good!' Rory called to Dym, who grinned and nodded enthusiastically. The surge of connection he usually found here, where the queer and queer-friendly just want to lift each other up, felt especially powerful tonight with Dym by his side. That they could share their appreciation of drag done well made the night even more fun.

At the end of the show, the DJ kicked off again and the crowd went back to dancing.

Dym turned to Rory and said, 'It was good to see you again, but I've got to go.'

His heart plummeted. He felt like he had only just found her again. Even if they'd spent over an hour together.

'But it's early,' he said, not bothering to look at the time to see if this was true.

'I know. I was only hanging around to see Judy.'

'Can I give you my number?' Rory asked hopefully.

She took out her phone, and he felt joy fizz in him like soft drink as she saved his number. Then she kissed him on the cheek and said, 'Bye for now.'

He caught himself before he called out, 'text me', because, clearly, that was the point. 'Bye,' he said.

When he turned back to his friends, they were all watching him.

'So, I'm guessing she's the one you've been going on about all week?' Ollie said. Their grin undermined the accusatory tone.

Rory nodded.

'I get it,' said Sara. 'She's a stunner.' She reached out and wiped something off Rory's cheeks. 'You inherited some of her lippy.'

Riley said, 'Yeah, she knows how to do her face, that's for sure.'

'Well, as penance for ditching us,' Ollie said, 'it's your round.'

Rory narrowed his eyes. He considered buying a round of cranberry lemonade just to pay them back for the teasing.

SATURDAY MORNING

Rory opened his eyes to see Ollie sitting up and reading a book.

'How are you even …?' Rory said.

'I couldn't sleep, and I'm not feeling too rough.'

Rory rolled over to check the time on his phone. There was a message from an unknown number. It said:

You can ring my bell.

Dym had texted. She had actually texted! His heart raced. His fingers jittered over the screen as he tried to work out what to reply.

He sent back the bell emoji and the wink emoji, then lay back in bed thinking about her for a solid five minutes before he realised he hadn't registered the time at all.

'You hungry?' Ollie asked.

Immediately, Bo came to Rory's mind. The bakery wasn't so far away.

'Yeah, I could do a cinnamon scroll.'

'Dude! You literally just got that girl's number and now you're chasing the baker, too?'

He panged with worry, his thoughts giving him whiplash. Was it wrong to not shut one side down?

'There's nothing set in stone with either of them,' Rory said. 'And I'm just being friendly.'

'Ha! *Friendly*.'

Rory got out of bed and pulled on his overalls.

Ollie didn't move, or even take their eyes from their book. 'Well, you won't want me there. Bring me back a sticky bun. And some fruit bread. I'm gonna put half a tub of butter on it.'

When Rory was on the street, he found the sun had the decency to hide behind a cloud this week. It wasn't too offensive.

Ordering what probably was too much bread-based food for a two-person breakfast, Rory asked the cashier, 'Is Bo working today?'

Rather than answering, they turned over their shoulder and shouted, 'Bo!'

His head appeared around the corner from the back room. He looked puzzled until he saw Rory. Then his easy smile spread across his face. 'Oh, hey.'

'Hey,' Rory said, suddenly feeling nervous. Why had he asked for Bo? What did he have to say? He only knew he had liked him right away.

He was saved by Bo saying to the cashier, 'I'll take my break.' Then to Rory, 'Give me a min.'

Rory stood on the street scrolling through his feed and trying to keep his mind from racing too far ahead of itself. Then Bo was next to him, saying, 'Going in for round two against my baking?'

Holding up his bag, Rory said, 'Yeah, I guess so.'

'Are you wearing clothes from last night again? I'm starting to think you come here on your walk of shame.'

Glancing at his outfit, crumpled from Ollie's floor and a night of dancing, Rory laughed. 'Oh, no, my friend lives just around the corner.' He pointed down the street.

'I'm teasing. You'll learn I do that a lot. Should we go to our usual place?'

I'll learn? Usual place? Rory would have to up his banter game.

There was a forwardness to Bo that Rory appreciated. He could hold his own when it came to flirting, especially when it was fleeting and casual. But coming to Bo's work, repeat meetings … that carried more *ooft* in his chest. Kinda how he felt about Dym. Was it weird he was thinking about them both at once? It was too soon to decide.

They made their way to the park. Bo sat down on one end of a bench, turning in a way that was an invitation for Rory to join him there, so he did.

'Feel free to eat your breakfast, don't not on my account.'

Rory didn't need telling twice. 'Do you want some?' he asked.

'No, I'm good,' Bo said. 'I baked it. I usually find myself craving *all* the fresh fruit when I get away from those ovens.'

Rory tore off a piece of scroll and put it in his mouth.

Bo took an energy drink from his pocket and cracked it with a fizz. 'Did you stay out late, then?' he said.

Making sure he'd chewed properly this time, Rory swallowed before saying, 'Average time, two or something. I wasn't keeping track.'

'That's not too bad, I suppose.'

'Do you go out much?'

A slow but deliberate smile grew on Bo's lips. 'I like to when I can. Get dressed up and everything,' he said at last. 'But it's hard to do late nights with baker's shifts.'

Rory said, 'Of course.' He was getting very self-conscious. Not at all how at ease he'd felt last week when he was choking on bread. Is that what it took? He was fidgeting and didn't know where to rest his gaze.

'Hey,' said Bo, softly. He met Rory's eye. 'Relax.'

The anxious feeling that was rising up Rory's throat eased. He nodded and took another bite of the scroll, feeling baffled at the butterflies. This was a boy he'd met once. But for some reason, Rory felt both calm and like an excitable puppy when they talked. He wanted to matter to Bo in some way, not be the random dude from the park.

Searching for some sort of concrete knowledge about Bo, Rory finished his mouthful and asked, 'How long have you been a baker?'

'I started soon after I got here, year before last,' Bo said. 'I've always enjoyed baking and I needed work, so an apprenticeship made sense.'

'Oh, you're not from here?'

The smile on Bo's face cracked slightly. 'I grew up in the country.'

Rory noticed the falter and knew not to press that further. Instead, he said, 'Oh, cool. I grew up here.'

Bo's twenty-minute break went faster than Rory could account for.

Rory was so caught up in the conversation that after they walked back to the bakery together and said goodbye, he was halfway to Ollie's place before he realised that they hadn't exchanged numbers.

But as he walked up the stairs to the apartment his phone buzzed with a message from Dym.

It was good to see you. Last night was fun.

His zippy high doubled. Having two people show an interest in you was exhilarating, even if it came with a tiny side of guilt. The most important thing was to be honest with them both if anything progressed.

Opening the door, he found Ollie had moved to the couch.

'That must've gone well,' Ollie said.

Rory's thoughts were tumbling between Bo and Dym. 'What?'

'Your face, and how long you've been gone. I'm glad you remembered breakfast.' Ollie stood and took the bag from Rory easily. 'Mmm, raisin toast with too much butter coming right up!'

FRIDAY NIGHT

Rory had spent a solid hour changing outfits until he was happy. A button-up shirt with a bright floral print that reflected his mood, dressed down with jeans. After gathering the courage to ask Dym out for a drink, he wanted to make a good (third?) impression. He'd made sure he'd gotten to the quiet bar they'd chosen early, so she wouldn't have to wait a minute, and scored some seats for them both.

Telling himself it wasn't a compulsion, he read her text again.

Sure. Let's meet up early on Friday before going to The Keyhole.

He looked up from his phone. Suddenly, felt like he may as well be wearing a hessian sack. Dym walked into the tiny room looking like the night sky itself had stepped in off the street. Her black dress had long sleeves and sat high around her throat. Tiny, sparkling black stones caught the light and flicked it back in unknowable constellations. It fitted her body perfectly and rested just above her knees, showing off her legs and another pair of impossible heels.

Dym walked to Rory with a precision he admired. He stood and greeted her with a light kiss on the cheek before they both sat down in the small booth.

'What can I get you?' Rory asked.

She looked amused. 'I thought you knew my drink of choice. Or have you forgotten already?'

'Oh, no, I remember. But you still get to choose every time.'

He got their drinks from the bar.

'So, tell me,' Rory said. 'Is Dym short for anything?'

She took a lengthy sip from her drink, then set the glass down on the table. 'Dymphna,' she said. 'What can I say? My parents were religious.' She rolled her eyes.

Rory's family wasn't religious, and he didn't know what she meant. 'Oh?'

Did she wink? It was hard to tell in the low lighting. It reminded him of something he couldn't place. Instead of answering, she said, 'What's Rory short for?'

He decided to be playful. 'Usually just cash.'

There was a beat when he thought his joke hadn't landed, and he was certain he'd just ruined the whole night with a dad joke. Then she laughed loudly and without reserve.

'Touché,' she said.

He pointed at her drink. 'Does this mean you're leaving early again tonight?'

She looked down at the glass before answering. 'Yeah. I work every Saturday.'

'But can't you sleep in before work?'

She chuckled. 'No, are you kidding? I shouldn't even stay out as late as I do. But sacrifices, eh?'

'What do you do?'

She looked genuinely surprised at the question. She put both hands on the table between them and stared at him. Her brow furrowed, and she opened her mouth to say something but then caught herself. She exhaled deeply. 'I … I think I better go.' Standing abruptly, she picked up her purse and turned for the door.

'What is it?' Rory called after her. He stood and jogged to catch up. He touched her arm very gently to slow her down, then took his hand away. 'What did I say?'

She turned to him, the joy he'd seen in her just moments before replaced with worry. 'You must think I look flawless.'

He felt embarrassed and off-kilter, like he had just stepped off a carnival ride. He couldn't see the connection and had somehow spoiled everything without even realising. What had he done? And how could he fix it? He gave a half-smile. 'I do. You do. Every night I've seen you.'

'What about when you've seen me in the daytime?'

Genuine bewilderment took over. Had he ever? He racked his brain. 'I … what?'

Dym gave a small shake of her head. 'It's fine,' she said. 'Let's just save ourselves from any surprises and call it a night.'

Rory scrambled for the right thing to say. 'But I want to get to know you, surprises and all.'

She took a step back from him, eyebrows high in puzzlement. 'Why do you think I don't drink alcohol when I'm out on a Friday night, then drink energy drinks to get me through work?'

'I didn't know you drank …' he stopped speaking. Things were beginning to click in his head. He could see it now. Behind the make-up and the hair were the same eyes that winked at him. Under the lipstick was the same radiant smile.

An intense relief and joy flooded him, which he couldn't explain. Without processing completely, he said, 'You're Bo.'

The tension in her seemed to ease. She rocked slightly back onto her heels, seeming less like a spring about to jump out the door. That tiny relaxation gave him confidence. 'You are, right?'

'Rory, I'm taking this as the biggest compliment ever. You only figured it out now?'

It was thrilling to feel both his crushes collide into one entity in front of him.

'All I knew was I liked what I saw, and I wanted to know you better,' he said.

'When I said I like to get dressed up to go out …' Her shoulders softened, and her smile returned. She gave a small shrug.

'You meant as Dym.' All this time he'd wondered what Bo liked to do on his nights out. Now he knew. And he already knew that he and Dym had a lot in common from talking with Bo. It was like winning the jackpot. He smiled and gestured back to the table. 'Don't let your cranberry lemonade go to waste.'

She walked with him back to their booth. As they sat down, she said, 'I mean, my drag name is Dym the Lights.'

He laughed and was pleased to see her radiant smile again. The knowledge that Bo was behind it made him blush.

'You know, in some ways, this is a relief,' he said.

She gave a laugh and said, 'Why's that?'

'Because I was crushing on both of you and didn't know how to not hurt anyone.'

Her eyes twinkled like her dress. 'The only thing you need to decide now, then, is where you're going to take me on our next date.'

MOONFALL

ALISON EVANS

The night the moon disappeared from the sky, Nyx was sitting outside the cabin they had built with their brothers. As they watched, the moon grew darker, more red. The moon blossomed pink as she slipped behind the shadow of the earth.

And then she was gone.

Nyx waited on the cold porch for their brothers to return from their night as swans. As the dawn's birdsong started around Nyx, Ealadha and Oisín came down the path, half-running.

'The moon.' Nyx stood, blankets falling aside. 'What happened?'

Ealadha ran his hands through his hair. 'We don't know.'

'I thought you might've seen something while you were flying.'

'We saw the eclipse, then nothing.' Oisín stared up at the lightening sky. 'Even swan eyes can't see in the dark.'

Ealadha yawned wide, Oisín did the same. When it first began they'd told Nyx the transformation back into human bodies always felt too heavy. Their interactions were more often than not brief, and so Nyx would talk to the moon at night instead.

'Do you want anything to eat before we go to sleep?' Oisín asked, but Nyx shook their head.

'I'm going to see what the forest knows,' Nyx said.

Their brothers went inside and Nyx pulled on a coat and left, the ground wet from the night's condensation. The forest was quiet as they walked, too quiet. Nyx realised they couldn't see any of the usual animals that surrounded their home. The sun rose higher, but still the silence remained.

As they kept going, a red deer walked across the path. Nyx paused, wondering why the animal didn't run from them, and started to follow the deer. A noise made them look up, and they saw a flock of birds above flying in the same direction. Nyx, shivering, kept walking, and the cold of the morning seemed to drop away.

Shafts of sunlight dappled the mossy ground and they heard a soft noise growing louder. A voice? Goosebumps raised on Nyx's arms but they kept walking, a fox

scurrying between their feet.

They came to a clearing filled with the forest animals, where someone with white, glowing hair sat on an old log, speaking in a language Nyx didn't understand. Her hair almost touched the ground and her round, soft frame was clothed in a simple grey dress that shone wherever the sunlight touched it. When their eyes met, a complete calm washed over Nyx and they knew that this was the moon, fallen to the earth.

Nyx couldn't help but walk towards her, and as they got closer it was like stars blossomed in Nyx's chest.

'I've heard your stories,' the moon said, her voice low but confident, full of power. 'Seen you look up at me.'

Nyx's cheeks felt hot. 'It's hard not to.'

The animals seemed to come out of a trance as the moon spoke, and soon each one had dispersed, gone back to their lives.

'Do you have somewhere to stay?' Nyx asked.

She shook her head. 'No.'

'My home is close by. I live with two of my brothers, but they're ... well, you'll see.'

The moon sat down at the table and Nyx didn't have a lot to offer her. They usually ate alone, and to prepare a meal for two seemed so strange, indulgent.

'What would you like?' Nyx asked. 'I have some eggs at the moment, and there are still plenty of potatoes.'

'I don't think I've ever eaten before,' the moon said, frowning slightly as she looked at something that wasn't there.

'Oh.'

'I'm not sure if I can.'

'Would you like to try?' Nyx said, smiling, and the moon laughed and nodded.

Nyx started to cook and boiled the kettle as well, just in case the moon liked tea.

At the first taste of the meal, the moon gasped. 'I've eaten before.' She had a few more mouthfuls. 'Yes. I've been here in the past.'

'Why'd you come back?' Nyx asked.

The moon held their gaze for a moment, as if deciding how best to put it. 'I fell.'

Nyx tried to picture it. 'Fell?'

'It's hard not to look down,' she said. 'When you've been up there your whole life.' She stared off into the distance for a few moments and then turned to Nyx. 'Your brothers are cursed, aren't they?' She looked like she was remembering a dream, feeling for words that weren't quite solid. 'It was cruel of your father.'

Nyx looked down, avoiding the moon's gaze. 'I'm working on undoing the spell.' Nyx took a bite of the meal, the spices warming them. 'They'll return to normal soon, and then we can go home.' Nyx cleared their throat and looked up, amazed at how the moon was just as beautiful in human form as she was in the sky. 'Is the food good?'

'It's delicious.' The moon nodded. 'Thank you. It's been a long time. It's so … I feel like I'm half of who I'm supposed to be, my whole mind can't fit into this body.'

'Did it have something to do with the eclipse?' Nyx asked. 'I was watching last night, when you fell.'

'Perhaps …' Her eyes clouded over for a moment. 'The first time, I was a baby. I screamed and screamed, I remember. My throat was raw with it.' She frowned. 'I don't remember anything else.'

After eating, Nyx went out to the shed to collect more firewood. It took a lot to keep a fire going through the winter. Nyx hadn't realised that before they were banished from the opulent, easy life of the castle.

Nyx could have used magic to light and warm the cabin, but they had sworn off it. Mostly. It was hard to resist the tug of it, the wanting. So instead, Nyx would find wood, either in the forest or in town, and split it in the shed when they needed to. As the axe fell on the log in front of them, cleaving it in two, Nyx wondered how long the moon could stay.

Maybe it wouldn't be so bad to have someone to talk to.

The fireplace was roaring and the sky was getting dark when Nyx's brothers woke. Nyx introduced the moon and both Ealadha and Oisín bowed their heads a little.

'It's a bit hard to see now when we're flying,' Oisín said.

Ealadha nudged him in the side. 'Just like a new moon,' he said with a pointed look. 'We'll manage.'

The moon nodded her head. 'Thank you all for letting me stay with you.'

The sun disappeared and a swirling cloud massed around the brothers' feet. Nyx had seen the transformation hundreds of times before – the abrupt shrinking, the shortening of their brothers' limbs, the explosion of grey feathers – but the moon looked on with wide eyes. Nyx opened the door for Ealadha and Oisín to leave.

The moon and Nyx moved to the porch and looked out into the night, the steam from their drinks curling into the air.

'It's all so different to last time … There's more forest, more life. It was all grey and glass then.'

'How long has it been?' Nyx asked, looking out at the dusting of stars above. They were brighter than usual.

The moon smiled. 'I couldn't tell you.'

'Do you know how long you'll be staying?' Nyx asked. 'Winter's coming, so we'll need food. I try to grow things, but I'm not a very good gardener.'

'I can't stay for too long,' the moon said. 'Otherwise I can't get home. I'll become part of the earth again.' She sighed. 'I'll tell you a story.' The moon moved to sit on the edge of the porch, her feet swinging back and forth over the grass, and Nyx sat beside her.

'I saw an old woman be bathed and put into fresh clothes,' the moon began, eyes glowing brighter. 'Her husband lay beside her on the bed and took her hand for the very last time as she left this realm. I saw him sigh, only slightly, and nod. He kissed her forehead as he remembered their life together. So long ago they had met.

'Through the day and the evening, her eleven children came to say goodbye. Her twenty five grandchildren filed in, and her fourteen great-grandchildren were carried in.

'There was wine, and there was a prayer. Her husband's voice wavered as he spoke, but he stood, holding hands with one of his sons.

'I saw the love this woman had tended through the years, sowing its seeds and helping it grow.

'I saw her love.'

The moon's eyes dimmed back to their usual glow, and Nyx put a hand over hers, and they wondered what it would be like, to grow old with someone. Nyx gave the moon their bed and they went to Ealadha's, but Nyx couldn't sleep for a long time.

'How did you get here?' the moon asked the next morning. 'This isn't your home. This cabin. I know you like it, I remember you told me that one night. It's like my life in the sky was a dream.'

Nyx wondered how much the moon already knew. 'I was ... I was caught using magic. My brothers knew about it. To punish them, my brothers were cursed by my father to turn into swans during the night, to be human during the day, too tired to live as men. He exiled us. I'm trying to find a way to get them back the way they were.'

'Why?'

The question felt to Nyx like slipping on ice, the ground suddenly not as sturdy as it should be. 'What do you mean?'

The moon paused, threading some of her hair between her fingers. 'Why can't you use magic?'

'Oh.'

'What did you think I meant?'

'Nothing. I don't know. Magic is for *commoners*,' Nyx said, shaking their head. 'Anyway.' They clapped their hands together. 'We'll have to go into town to get more food, best make it quick.'

They got up and unfolded the trolley they usually took to the markets, wheeled it to the door, started to shrug on their jacket.

'What's wrong with town?' asked the moon from her perch on the couch's arm.

'I'm the disgraced princen,' Nyx muttered. 'Not worth knowing.'

The moon thought for a moment. 'Well, I think it'll be fun. It must look different from the ground. There's always so much going on.' She stood, light on her feet. So light she was floating just above the floor. Nyx hadn't realised yesterday, but now it was so obvious they didn't know how they could have missed it. Of course the moon would float.

'Right.' Nyx went outside first, grabbing a basket of seed potatoes along the way, and the moon closed the door behind herself.

As they walked the track through the forest, the birds around them were singing, songs pealing out like bells, like pond-skipped stones.

'Do you miss using magic?' the moon asked.

Nyx shrugged. 'Sometimes,' they said, but they didn't meet the moon's gaze. 'Town isn't too far. It's a small one, we chose that on purpose.'

As they walked, Nyx saw more animals than usual, but they didn't come closer like they had yesterday. They just walked alongside for a while, dropping off the further Nyx and the moon travelled.

When they reached sight of the first buildings, Nyx took a deep breath and walked a little faster. They felt the moon's eyes on them and though Nyx's cheeks reddened, they faced forward. They went straight up to the shed where farmers sold their crops. It was always the busiest part of town, and Nyx hated that, but they had to go.

'Princen, you heard about the moon?' asked the shopkeeper as Nyx came to the counter.

Nyx didn't wince at the title but they felt the discomfort bubble in their gut. 'I saw it happen.'

'Old Niamh reckons that it's a sign of the end times.' The shopkeeper leaned in as they spoke, raising their eyebrows.

'I don't know about that.' Nyx looked around to see where the moon had gone. She was over by Ethan, the mushroom-monger. 'Thank you.'

Nyx traded some seed potatoes for bundles of willow branches for the garden, then went about trading for more things: eggs, milk, seeds. When their basket was full, Nyx saw the moon was still talking to Ethan.

'Let's go,' Nyx said quietly from behind her, but Ethan's face lit up.

'Princen!' ve said. 'Always a blessing when you deign to visit my stall.'

Nyx didn't know what to say, and so said nothing.

'I love this one,' the moon said, picking up a large, flat mushroom, bigger than the palm of her hand.

'That one's a goodie,' Ethan said. 'It's a portobello, perfect for roasting. One of my favourites.'

'Fascinating,' the moon replied, holding it up to the light that streamed through the big windows.

'We'll take this, and these,' Nyx said, getting a small pile of mushrooms together with the portobello. They traded for them without saying anything else, and then speedily walked back into the open air. 'Glad that's over.'

'I think Ethan was just teasing,' the moon said. 'Ve was very nice when we were talking.'

'Let's just go home,' Nyx said, and they started walking back home.

'Should I call you Princen?' asked the moon when they were amongst the trees.

Nyx snorted. 'Please no.'

In the garden, Nyx bundled the new willow branches together so they stood, making a tent shape, and started to weave the thinner, water-soaked sticks through to keep it sturdy. The sky rumbled and they looked up at the dark, plump clouds that threatened rain.

As they looked away, one of the willows whipped around and hit them across the face. Nyx shrieked, stumbling backwards. As they let go of the structure, the whole thing slumped to the side.

Nyx swore under their breath.

'What's this for?' the moon asked, and Nyx started.

'I forgot you were there, sorry. It's for the beans to grow on. They need something to hold onto.'

'Beans are something you've been able to grow every year,' the moon said, her voice faraway as she looked at the birds nearby.

Nyx stood up straight. 'Yeah. It's weird that you know that stuff sometimes.'

'Sorry.' The moon smiled regretfully. 'It's like all the knowledge I have is just simmering below the surface. Sometimes it breaks free.'

Nyx looked at the bundle of sticks they'd been trying to put together for the last half hour and sighed. 'This is hopeless.' They took off their gloves and let them fall to the dirt. 'I have to go get some brambles at the graveyard, if you want to come for a walk up the mountain.'

'At the graveyard.'

Nyx laughed and shook their head. 'Yes.'

The path was up the mountain, the stone steps slick with overgrown moss and the overnight rain. The walk was always quiet and smelt of humus, the branches of trees covered in ferns and lichen, rabbits darting silently across the leaf litter.

Nyx shivered as they opened the graveyard gate. The place was old, names faded from the stones, and the brambles grew on the other side of the graveyard so that Nyx had to walk through the whole of it to pick them. The brambles were enchanted to grow slowly so Nyx could only harvest them every few months. Nyx reached down and muttered a spell that would cut the branches and winced as the thorns drew blood.

'Was that magic?' the moon asked.

Nyx couldn't look at her. 'Nothing else cuts them.'

'But weren't you punished for—' The moon stopped speaking when she saw the face Nyx was making. 'Do you need help?'

Nyx shook their head. 'I can't be helped, otherwise it won't work.' They gathered the brambles and put them in their pack, only getting cut once this time. 'The blood is a part of the curse,' they said, as they saw the moon watching.

Back in the cabin, Nyx grabbed out the bramble coat they'd been working on for three years – not even half done, only the first of two – and sat on the couch. The thorns were already opening new cuts in their palms. They winced at the stinging but there was nothing for it but to grit their teeth.

The moon went to the stove and put on the kettle. 'I think I remember how to make tea now,' the moon said brightly. 'And a fire?'

Nyx nodded and the moon got to work at the fireplace. Soon enough, the warmth glowed to Nyx's feet, and the moon made tea.

Nyx paused and looked out at the forest through the window, enjoying the way the dew left by the rains sparkled in the sunlight. It was nice, this place, and Nyx not for the first time wondered if they actually wanted to go back to the castle, to their life there.

But they had to weave the coats for their brothers anyway, so they bent back to their work with a sigh. Better to try and focus than to let their mind wander where it shouldn't.

The moon sat on the ground and started to read a book as Nyx wove. The silence was a comfortable one, and Nyx realised how different it was from being alone.

The moon put down the book and watched Nyx weave the thorny coat. 'Why are you making that?'

'For Oisín and Ealadha. Once the coats are done, they can wear them and the curse will break. But this is only the first coat. It'll take years to finish two. It's been years already.'

Nyx and the moon were silent then, sipping their drinks and watching the steam curl in the morning sunlight streaming through the windows.

'If there's anything I can do while I'm here, let me know,' the moon said. 'Though I don't know how long I'll be able to linger … Can I keep staying here?'

Nyx looked at her and thought about food in the winter and how they'd struggle.

But then thought of all the days alone while their brothers slept.

'Of course.'

'I can never make the garden ready in time for winter,' Nyx said as they stood over the vegetable patch that was covered in weeds. 'But we can get ready for spring a little bit. Over there are lots of potatoes, carrots, onions. I would love to grow mushrooms but I can never make it work.' They sighed. 'Maybe together we could make something come of it.' Nyx blushed when the moon's eyes met theirs. They coughed and looked away, trying to ignore the way their heart fluttered. The moon couldn't stay. They knew that.

'I don't think I've ever gardened before.' The moon bent down to pick up some of the wet dirt, rubbing it between her fingers. 'It smells so real.'

'I think that's a good sign,' Nyx laughed. They couldn't remember the last time they'd laughed. It felt nice, and the moon's hair seemed to sparkle at the noise.

A few days later the moon came back from a walk with someone, and Nyx's heart jumped into their throat. They watched from the window, thinking the person would leave, but the moon poked her head in and waved at Nyx to come outside.

'Ethan's going to help with growing mushrooms,' the moon said excitedly. 'Ve said you just need a shed, or something like that. And we – you – have one of those!'

Nyx's face heated up and they considered pretending to be very ill. 'Oh.'

'I'll make the tea, you go outside,' the moon said.

'Okay.'

And before Nyx could think too much more about it, the moon pushed them out the door and onto the porch. There were three seats – two for the brothers who never sit there.

'I'm Ethan, Princen,' Ethan said. Ve brought a few things on a trolley, pulled gently behind ver. 'Serena said you wanted some help with growing mushrooms.'

'Did … Serena,' Nyx said, almost to themself. 'You don't have to call me Princen.

I'm just Nyx now.'

'She did. Nyx.' Ethan shifted on ver feet.

'Please have a seat,' the moon said, bringing out the teapot and three cups. 'So what will we need to do?' Her hair was glowing brighter than usual as she looked between Ethan and Nyx.

Ethan talked through the process, and Nyx could see how it might work. A few logs in the woods they could set up easy enough, and then with the tubs in the shed they'd have more mushrooms than they'd know what to do with.

'The best thing is that the ones in the shed aren't weather dependent,' Ethan said. 'So you can get protein all year, if you do it right. The ones we put in the logs will vary with the seasons.'

When Nyx showed Ethan the shed, ver smile widened.

'It's perfect,' ve said. 'I prepared one bucket, but we can do one together.'

Nyx's heart picked up a bit, but the moon gave them a little nudge and Nyx breathed out. They copied Ethan as ve showed them how to pack the straw into the bucket and spread the spores.

'It's good to keep them warm and damp,' Ethan said when ve put the lid on the finished bucket. 'It might not be warm enough in here for them to thrive, but they'll manage.'

'It's okay,' Nyx said, and they closed their eyes, focusing on their heartbeat. This was what their father forbade them to do, but maybe it was okay. For the mushrooms. They pulled from within them a small, glowing ball of heat, and as they rolled it back and forth between their palms, the ball began to float. This was one of their favourite spells to do, back when they had been practising daily, and as Nyx placed the ball in the air it felt like greeting an old friend.

Ethan didn't bat an eye, but the moon gave Nyx a smile that made their cheeks redden.

They all walked through the forest and set up a few spore logs, and soon the sun was setting.

'Would you like to stay for dinner?' the moon asked, and Nyx was surprised that they didn't mind.

As they got cooking, their brothers woke from the smell and came out to eat. It was more people at the table than they'd ever had, and the night crept closer as they spoke.

When the time came, Oisín and Ealadha excused themselves, turning into swans outside, away from Ethan's eyes.

'Should I call you Serena?' Nyx asked the moon, once Ethan had left.

She laughed. 'No. I made that up for Ethan's sake.'

Nyx and the moon sat together on the porch and watched as the stars started appearing in the darkening sky.

'Thank you for inviting Ethan,' Nyx said. 'I'd been wanting to know how to grow mushrooms for so long.'

'I knew you'd like each other,' the moon said. Her hair had dulled, and wisps of something sparkling escaped from her mouth as she spoke.

'Do you have to go back?' Nyx's heart ached at the thought.

The moon sighed and more glitter escaped her, and Nyx realised it was stardust leaving her. 'I came from earth, birthed from here long ago. If I stay here too long, I won't be able to go back. And the earth needs its moon.'

Nyx put their hand on the moon's, chest aching. 'Do you want to?'

'That's a complicated question.' The moon looked away. 'I miss the sky,' the moon said. 'Looking down on everything. I could see so much. Now, I've only got what's right in front of me. It's stifling.'

Nyx paused for a moment. 'Maybe you could tell me more of the things you've seen. I liked your story from the other day.'

The moon stayed silent, so Nyx cleared away the plates from dinner and left them on the bench to clean later. They found some biscuits for dessert and returned to the porch. 'I saw a traveller,' the moon started, sitting so her thigh was pressed against Nyx's. She leaned her head against Nyx's shoulder, and Nyx moved closer so she'd be more comfortable.

'The traveller was always going to new places and meeting new people, and they were looking for something, but they didn't know what. It was like there was a hole in their torso, something missing.

'They tried to fill it with friendship, with new foods, new loves. The hole remained. After many years, a relative had taken ill and so they returned home. Everything had changed, but they recognised the birdsong, the shape of the hills, the smell of the trees.

'And it was like they had never been away, and as they remained there, the hole in their torso lessened. And they knew they were home, and where they were supposed to be.'

A bat flew overhead. Nyx listened to its clicks. 'Do you want to go inside?' Nyx asked, brushing their fingertips over the moon's forearm.

She shivered. 'Yes.'

As winter started to take a firmer root in the days, Nyx and the moon went to the markets and came home, and Ethan came for dinner a few times. They shifted meal times so the brothers could have breakfast or dinner with Nyx and the moon.

The beans sprouted when they were supposed to, their delicate tendrils grasping a hold of the willow branches. Sometimes the moon helped tend the garden, but mostly Nyx was out there on their own, dirt under their nails, rugged up against the cold.

Nyx started wandering the forest a little just after their brothers turned to swans some nights. They'd walk home as the forest animals slept, and Nyx would pull a small ball of light into existence to illuminate their path home. Every time the joy in using magic grew.

Inside the cabin, Nyx and the moon orbited each other. Together in front of the fire, on the porch, curled up under the blankets of Nyx's bed.

'You really don't belong here,' Nyx said into the cold morning air. 'Do you?'

The moon turned to look at them, and her eyes were dim. She sighed, and Nyx could see stardust, barely there, escape from her mouth. 'I do want to stay, but …' She trailed her fingers down Nyx's arm, raising goosebumps. 'I have to go.'

'You could visit every night. Tell me stories from the sky.'

The moon smiled sadly. 'If my voice could reach you.'

'I'd hear you, regardless.'

Nyx dreamt that night of a spell that would let the moon return to her home in the sky. It needed their brothers, the mountain, a fire, a story and a kiss.

The day after the dream, Nyx didn't talk about the moon leaving. And the day after that, and the day after that. A fragile silence hung over everything until one day the moon stood and said, with tears trickling down her face, 'Wake your brothers early, we have to go to the mountain.'

Later that day, they started up the mountain. Nyx's brothers lagged behind, their human bodies much heavier to walk in than their bird ones. They didn't complain, though, and Nyx was grateful. It was almost time for them to transform and they could have just waited, flown up to the mountain as swans, but they didn't.

'Everything looks different on the ground,' Oisín said. 'I wish I could fly you up, Nyx. You'd love it.'

'I'm very content here.' Nyx laughed, thinking of the green of the moss and the rich smell of the soil. The way the leaf litter sounded underfoot. The mushrooms that had started to sprout.

The moon walked steady and sure, but she smiled at Nyx, and Nyx reached out for her hand. It was cold, and the air grew colder as they travelled up.

The moon's eyes were dim and the shine in her hair almost gone when they got to the highest point they could, a clearing with a view over the valley. Down below, a few chimneys poked out between the trees, smoke curling into the air.

'That's ours,' Nyx said, but Oisín shook his head.

'Wrong colour.' He grinned. 'Over there – it's further than you think.'

The moon moved away from the others, and Nyx followed. Ealadha pulled out the kindling from his pack and, with Oisín, started to build a fire.

'I guess this is it.' Nyx's tongue felt heavy in their mouth, weighed down with words too heavy to say. 'I'll miss you.'

The moon took their hands. Her skin was cold. 'I saw a forest, brimming with life, and the ones who lived there. I saw how this forest changed through the ages, regenerating from the brink.

'I saw the way a princen and two princes made it their home, too, and they cared for each other because there was no one else. I saw them become a new family, a better one.

'And I saw,' her voice cracked, but she went on, 'how they could keep going.'

'Thank you,' Nyx said, their voice wavering as the moon looked at them. Tears pricked in the corners of their eyes, spilling over down their cheeks.

The moon pulled Nyx close and pressed her lips to theirs. She tasted like the salt from their tears, like the ocean pulling and pushing at the shore.

The day slipped into night. Ealadha and Oisín twisted into spirals of feathers, emerging as swans. Nyx and the moon let go of each other, the space between them widening, and Nyx wished they could leap forward, take the moon with them wherever they went, but they stood still, and the moon stepped away from them. Ealadha and Oisín took flight and the moon held out her arms as she floated above the ground. Nyx looked away and listened to their brothers' wings as the moon was flown away.

Nyx didn't move for a long, long time. Their feet began to freeze in their boots and the fire turned to a glowing ember.

Eventually, when the sky cracked open and rain fell down all at once like a sheet, they pulled out a ball of light and picked their way along the path down the mountain.

This time the tears were strong and hot despite the freezing rain, and Nyx howled into the night air as they walked all alone. The sky flashed pink, and Nyx looked up. There was no moon yet, but they could see two swans flying towards them in the rain.

One swooped close, feathers brushing their hair. The other flew above, squawking.

'Thanks for coming back,' Nyx said quietly, unsure if they could be heard over the rain. Together, they went back to the cabin.

Nyx waved them away when they opened the door, needing now to be alone. Nyx changed into dry clothes and crawled into their bed, sheets cold, teeth chattering, and wrapped their arms around themself to try and get warm. They cried silently as the rain roared on the cabin roof.

'You don't want to be human again, do you?' Nyx asked Ealadha when the brothers returned at dawn.

Ealadha looked at Oisín before replying. 'I can't begin to describe it to you. It's like nothing else. Whenever we have to come back down to earth, before the sun rises ... we feel so heavy.'

'Do you wish you were birds all the time?'

'Well, then I'd never get to speak to you, would I?' Ealadha pulled them into a hug. He smelt like wood smoke. 'The night is enough.'

They released each other and Nyx looked down at the bramble coat. They always hated making it, the thorns pricking their fingers constantly. Nothing about the coats was comfortable, and the thought of making their brothers wear the garments brought them no joy.

'I don't want to go back to Father,' Nyx whispered.

Nyx looked around at the cabin that they had all built. They thought back to those first few weeks, trying to find places to sleep out of the cold and the rain ... 'How could he do that to us?'

Oisín shook his head. 'It doesn't matter now.'

'I don't want to go back to the castle,' Nyx said. 'The thought of the luxury, the servants, everything of it makes me sick.'

Oisín and Ealadha smiled at them, and they sat down to eat.

The brothers went to sleep for the day and when they woke, Nyx had built a fire out the back of the house. The three of them stood there and watched the half-finished bramble coat burn, and a different curse was broken.

After their brothers took off into the night again and Ethan had cleared the dinner plates and walked back to town, Nyx put on their coat. They took a deep breath and opened the door, leaving their lantern inside.

Up in the sky, the moon was full, bright and glowing.

Nyx thought they'd feel sad, but happiness bloomed in them, pink and warm, as they looked up at her and spoke, 'Do you have another story for me?'

ACKNOWLEDGEMENTS

There are *so* many people to thank when you make a book. That's even more true when you have a lot of contributors. I'd like to start with them. Thank you to Alison Evans, Helena Fox, Amie Kaufman, Will Kostakis, Jes Layton, Gary Lonesborough, Amber McBride, Abdi Nazemain, Meagan Spooner, Maggie Tokuda-Hall, Alexandra Villasante and Lili Wilkinson. You are the heart of this project. Special thanks to those who wrote me a story so I could pitch the idea, and those who jumped on board to complete the set, writing brilliant stories in a hurry. Readers, pick up all these authors' books! They will captivate you.

Thanks also, Kit Fox, who breathed life into our stories with her beautiful art! I'm thrilled you're part of the family.

An enormous thanks to my agent, Linda Epstein, and everyone at Emerald City Literary Agency, as well as the team at Abner Stein.

Thanks to Meg Whelan, editor extraordinaire and faerie godmother! The Affirm Press team is so lucky to have you. The work you put into this dream of mine can't be overestimated. I'm certain that this book is as much yours as anybody's.

Thank you to Tash Besliev, Coral Huckstep, Dana Anderson and everyone else at Affirm. You're all champions, and it's surreal that I get to work with you all. (This book found its home with you more than a year before I did.)

A humble thanks to both of my writers' groups – *Scribblemaniacs* and *Queer AF (Author Friends)* – who listened to me rabbit on about this book for four years.

It would be remiss of me to not thank the booksellers who now usher it into the hands of readers, as not that long ago I was one of them. Thanks also to the librarians who curate incredible collections. I see the fantastic work you do for creatives and the change it makes in people's lives.

This list of people who brought the book to life is incomplete, but please know everyone involved makes my heart sing … just like the stories in these pages.

had not seen anyone leave except a girl who was poorly dressed and looked more like a peasant than a lady. *Cinderella*, Charles Perrault · Off they started now upon the highroad; but it being very warm weather, they had not walked far, when, as they came to a corner, the Dog said, 'I am tired and must go to sleep.' *The Dog and the Sparrow*, Jacob and Wilhelm Grimm · She was unable to resist, and, trembling, she took the little key and opened the door. *Bluebeard*, Charles Perrault · The old man's garden was suddenly transformed into a beautiful picture of spring. *The Old Man Who Makes the Trees to Blossom*, Yei Theodora Ozaki · Rapunzel's voice had stirred his heart so powerfully that he went out into the forest every day to hear her. *Rapunzel*, Jacob and Wilhelm Grimm · Mirror, Mirror, on the wall, who's the fairest one of all? *Snow White*, Jacob and Wilhelm Grimm · 'I don't like the sound of that. Come with me,' said the mermaid. *Mary Belle and the Mermaid*, Virginia Hamilton · But it's delightful not to be forgotten! *The Old House*, Hans Christian Andersen · Just this. When bad boys become good and kind, they have the power of making their homes gay and new with happiness. *The Adventures of Pinocchio*, Carlo Collodi · Tomorrow, at the crack of dawn, let's take the children out into the deepest part of the forest. *Hansel and Gretel*, Jacob and Wilhelm Grimm · By chance he put his eye to the keyhole. *Donkeyskin*, Charles Perrault · Here was a well-known face at last – a round, friendly countenance, the face of a good friend I had known at home. *What the Moon Saw*, Hans Christian Andersen · She did not mind as long as it meant that she would be able to free her beloved brothers. *The Wild Swans*, Hans Christian Andersen · They said they had not seen anyone leave except a girl who was poorly dressed and looked more like a peasant than a lady. *Cinderella*, Charles Perrault · Off they started now upon the highroad; but it being very warm weather, they had not walked far, when, as they came to a corner, the Dog said, 'I am tired and must go to sleep.